THE PIPER'S DANCE

A Novel

THE PIPER'S DANCE

Maxim Jakubowski

Also by Maxim Jakubowski

NOVELS

It's You That I Want To Kiss (1997)

Because She Thought She Loved Me (1998)

The State Of Montana (1998)

On Tenderness Express (2000)

Kiss Me Sadly (2002)

Confessions Of A Romantic Pornographer (2004)

Skin In Darkness (omnibus edition of revised versions of *Because She Thought She Loved Me, It's You That I Want To Kiss* and *On Tenderness Express*) (2003)

I Was Waiting For You (2010)

Ekaterina And The Night (2011)

The Lousiana Republic (2018)

SHORT STORY COLLECTIONS

Life In The World Of Women (1998)

Fools For Lust (2006)

A Washington Square Romance (2011)

The Music Of Bodies (Ebook only) (2011)

We Mate In The Dark (Ebook only) (2011)

Hotel Room Fuck, The Best Of Maxim Jakubowski (Ebook only) (2012)

First published in 2021 by
Telos Publishing Ltd,
139 Whitstable Road, Canterbury, Kent, CT2 8EQ,
United Kingdom

Telos Publishing welcomes feedback
feedback@telos.co.uk

The Piper's Dance © 2021 Maxim Jakubowski

Cover © 2021 Mark Stammers Design
markstammersdesign.myportfolio.com

ISBN: 978-1-84583-186-8

The moral right of the author has been asserted.

British Library Cataloguing in Publication Data. A catalogue record for this book is available from the British Library.

This book is sold subject to the condition that it shall not by way of trade or otherwise, be lent, resold, hired out or otherwise circulated without the publisher's prior written consent in any form of binding or cover other than that in which it is published and without a similar condition including this condition being imposed on the subsequent purchaser

PART ONE

The Memory Of Absence

'There's no absence, if there remains even the memory of absence.' Anne Michaels, *Fugitive Pieces*

1

Today, I am 750 years old.

And I can no longer recall my mother. In dreams, I catch evanescent glimpses of her face, her hair, her smell, but nothing ever comes properly together as sleep encroaches on the memories and tears them to minute shreds, scattering them on the wings of the invisible night breeze. When I wake, no images remain, just shards, filaments, shreds of thoughts and visions that I can't even trust to be true.

Of my father, I remember even less, but then he disappeared when I was only six, lost in the wars I was told by some, lost at sea, I was told by others. Or, more likely, he abandoned us to our fates, my mother, my sister and I, as so many men were known to do in those ancient days of strife and poverty.

Ages back, I would often question my sister Claudia about our parents, and more particularly my mother, but her memories were even more fragile than mine as she was three years younger when we were taken and, for her, the Island is all she knows, her attachment to the faraway past in no way as cumbersome as mine.

Some nights, I imagine my mother had long, wavy darker than dark hair which fell to her shoulders, and that she was beautiful in an eerie, distant, exotic way, but then I am reminded that both Claudia and I are fairer, our colouring veering from outright blond to ash blond depending on the time of year and how long we have spent in the sun. But I am certain that her eyes were blue, and kind. And that she often sang us to sleep when the thunder and lightning outside roared, and the wind blew through the fragile walls of our small wooden house, windows shaking, sometimes drops of water leaking through the patched-up ceiling.

And I blame myself for not even remembering her name.

I don't think that Claudia even resembles our mother. Do I? The two of us don't look like brother and sister. We have long lived separate lives, have few interests in common. Could we have had different fathers?

As I mentioned, Claudia is younger than me, of course, but she also looks it, still presents the appearance of a teenager about to shed her puppy fat, while I am already beginning to sprout grey hairs, have dark crescents under my eyes and what I think are worry lines criss-crossing my forehead. And that gap in age and appearance appears to be growing ever more acute.

I once asked our Master about it.

'They think I have control over everything,' he responded, pondering his answer in his customary, deliberate manner. 'But even I am still a novice in the ways of the Bubble.'

The Bubble is what he always calls the Island where he has stranded us.

'But didn't you create the Bubble?'

He was evasive. 'Yes, I did, for the purposes of the experiment, but in a sense, it's always been here …' He looked thoughtful.

A century or so later, I rephrased the question and queried the Master again about the curious fact that us children were beginning to age differently. This must have been after we'd celebrated our third century on the island.

'Ah,' he said. 'That's a most interesting point. He passed his fingers through his beard as he pondered his answer, or at any rate tried to fetch the right words to explain something so complex to someone like me.

'It's the shadow of sin that lurks over all of you.'

I must have no doubt looked puzzled.

He continued, 'You could call it an experiment. I had to make compromises, do a deal with the other side …' His voice tapered off as he became more pensive. 'There were … conditions.'

I could but remain silent.

Eventually, both of us were facing each other through the pause in the desultory conversation, he elaborated, for all that I couldn't understand.

'A deal was done. They're supposed to be on the side of light, but they weren't bothered in the least if I had led all you children straight over the cliff ... Who's to reason why?'

And then he walked away.

He didn't return to the island for many years following that conversation, leaving us to our own resort and some of us continued to remain youthful while others, including Katerina and I, began to mature at a faster rate, gradually shedding our childlike appearances, becoming adults, of sort. Claudia was one of those left behind in the process, which I feel further alienated what little closeness of relationship my sister and I had ever enjoyed.

Standing outside time makes you act and think differently. None of us have birthdays any longer, not that most even recall the precise date of their birth. We have no calendars. We just tick off every new year that passes on the bark of a tree, on a piece of paper, in the recesses of our minds. No celebration is involved. Over the centuries, we have become outsiders, looking in as we follow the travails of the outside world on our impossible island, allowed to use the Great Library – which few of us actually do, and not coincidentally the majority of us readers, searchers after truth happen to be amongst the so-called older looking ones of our group, the children of Hamelin. I don't blame the others and their multitude; they are happy even in their relative ignorance and have little to worry about. But us, those that the Master would define as 'touched by sin', know this is not the real life, that somehow we have been cheated. We appear to be immortal but we have no life to speak of.

I miss my mother and I miss the real world, not the one I have so few memories of but the one we are denied.

I woke early before dawn on the day I became 750 years old and walked down to the nearest beach. I was barefoot, and the damp sand warmed the soles of my feet as I left a trail of footsteps in my wake while I strode along the thin stretch of land that separated the wood from the open spaces. Katerina was already there, sitting by our familiar tree, with her back to me, and looking out at the sea.

I approached her silently but she knew it could only be me, the elaborate slowness of my movements possibly causing a slight vibration, disturbing the morning air, betraying my presence.

'Tristan,' she said, her voice like honey.

'Katerina …'

She didn't look up at me.

'I love it here, when it's so quiet and peaceful,' she said.

'I do, too, but there must be more to life than this, no?'

She nodded.

I sat down next to her. The dampness of the sand rapidly soaked my thin linen trousers. She was naked. A spectacle I would never tire of.

Her back straight, her shoulders tanned, her hair pulled forward, forming a curtain around her small breasts. Her legs were crossed, and her toes dug into the sand, forming intricate patterns of disturbance in the beige carpet of the beach. Many of us, thanks to the clemency of the weather, often went around in the nude, particularly the children who showed no perceptible signs of growing old. When you've been together so long, there is little curiosity about the mystery of bodies any longer.

The Master never commented upon this, nor objected, as if he wanted us to believe we were in Paradise, maybe, and that our innocence protected us.

'You beat me to it, this morning,' I said.

'I couldn't sleep.'

'Till?'

'He's still sleeping in the room. I wanted some space. Did you know he snores?'

I smiled.

She had been living with Till for a few years. Once she had been with me. Actually, we had all lived with a variety of partners over the centuries. It made sense. It was complicated but the weight of years is not conducive to monogamy. Those of the original children who had not markedly aged were spared the agonies and epiphanies of sex, and sometimes I envied them. I was now with Maria. Before me, she had been with Johann the older, while Katerina had once mated with Johann the younger. And prior to that, we had briefly been together. That had been during the years of the Plague in the outside world. It felt both like ages ago and yesterday.

We quietly gazed at the horizon, the line where the sky blurred effortlessly with the far reaches of the sea, until your eyes watered and you began to question what you were actually watching. There were few clouds today, no imaginary shapes to invent by way of a game, comparing their shapes to animals and daring each other to locate a giraffe or a whale in the immensity of the sky. Not that either of us had ever seen any such animals, unless they had featured inside in books.

The only animals we knew of, had seen, were the rats who had invaded our small town before the Master appeared and rid the land of them. And then made our parents pay a terrible price.

The other unnatural thing about the Island where we live in isolation is the fact the weather never changes: it's warm, but not too hot as to ever prove uncomfortable, and we no longer experience the sometimes bracing cold that would embrace our old Lower Saxony town in winter.

'How are the two of you?' I asked Katerina. I seldom came across Till these days. He always seemed too busy foraging in the fields. Couldn't in truth relate to him much. I knew he was a generous soul, assumed he was a good lover, but he was not a man who questioned the world, nor our situation. I was certain he had never even set foot in the Great Library. He had no curiosity. I knew he sculpted but I found his creations simple, uncomplicated. Like him. Made of wood or clay, abstract representations of who knows what. To me they just looked like random shapes.

'I think our time together is nearing its end,' she said. 'You know how it is ...'

I did.

Should I tell her that Maria and I had reached a similar point in our association?

'Swim?' I suggested.

Katerina pondered, as if torn between alternatives, her mind stuttering between possibilities, unsure of what she should say next, what decisive step she should take.

I remained silent and immobile, not wanting to precipitate whatever she would decide to do next. There was an unusual tension in the air, surrounding us, insidiously penetrating our respective thoughts.

Finally, I had to say something.

Anything.

'You know what's wrong about this?' I asked her.

She turned her face towards me. Her eyes were the colour of the deep sea.

Their gaze paralysed me.

I recalled a time long past when we were mating and in the throes of mutual pleasure, I would notice she kept her eyes wide open, and their shade appeared to move uncontrollably between every stage in the spectrum between bottle green and azure punctuating the rise of emotions and chemical reactions running though our bodies.

'No.'

'In all the books I've read, there are always birds flying above the sea, swooping across the shore, hopscotching above the canopies of the trees. Here, there are none. We're living in an artifice. It's not real.'

'It's the Island …'

'I know, but …'

She interrupted me.

'He's always told us we were living in a Bubble, outside of time and space, hasn't he? That it was for our own good.'

'Is it?'

'I have no answers, Tristan.'

'Damn it, I want answers,' I said.

It had been some time since the Master had visited us last.

But whenever we had conversations, his words were always enigmatic, his explanations unclear, obfuscated. I wasn't sure whether he wished to keep us deliberately in the dark, or if he was actually embarrassed because even he, with all his powers, was unclear about his aims, the situation we found ourselves in and how much other forces beyond his control were involved.

'Don't come to me for them,' Katerina said.

She rose, sweeping her waist-length hair back across her shoulders, baring her chest.

I thought she was now about to tread her way towards the water and go swimming, but she stood on the spot for what felt like an eternity of utter quiet.

I remained seated, with my legs crossed.

Finally, she approached and I could feel the warmth of her breath gliding across my skin.

'Get up,' she ordered me.

I did.

We now faced each other. A faint breeze rustled the leaves of the tree under which we were half sheltering.

Her lips parted.

'Take me,' she said.

We embraced at length, still standing, our footing at times uneasy as the sand shifted between our toes. Behind us the tremors of the forest multiplied, a faint wind streaming through the branches, leaves fluttering like a discordant ballet as the air moved in subtle variations of speed and strength. Even silence has a sound.

Finally, we slipped to the ground and we made love.

Slowly.

Hesitantly at first, dredging up the memories of our previous times together, familiarising ourselves with the respective taste of our skins, adjusting positions anew like building a jigsaw we'd already formed so many times but thought we had forgotten to assemble, orchestrating the way we breathed, alternately fast, then slow, then fast again and once we had pinpointed our right rhythm in unison, we at last became one and our bodies and thoughts merged into a single entity.

How could I have ever allowed us to drift apart, and moved on to others? How could she?

Later, we lay in the warm sand, having rolled along, no longer under the protection of the trees bordering the beach, as the sun rose on the distant horizon, the thin sheen of sweat enveloping our bodies not so much drying against our skin but now merging into some form of soothing lotion to keep our flesh alive as the heat from above tick-tocked along in intensity as the day grew.

One of our favourite pastimes: looking out at the sea.

The shimmer of the faraway waves, closer to the event horizon, the subtle changes in its colour depending on the depth of the water or the position of the sun as it passed above in sublime indifference, seemingly in infinitesimal motion, the microscopic variations in the texture of the gleaming surface. So many mysteries and elements of beauty.

'There are no tides,' I pointed out.

'What are tides?' Katerina asked.

Just useless information I had gathered in the Great Library about the place where we all lived and how it differed in curious ways from what I had learned of the outside world. Tides. Animals. Birds. So many mysteries to contend with.

A long time ago -I wasn't one of them, whether out of caution or because I knew the attempt was doomed to fail – a group of children had painstakingly built a fragile raft and paddled out to sea, hoping to breach the line of the horizon, in the hope of reaching whatever the outside world consisted of. It had taken ages as the tools at our disposal were minimal and elementary their fragile embarkation constructed from possibly unreliable information in books and documents we had little true understanding of. Three of them, two boys and one girl, Mathilda, I think her name was, shipped out on the absurd craft and rowed out until they had become just a dot in the immensity of the landscape.

We actually took bets on the outcome.

Whether we would ever see them again?

Whether they would succeed and return one day with answers to our questions, finally liberating our curiosity?

Whether, in that case, they would be punished by the Master when he discovered what they had attempted?

None of those things happened.

We had almost forgotten them, believing them dead – drowned, succumbing to starvation or other sinister scenarios – when one early evening as dusk was painting its more sombre colours over the Island, the raft reappeared and they made their way to the shore, and we effusively greeted them.

By our reckoning, and the rise and fall of the sun, they had been absent for almost six weeks. As far as they were concerned, their unsuccessful attempt to breach the physical laws under which we laboured had barely lasted three or four days. They had found nothing; just more sea, an endless horizon that never grew nearer, the ever-repetitive canopy of an unchanging sun, and it appeared they had just navigated in circles all the time they had been away, making no progress, as if there was actually nothing out there and the Island and its surrounding waters was all the world contained; it never even had barriers, a wall to stop their advance into the becalmed waters, it just was.

A strange thought occurred to me.

If there was no escape by way of sea, could there be another road out?

From land?

'What do you think?' I asked Katerina.

She frowned.

A mask of gravity I had seldom seen draped across her face, her high cheekbones highlighted by the angle of the sun above us.

'The Master.'

'What about him?' I queried.

'He comes and goes.'

'That's true.'

Not that it happened that frequently of late, but he arrived out of the blue and when his work – whatever work he was actually engaged in aside from supervising us and seeing we were all fine and not up to some mischief or other – was done, he would similarly depart, with no word of warning. One moment he was here, then brusquely after he was gone.

'Does he just disappear into thin air?'

'I wouldn't put it past him.'

'Or is there another way in and out; one that only he knows.'

We eventually walked back to the Island's huts, then separated.

Later that morning, I told Maria that I thought it would be better if we parted. It came as no surprise to her, as if she had long been expecting my decision, or I had in fact beaten her to it. I offered to move out, but she declined. She had fewer belongings to carry, as I'd for some time been hoarding notebooks, papers, documents I'd borrowed from the Great Library and it was less cumbersome that way. In the matter of relationships, us children of Hamelin are not very sentimental. How could we be?

Unbeknown to me, that same day, Katerina and Till also amiably parted ways. Whether anyone made a connection between the two separations, I don't know. Again, few of us are very curious about things. Probably because the weight of years or something in our wiring that was adjusted when we were brought here. Who knows? Who cares? She didn't move in with me either.

We remained in theory apart, just crossing paths at dawn on the beach.

Not that anyone else was much bothered about matters of the flesh any longer in this strange territory we occupied. Some of us were still children and quite unphased by the situation; others had grown to this strange state of adulthood that Katerina, I and a handful of others shared, but even then the status quo remained the order of the day.

We both separately began enquiring around, whenever the opportunity presented itself, if anyone knew much about the

Master's activities when he was among us. And soon realised we knew so little. Where did he geographically arrive when he was on the Island? From which part did he normally depart? Few had any ideas, let alone concrete answers. He was elusive not just in conversation, but also in his actions and wanderings. We had grown too accustomed to his evasive presence to pin him down to one hut, a specific area. He roamed freely amongst us, as if our needs and whereabouts dictated his movements, and he was in some way dependent on us, at our beck and call.

'This isn't getting us anywhere,' we concluded one morning. I think it was a whole two weeks after I'd ushered in my 750th year.

'Let's concentrate,' Katerina said. 'Where he is most often seen, or do we ourselves see him?'

'Well,' my initial reaction was, 'we know he doesn't reach the Island by sea, so there must be somewhere inland which has some form of what could I call it ... portal, maybe? But having been here so damn long, don't we collectively know every inch of the Island?'

Katerina nodded.

Then it came to me that very instant.

The Great Library.

When we first arrived here, after being led away from Hamelin, there was no such library in situ, just the random collection of thatched huts spread out in concentric semi-circles from a centrally-situated square, where a deep well formed the geometrical focal point of what was to become our village. Many years had already gone by when we woke to a changed landscape, with the well now covered and a squat brick and stucco building encroaching on its previous space, which the Master ceremoniously led us too and introduced to us as the Great Library. The building had no windows and over two floors just ceaseless, flowing walls bursting with books, old and new. When you were inside, the library felt so much larger than you would expect from the outside. Its overnight appearance (or had we slept longer than usual to facilitate its construction?) and the contradictions between its outer appearance and its inner sanctum spoke of the supernatural. But then supernatural matters were no novelty for us, having been at the very heart of our journey here.

Even though the Master encouraged us all to frequent and use the Library, few of us did after the initial burst of interest.

'Knowledge is not only power, but it will also illuminate your lives,' he proclaimed. 'This will be called the Great Library, as it houses some of the treasures I succeeded in retrieving from its Alexandrian counterpart. Make good use of it.'

I had no desire for any form of power, but I certainly felt I needed more light in my life.

The following night, Katerina and I agreed to meet up by the entrance of the Great Library.

2

It was on St John and Paul's Day that we followed the music, dancing ourselves into a joyful trance as we first hopped along towards the Weser River.

It's strange reading about yourself as if you were a character in a story or indeed, as it became, a legend.

In some accounts I've come across we were led to Koppenberg Mountain, in others we drowned, and yet further tales erroneously declare we fell to our doom, all 130 of us, over a tall cliff, plunging downwards in the thrall of gravity like lemmings racing to their destruction.

The three children who did not join us and were left behind could shed no light on our fate. One was lame and could not follow quickly enough, the second was deaf and therefore was immune to the hypnotic effect of the Piper's music and the last was blind and consequently unable to see where he was going; his name was also Tristan. The inhabitants of Hamelin had a limited imagination and many of us shared similar names.

It was in 1284.

I have read countless versions of what happened to us. Early on when I was still exploring the treasures of the Great Library, I came upon a facsimile copy of the famed 15th century Lüneburg manuscript, where our tale was rendered in the form of an inscription on an edifice known as the Rat Catcher's House, stating that in Hamelin on 26 June 130 children born locally were led away by a piper clothed in many colours to (their) calvary near the Koppen, (and) lost.

Koppen means a knoll or domed hill.

It's accurate that after crossing the river our merry group then made its way, in the footsteps of the Master, to one of the many hills surrounding Hamelin, but no account I've had leisure to examine ever recounts what occurred afterwards.

The Piper's Dance

The whole village had attended mass that morning, and following the service Claudia and I had been allowed to go play on our own for a few hours and had immediately headed for the park on the border of town, where we knew we would come across many friends, children from our school and others. It was a custom in Hamelin that kids would be set free on Sunday afternoon, providing parents, carers and grown-ups with an opportunity to relax and enjoy each other's company while we gallivanted with the vigour of youth. Now that we were all free of the curse of the rats.

There had been a terrible infestation. Initially, it was just a case of a couple of rodents seen racing across the cobbled streets as the morning dawned and the town began to go about its business. No one took it very seriously. But within days, more rats were spotted, including some gnawing their way into sacks of flour and food supplies in some of the warehouses where the grain was being stored. The growth of the infestation was exponential, with the nasty creatures encouraged by our lack of response and all too soon running amok in packs of five or six, as if inviting us to react with violence. Some of us children took much amusement in aiming stones at the parasitic animals whenever they ran before us, but our small projectiles seldom reached their intended targets; they were too fast and nimble.

Within a month of their first manifestation, the situation was racing out of control, with the rats seemingly hunting in packs and openly defying us denizens of Hamelin, taking over our small town, calling it their own, stealing our food, infecting not just our goods but preying on our minds. Should anyone stray into their path, they risked being bitten and the town apothecary was soon running out of balms and medicines to treat the victims of the roaming rats.

The town council gathered, and the Burgher, an obese individual whose wealth had been inherited from his forefathers and acted as if he owned the town, first offered rewards to each individual who could catch a brace of rats to be summarily drowned or burned. Few of the men and women of Hamelin proved more successful in this endeavour than us children with our improvised cardboard and string traps or our slings and stones.

Another meeting was called, at which the Burgher, or was it one of his acolytes, mentioned having heard of a nearby village which had suffered some years previously from a similar plague of rodents and had been obliged to employ a professional rat killer to rid themselves of the nuisance.

Enquiries were made and it was agreed to summon the Piper.

A deal was agreed.

He made it clear to our council members however that he must operate out of sight of the Hamelin populace, and every inhabitant of the town must be in church with the doors firmly closed while he was allowed to do his hunting outside, free of interference. Some said it was because he used magic, others speculated that he just wanted to spare us of the likely spectacle of devastation that might ensue, shield us from the disgusting spectacle of hordes of rodents lying dead in pools of their own blood, stomachs bloated and burst open, eyes gouged and whatever other horrors mostly us children conjured in our conversations about the coming day of the rat catcher.

At any rate, we exited the church on the day, adults apprehensive, children excited and pruriently curious, looked out at our small, cosy town further down the hill and all peering out anxiously to see if there were any rodents. None were ever seen again. The Piper had done his job, as he had promised us.

Actually, half a dozen souls had not attended the church because of disabilities, long term illness or just cussedness, and the word soon spread from their mouths that the Piper had been spied through the thin gaps between carefully drawn curtains or shutters wearing a garish outfit of many colours and had lured the rats away from all points of the compass by creating some entrancing musical tune on his instruments. The rodents had congregated in a docile manner at his feet and then followed him away. The possibly unreliable witnesses outfought each other to boast of the stupendous number of rats that he had charmed out of their lairs, their uncommon sizes, the colour of their fur and how captive they had been once the Piper played, evoking the power of his magic in both wonderment and awe. But no one, when asked, could provide any indication as to what the Piper looked like. For some, he had appeared young and sprite, for others old and stooped, he had a beard or was clean-faced, his hair was long or else he was bald, no details coincided. This just added to the mystery; his features had been masked, a thick, brown scarf pulled across his face, with just his eyes visible when he had met the Burgher and the council members so every minute fact was up for speculation.

But prior to the rodent infestation, the region had suffered a bleak and harsh winter that had left the town coffers perilously bare and our officials' initial reaction was to instruct every inhabitant to meticulously scour the streets, cellars, warehouses and storage rooms to maybe find if only one remaining rat had been left behind which would allow them to use this as an excuse to delay or avoid payment to the Piper. Naturally, this amounted to nothing.

So he wasn't paid on some pretext or other, and issued dire threats which the Burgher blithely ignored, possibly compounding his mistake by insulting the rat catcher and accusing him of being responsible for the plague of rats, which he had supposedly set in motion in order to make his fortune.

The Piper walked away from the meeting in a huff, promising he would be back and that Hamelin would bitterly regret its lamentable actions.

Us children were naturally unaware of what had taken place but I vaguely recall it must have been no more than a week or so before the Piper's return on that fateful day.

In the communal park, Claudia had been involved in a minor scuffle with Johannes and Mathilda, the children of the town's locksmith and in running away from them (or maybe she was running towards in fierce attack; at that age the truth is flexible according to the person asked …) she had stumbled to the ground, superficially grazing her knee and I had been called over to attend to her wound. I was bending over and cleaning away the grit with a cloth I had wetted close by in the fountain in the town square when I first heard the strange sound that was to change our lives.

It was like an unformed, swirling melody played on a distant pipe, insinuating its way through the breeze, floating above the roofs of the houses, gliding over the narrow streets, both melodic and somehow angry with a confused back-note of dissonances. Music we had never heard before, so different from the hymns in church or the small songs we sang to each other at school or in our homes to please our parents.

We all raised our heads to the sky, peering at the low banks of heavy rain clouds roaming across our horizon.

Small voices began questioning.

'Did you hear that?'

'What is it?'

At first the sound was indistinct, broken up, fragments emerging from nowhere and close by at the same time, but soon its proximity and intensity began to steadily increase until every single child was standing, games abandoned, looking out for its point of origin, faces creased with either anxiety or excitement.

The slithering music wormed its way towards our group, dancing through the afternoon air with a jaunty confidence, playful and menacing, hypnotic and full of silenced fear, until we were literally enveloped by it.

Soon, we all fell silent, just standing there transfixed. This was unlike any sound, any melody we had ever heard before. Its cadences somehow clashed with our understanding of song or liturgy, it's now uninterrupted flow like a veil descending to cloak us in its alien beauty.

I think all of us had reached the stage where all we could do was hold our breath, in expectancy of something momentous, eyes glued to the shifting shapes of the clouds in the sky, which seemingly danced along to the rhythm of this new kind of music.

Then the Piper appeared.

The Piper's Dance

He was no longer dressed in his familiar multi-coloured clothing, as he had been on his initial summons to Hamelin and the day he had spectacularly freed us of the rats, but was now clad all in green, like a hunter. His shoes were red and he wore a dark cap in the muddy brown shades of the rotten leaves that could often be seen littering the border of the nearby forests. He held a pipe in his hands, as his voluptuous lips caressed its stem. The pipe shone with fantastic light. As if the gold it was carved from had caught fire, the music he was expressing through it a conduit for invisible but supernatural will o'the wisps, leading the melody through a subtle dance blending the eddies of the wind and the invisible wings of a song with no name.

He reached us, as we congregated at the centre of the park, our feet stamping the thin, sparse grass. Our circle opened up to let him through until he stood surveying all of us, our eyes unable to look away from him, let alone blink. Mathilda began sobbing.

He opened his mouth, but the music from the pipe continued uninterrupted as if by magic, its waves washing up around every one of us.

He spoke.

'Children,' he said, 'from henceforth I shall be your Master and you will have no other.'

We all remained silent.

He brought the pipe back to his lips and the melody blanked out our surroundings.

The tune twisted and turned, it danced and skipped, it soothed and hopscotched.

'Follow me, follow this pipe of truth, follow the music,' he ordered. And stepped away from us, inching his way towards the borders of the park.

Hesitantly, but steadily, we complied with his orders, one foot forward at a time, following the map of his footsteps. The smaller children went ahead and the older ones further behind. I was separated from Claudia.

All the while, the magical melody of his pipe insinuated

itself inside our heads, playing a merry gavotte across our thoughts and feelings as we ambled along, eyes fixed on his moving silhouette. The music was a thing of beauty and dread, it hypnotised us with its alien powers, turned us into willing puppets, banishing all thoughts of home, parents and reality as we soon reached the outskirts of Hamelin and our motley group, led by this strange piper who called himself our Master, began the short trek towards the river.

Later, I would compare impressions with some of the others but every single one of us experienced things slightly differently.

Claudia told me that the music we followed was like a long scream, full of sorrow, that it travelled across her skin like a scouring wind, polishing her soul until it yearned for the coming of sleep, of nothingness.

For Johannes, the melody had been suffused with irrepressible anger, like a cauldron swirling with terrible memories of both past and future, a tune that controlled every muscle in his body, stretched sinews, making his blood boil.

For me, it was just beauty incarnate.

Both a melancholy and dionysiac sound. The sum of opposites.

A tune serene, peaceful like the sky at night in repose, full of distant stars like lights at the top of the world, summoning me to fly, to float on its slight breezes, swoop up and down like a bird, metamorphosing into a creature of air. It lullabied my heart with a joy I had never experienced in my brief life so far. Even now, if I close my eyes, I still hear those diaphanous sounds again with crystal-like purity and they effortlessly transport me back in time, and trigger my heart to skip several beats and my head to go dizzy. Listening to it was like entering a whole new world; which was not that far from the truth at the outset of that crucial day, of course.

As we began our winding march, our column stretched as we walked four or five abreast. I'd managed to reunite with Claudia and instinctively held her hand as we slowly advanced first through the desolate, almost grassless plains surrounding

Hamelin and later through rougher bracken which slowed our pace. Somehow, never ever looking back, the Piper at the front of the long line adjusted his pace to suit us, so that at no time was there a significant gap between his shimmering silhouette and the entrancing music flying from his pipe and dissolving in the air in our direction like invisible threads of smoke.

It came to mind that this was the very same route that he had adopted to lure the posse of rats to their doom, but the thought somehow didn't feel concerning.

Occasionally, one child or another would stumble, as we all advanced in a daze, captive of the unceasing melody that emanated from the golden pipe, but there was always another child to help him or her up and avert slowing down our mysterious journey.

Finally, we reached the river and the tone of the piper's melody appeared to change, moving away from what to me sounded like melancholia and adopting a jauntier rhythm. The piper in his green hunting garb turned right as we approached the bank.

We did the same. Sharply changing direction and now beginning to journey alongside the muddy approaches of the rumbling thunder of the stream. Spring was approaching and the waters of the mountain river were swollen from the rains caused by the melting of winter snow from the faraway peaks and hills, the recurring punctuation of the change of the seasons in Lower Saxony.

Very soon, the sky began to darken but our pace continued, steady, automatic, led by the music, captive inside its net of charms.

It felt like hours and we were now journeying in total darkness when we finally bifurcated away from the river and entered unknown territory, through trails and copses, distant enough from Hamelin to guarantee that none of us had ever ventured so far.

It was a slow climb up the nearest hill, its gradient gentle but progressive. By now, as the altitude rose, it was getting much colder, but no one complained, as if our minds had been switched off and we were puppets, manipulated by the pipe's ethereal strings. An endless carpet of dead leaves and scattered twigs crunched under our feet as we progressed halfway up the hill until we reached the end of our trail, a hidden gorge initially obscured by a curtain of thick trees where the higher part of the forest took root and spread downward towards the plain where our town resided.

Still unconcerned, confident we were still completely in his thrall, the Master, with nary a look across his shoulder to check we were still present and complete, squeezed himself, the sound of music quite uninterrupted, through two ancient oak trees, or maybe they were chestnuts. We changed our formation and followed him, one at a time, through the narrowing between the venerable trees. There was a brief interval of darkness as we advanced blindly ahead and then, we emerged into the light of day. Which made no sense as just a hundred metres behind us we had been travelling through the gloom of dusk.

We all blinked and once again, the volute of the music that led us changed in tone, reaching elegiac and almost religious tones, as if its shapes were dictated by the landscapes we wandered through.

It was a valley. Verdant and fertile.

We began our descent.

Time froze.

Marching downwards to the strings of the melody that controlled us, one step, one note, one step, one further note of exquisite beauty carrying us along in its coat of wonderment, and inexorably onwards.

Finally, we reached the heart of the valley. The light of the sun above us was still unblinking. The music stopped. It came as a shock, the breaking of a spell, leaving us bereft, abandoned, frightened, disoriented.

We all looked at each other beseechingly, disturbed by the circumstances, unsure of our future, hungry for the music that had sustained us so far.

We gazed at the piper who was now standing, his arms by

his side, at the very centre of our motley group of children, his green hunting garb still pristine while our clothes and rags were soaking with sweat and littered with dirt from the journey we had completed.

'No, children,' he said, his basso voice no fair replacement for the music we had just lost and loved more than anything else in the world, 'This is not the end. It's only the beginning.'

I was still holding on to Claudia's hand, a longstanding habit of having to protect her from all and sundry and life itself. I let go, knowing there was nothing I could ever control from herein.

He held the golden pipe in his fist and secreted it away in an hitherto hidden pocket of his green leather trousers. I noticed how clean his red shoes were, despite the rigours of our march.

I sighed. Guessing I would hear the music no more, and felt a terrible loss, as if it had become a part of me, sewn into the fabric of my life.

Then he raised his hand and the world came to an end.

Our consciences closed down and, I assume, we must all have fallen to the ground.

How long we remained that way is impossible to know.

When we awoke – had it actually been sleep? If so, there had been no dreams – we were on the Island.

There was a scattering of huts at the centre of what we soon referred to as the colony, at the suggestion of the Master on one of his early visits, enough for each of us to have his own, private abode, although brothers, sisters, relatives and friends initially chose to stick together as the habitations were large enough for several to occupy. We were all safe and well.

Our immortal lives were about to begin.

3

'Are you truly happy here? Where we live?'

Most present at our gathering nodded, visibly puzzled by our question.

Those who, like Katerina and I, increasingly suffered the angst of wanderlust or existentially questioned our longstanding state of affairs looked more thoughtful.

Mostly folk who were known to frequent the Great Library, displayed a spark of interest.

We had called a semi-clandestine meeting, inviting some of those we suspected would feel like us about the colony to a small extent, mostly those who had somehow turned into adults and had not physically aged much over the centuries of our isolation here. Till had willingly come along, despite his rift with Katerina. There was also Hans the older and Hans the younger, the Schlück twins, Brunhilde, Albrecht, Bertoff, Agathe, Ennelyn, Rüdeger, Apollonia. Sophie the mute and Rudolf. Konrad the cook – named as he'd been the one who enjoyed that chore the most and, for lack of rivals, had evolved into the principal member of the colony in charge of all matters digestive; foraging, planting crops, organising storage, devising dishes from the many resources at our disposal, cooking – had expressed a willingness to attend but did not turn up on the night.

Katerina took the lead.

Heads turned towards her, a general air of suspicion lingering in the air.

'Surely, there must be more to this, no?' she asked them.

'Would the Master approve?' one of the Schlück brothers asked, the one with a deep scar across his chin, which was the way we told them apart, as they also combed their hair in identical style and wore matching clothing.

'Probably not,' I interjected. 'But we deserve answers. We have to find out if there is another way of life. Out there. Somewhere.'

A few of them lowered their eyes, as if embarrassed by what I was saying, realising it resonated with something buried deep inside them but that they did not have the courage to express.

'He looks after us ...' a plaintive plea.

'Does he really?' Katerina showed signs of anger. She had never been a quiet one. 'We only see him rarely. He pontificates when he talks to us but how do we know if he is to be believed.'

I took over her argument.

'He brought us here to punish our long lost parents for their sins. But isn't being captive here a form of punishment? We know from the books there is another world beyond, which is moving, changing, wondrous even and all we get is hints of it, of what is the true life.'

'But he also protects us,' Till objected.

'Does he really? Do we truly need that protection? Can't we think of our own accord, do what we please?'

The debate went round in endless circles, but I could read both the fear of the unknown and of authority in their downcast eyes.

Eventually, some stormed off, then others peeled off when the conversation becalmed, leaving just a handful of us repeating ourselves again and again.

And then, inevitably, it was just Katerina and I. The instigators, the troublemakers.

She returned with me to my hut. We lay in silence after our congress, the air heavy with a welter of unexpressed thoughts wrapping their frustration around our resting bodies.

'Do you think any of them will tell him what we have said?' she asked me.

'Maybe ...'

'But what can he do, eh? Punish us? That would be unprecedented. Anyway, nothing could be worse than the way things are right now, don't you think?'

I agreed.

'Anyway, he hasn't been among us for ages. As if he has lost interest in us, his experiment. Has better things to do in the real world.'

I'd read the encyclopedias and countless books whose weight buckled the shelves. I'd even taught myself English to facilitate my hunger for knowledge. So full of tales of war, misery and dreadful horror I found it difficult to picture in my mind. But also enlightenment, progress, natural disasters and tragedies, victories of the soul, impossible machines, epiphanies of knowledge I aspired towards. But, more importantly, full of other folk who lived their lives in a different manner, guided by their mortality and the rush to live a life fully.

A different world. The real world. One bursting with pain and love. The very reverse coin of what our pitiful colony had come to represent.

A world where time was an unending stream and things happened, every single day an adventure in the making. There were unaccountable wars, kings decapitated, countries destroyed and created, industrial revolutions and machines we could but dream of: engines, electricity, motorcars, aeroplanes, hot air balloons, radios, moving pictures, space satellites. One where people actually died, as they used to do in Hamelin all that eternity ago. A whole, strange universe where men had even landed on the moon and appeared to be shooting for the stars. To think that when we were children, before the Piper, we had been taught that the earth was flat! It was all there in the thousands of pages Katerina and I had assiduously studied. Why had the Master allowed us insights into such information? Was it part of his grand plan? Had he a grand plan?

The sun fell and rose on another twenty occasions before Katerina and I convened again, having agreed to explore the Great Library beyond the immediate stacks in an attempt to determine whether the curiously unnatural space concealed any secrets as yet uncovered in our timid explorations.

'Read, wander through the million pages, absorb, digest,

reflect,' the Master had suggested to us. 'You don't know how useful it might one day prove.' Was he already in some devious way preparing us for this day, encouraging our eventual betrayal, sowing the seeds of escape in our minds?

There were sections of the library where the shelves were still cocooned in blankets of dust, laden with ancient manuscripts in languages we couldn't read or where the jumble of hieroglyphs on crumbling sheets of vellum defied our understanding, places we had seldom set foot in.

We were systematic and determined, investigating every nook and cranny, emptying shelves in search of hidden recesses, in search of anomalies, clues, answers to our nagging questions. There was a random element about the way the library was organised which I had never quite fathomed, some sections mapped by eras, others by subject matter while yet others were a topsy turvy pandemonium of conflicting books in a variety of sizes, thickness, languages, which didn't appear to have anything in common and might as well have been thrown together by a blind person who could only judge the books' contents by passing his thumb across their binding and crisp pages and then scattering them to the winds relying on the forces of gravity.

We reasoned that the library and its impossible space must have some form of heart, a centre. But we didn't appear to have the right compass to point us in that direction amongst its labyrinth of knowledge.

Katerina sighed, replacing a pile of heavy, rolled-up, beribboned antique, illuminated manuscripts from a dark corner where they had been lying for possibly centuries, full of fantastical images of flora and fauna we had never yet encountered even in our wildest dreams, just the tip of the iceberg in our own map of ignorance of the world that lay beyond.

'This is not working,' she remarked, her fatigue and disappointment all too clear as it darkened her beautiful features. 'He's too clever for us. Has been ever since he first set foot in Hamelin.'

My back was hurting, from all the bending and moving heavy piles of books.

Her words echoed through my mind.

Hamelin. The circumstances of our disappearance from our own, long forgotten world.

'Maybe …' An idea had flashed through my mind. 'Just maybe …'

I trooped over to the other side of the book stacks, almost stumbling across piles of volumes we had not yet replaced in their proper place.

Reached the section where I had, aeons ago, out of curiosity, consulted the extant documents and read all I could about our own legend, the story of the Rat-Catcher, the Rattenfänger von Hameln. Strange how we had become part of history, a tale whispered at night by children who feared the dark, something buried in the sands of time which by now no one knew the actual truth of.

I'd almost forgotten how much had been written about the event.

One by one, I carried the musty volumes and papers from the shelves to a nearby reading table.

There they all were, these pages I had poured over without ever truly understanding what had happened and how the Piper had effected his magic and entranced us so. The 14th century *Decan Lude* chorus book, the 15th century Lüneburg manuscripts, Count Froben Christoph von Zimmen's disputed account, Johann Weyer's *De praestigiis daemonum*, the uncountable collections of myths and fairy tales which had passed through the ages from hand to hand until they were actually written down.

At last the shelf was empty, just the outline of the past presence of its contents drawn across the wooden base of the shelf, patterning the dust.

I pictured the outside geography, the configuration of the Great Library and tried to situate in my mind where the section of wall which had backed up to the Hamelin texts was located. I must have looked somewhat deranged, rushing through the shelves to frantically empty this particular one in total silence, brushing volumes aside. just the excited sound of my breath punctuating my hurried movements, while Katerina gazed at me strangely.

I was trying to mentally reconstruct the inside space and how it connected to the outside periphery of the building. We'd always been aware the library appeared to be so much larger from the inside, but had never seriously bothered to draw up a plan, make any measurements.

I extended my arms across the empty shelf and tapped the wall.

The sound I made was hollow. My heart stopped. Watching me attentively, Katerina's eyes widened.

'There's something there,' I said. 'It appears hollow.'

She nodded in agreement.

Our determination had paid off.

We agreed to postpone our investigation to that evening, as very soon there was a strong possibility others might enter the library as the day progressed and we knew at heart this was a venture we had to keep from our fellow islanders.

The library was well-lit at all times, the oil lights we used generously scattered across its walls and ceiling always firing away, their flaming heart never extinguishing, another of the many anomalies we had learned to unquestioningly accept.

So, working after the fall of darkness would not prove any more perilous than during daytime.

In order to avoid attracting undue attention to ourselves, we agreed to spend the day apart. Katerina went swimming and assisted with the communal cooking, while I spent much of the day in the library, continuing my research, unconsciously already planning for what might turn into our great adventure if we succeeded. I spent so much time as it was in the building that no one would become overly suspicious. If we did escape, I already knew all too acutely that adapting to new circumstances, another world, would not prove easy and we would have to be prepared. I'd taught myself a handful of languages over the thousands of hours I'd poured over the many pages, and was acutely aware from the reference volumes and encyclopedias that the world had moved on in leaps and bounds while we were stuck in our closed bubble, and matters practical would quickly arise should we somehow miraculously emerge into it. There would be sea tides, animals, new ways of seeing and acting, machines and technology we would not know how to use properly; it would be a universe and more away from the Hamelin we once knew, in what I had quickly come to learn was now called the Middle Ages. It would be perilous in the extreme; we would have to fit in, take extreme caution not to betray ourselves as strangers or potentially enemies. Humanity had progressed but its ills remained.

That night I borrowed some tools from the forge and Katerina and I entered the library building under cover of dark.

We quickly pulled some of the shelving away from what appeared to be the hollow wall and sought possible points of purchase for the pick.

There were none. It was uniformly flat and regular along all its surface. We tried another way. Extinguishing the lights in the nearby sconces, we began to slowly pass our hands across the wall, moving systematically from side to side and top to bottom, seeking irregularities, a break in the uniformity of the wall's texture.

'There!' Katerina exclaimed. 'Something …'

I approached her. Her thumb was pressed against a minute indentation in the wall at waist level in the far right quadrant of the area we suspected of concealing an unknown space.

She pulled her hand away and I stuck my own finger into the miniscule gap. It barely fitted in. I twisted my finger around. There was an eerie smoothness assaulting the pad of my delving finger, as if the wall had become flesh, warm, malleable.

I pulled out my forefinger and now inserted my thumb. It fitted the indentation like a glove. I pushed hard. Nothing happened. Harder. Still nothing.

I then twisted my thumb, one way and then the other.

There was a muted click.

I held my thumb there. We held our silence.

'What is it?'

'Wait ...'

A hiss, the wall imperceptibly shimmering. moving, as if it were breathing.

A gap appeared. Growing larger, until there was a definite opening, the size of a door, and total darkness beyond.

We hesitated.

Might the Master reside there? Could there be traps awaiting us beyond?

I reignited one of the hand-held torches we had brought along and advanced it through the gap, revealing a small, cosy area, not unlike the rest of the library, but on a smaller scale, like a carefully-designed miniature version of it. Walls laden with shelves and books, a sturdy rattan chair, a desk, a wooden cabinet.

We ventured through.

My first thought was to examine the books the Piper kept here, to ascertain what they were, whether they possibly held forbidden knowledge he was deliberately keeping from us, but I quickly realised I had come across most of them before; they were just volumes borrowed from the main library, on a diversity of subjects, with few visible links connecting them. I heaved a sigh of disappointment.

In the meantime, Katerina was roaming all around the enclosed space we had unveiled, seeking a form of exit, a way whereby the Master could come and go, hidden from our eyes.

'There is no other way in or out,' she stated, a puzzled frown spreading across her face.

This was not what we had expected.

We both felt deflated.

My eyes were drawn to the desk. Its top was quite dusty, not having been used for some time. The Master's last visit went back months.

There was a small drawer. It didn't appear to be locked. I approached it and warily pulled the drawer open.

No sheets of paper, no books. Just a pipe. One that looked ever so familiar.

Intricately carved like an instrument of ritual, its six holes like small gills, scattered across the tubular length of the primitive instrument.

I gingerly extended my hand and picked it up, wondering what it was made of. I had read that shepherds' pipes, of which this seemed to be an example, were normally carved from cane, ivory or wood and since Hamelin days had evolved and were presently made of metal and of plastic.

There was nothing traditional about this particular pipe, however.

I recalled with a pang of anxiety when we had been lured away from the town and how it had caught the rays of the sun and looked as if it was on fire, burning brightly with both menace and sheer beauty.

This pipe, THE pipe was made of gold.

It was heavy, solid.

I brought it to my lips. The mouthpiece inviting my breath.

Katerina gazed at me with concern, worried that I might be crossing a metaphorical Rubicon from which there could be no way back.

I blew.

A plaintive sound emerged. Nowhere near a melody, barely a note.

Gold.

The one constant in the old world and what I knew of the new one.

The most valuable of commodities.

'Can I try?' Katerina asked me.

I handed the golden pipe over and she raised it to her mouth, a look of determination on her shadowed face.

'I didn't think it would be so heavy,' she said, weighing it in her hands.

'Neither did I. It's the gold.'

'There's a tune I know. It's the only thing I remember of my parents. They would lullaby me to sleep with it, all those million days ago.'

Her fingers cautiously moving between the pipe's holes, as if trying the instrument for size, she attempted to play, the ancient song punctuating the in and out of her breath. At first, it was a clutter of clumsy sounds as if the translation between the air flowing from her lungs in memory of the tune she remembered, and the resonance engineered by the pipe was out of sync.

Somehow encouraged, she continued to blow through the mouthpiece, while her fingers fluttered faster between the holes. I began to recognise the tune, as it moved slowly from mind to lungs to mouth to pipe.

Its sound grew in power as Katerina found her equilibrium.

And soon the melody was dancing through the air, distinct, recognisable, stumbling at times but reaching for our familiarity.

She had a hitherto hidden talent for the wings of song.

Already the charm of the pipe's notes was beginning to percolate into my brain and I felt instantly lighter, relaxed. I gazed at Katerina in wonderment.

There was hushed sound, a counterpoint to the clumsy melody she was helping rise from our distant, childhood past.

The wall behind her briefly blurred, shimmered and then miraculously faded, allowing us a grand view of a verdoyant valley. A familiar one. Deeply buried memories stirred.

Katerina turned round to take in what had just been revealed, but kept on playing, recognising the connection between the golden pipe's sound and the dissolving wall.

I extended my hand forward beyond the line where the wall had stood, fingertips making a shy incursion into the other world, the real world. Nothing happened; my hesitant digits neither burned nor froze. I heaved a sigh of relief, winked at Katerina. I moved forward and crossed the threshold. Immediately, the temperature dropped. It must have been winter there. I stood outside, unharmed, drinking in the crispness of the air, watching the canopy of the forest trees flutter in the distance. I indicated to Katerina to follow. Which she did.

We were now off the Island where we had been marooned for centuries.

Finally, she held the golden pipe away from her lips and the tune she had been improvising died. At the very same moment, the wall of air behind us quivered for a second or two, its barely there tides trembling imperceptibly and the door we had unwittingly created between the colony and here closed, leaving us standing stranded in the green valley. The low peaks in the distance looked familiar. Were we back in Lower Saxony? Did Hamelin still even exist?

The realisation we had succeeded was no consolation for the fact we were alone, with just the golden pipe as a hostage to fortune.

'Hold on to it for dear life,' I asked Katerina.

'Should I try playing it again?' she asked me.

'No.'

We had somehow found a way out. Now was not the time to experiment again.

I remembered the path through the hills and the road to the river.

We set off for Hamelin.

We were apprehensive. We were elated. We were alone and both old and young. I had a brief thought for Claudia, left behind.

As we trekked through overgrown banks of grass, I wondered what year it would turn out to be. Had we returned to our point of origin in the 13th century or would it be the wondrous future. In the encyclopedias I had read in the library the real world had already reached the 21st century. Which would it be?

I looked round at Katerina as she took long strides along our route.

My heart skipped a beat.

Just the two of us.

4

The pawnbroker looked up at us suspiciously. He was an unhealthy creature, his features oddly asymmetrical, his cheeks pockmarked, the bags under his eyes folding over each other, and it looked as if he had lived and slept in the same clothes for too many days in a row. He sat behind his counter, his imposing bulk spilling over its edge. The back of the store where he officiated was cluttered, shelves laden with clocks in all sizes and shapes, cameras, watches and the whole paraphernalia of pawnbroking. The alley where his business resided was in the shadow of the massive shape of the stone cathedral, whose bulk dominated the city like a sleeping mastodon.

We had reached Hannover.

Hamelin, or Hameln as it was now, had totally changed, with not a single building any longer familiar to us, all our memories erased. A place now cut off from its past and ours. We had wandered through its streets in a state of confusion, slowly adapting to our new reality.

We had become stowaways of time. We had no money, just the clothes on our back which were not too old-fashioned as to make us stand out as summer strangers; we were hungry and, despite all our reading about what we might have expected here, quite disoriented.

We had stolen fruit from market stalls and a loaf of bread which had partly gone stale and which someone had abandoned on a trestle table on the edges of the church. We had caught a few hours' sleep in a courtyard where a tiled steeple concealed us from passers-by, when it had become dark and we had felt tiredness spread across our bones.

In the morning, we had weighed our options. They were limited in the extreme. In fact, there was only one thing we could do to survive without throwing ourselves at the mercy of strangers and likely ending up in an asylum for the insane should we try to explain our presence.

It boiled down to what was now our only possession.

We could have held on to it and returned to the valley, attempting by playing the pipe again to rejoin the Island we were so familiar with, but both of us agreed this would be an admission defeat, aside from the fact we would eventually be confronted by the Master there and knew no good would come of such an altercation.

Since reaching the city we had rapidly established the year it was: 1984. It had taken us by surprise, secure in the knowledge we had gained from the Great Library that the world had at least reached the next century. The germ of an idea had taken root as to how we could exploit our thin remembered knowledge of what was still to be the future. But we required capital to do this. We had to proceed one step at a time.

'We have something we wish to sell.'

'Most folk who pass through these doors say the same thing.'

'We think it's valuable.'

'We KNOW it's valuable,' Katerina insisted.

'That's what you all say,' the pawnbroker said, unconvinced.

Katerina pulled the golden pipe from the folds of her skirt where she had been keeping it, wary of traversing the city streets with the instrument in full view.

The pawnbrokers' eyes widened. He bent forward.

'Surely not,' he remarked, 'it isn't gold?'

'It is,' I confirmed.

'Hmm ...'

He gestured toward us, suggesting we hand it over. Katerina paused a while before doing so.

He took hold of the pipe in his left hand with unnatural delicacy. Pulled out a magnifying glass from the drawer of his desk and carefully examined it from every conceivable angle, turning the instrument round and round between his fat, stubby fingers.

'Where did you get this?' he finally asked, sighing heavily.

'It's an old family heirloom,' I improvised.

'Is it really?'

We both nodded in unison, suspecting he could read the lie on our faces with ease.

'It's very old gold,' he stated. 'I have never seen such a degree of purity.'

The Master's pipe gleamed in the penumbra of the store's front office. Considering how long it had been around, it had not a hint of a scratch, every inch of its golden surface carved from the precious metal with shiny perfection.

'I don't know,' the pawnbroker said, 'it feels … looks like it should belong in a museum. Under some sort of glass case …'

Was he saying he wouldn't take it?

He gazed at us questioningly, taking in our tired appearance, our old-fashioned, simple clothing.

'What is it worth?' I asked impatiently.

He leaned back in his chair and it creaked under his weight. Paused.

Dragged his fingers around the pipe's stem.

Reflected. Then finally came to a conclusion.

'I think I would require more information about the object's provenance.'

Katerina moved forward, indicating she wanted the pipe back.

'In that case, we'll take it elsewhere. I'm confident someone else will appreciate it better …'

'Not so fast …'

He stood, stepped back to a wooden commode and picked up a small burnished copper set of scales and placed the pipe on its left plate and began to weigh it.

His eyes widened when he realised how heavy the instrument actually was.

He picked the pipe up again and set it down on the desk separating us.

'Fine, I will make you an offer, but in the absence of any precise information about the object, I will have to act in a conservative manner.'

I smiled inwardly. This was the beginning of a negotiation. And we had earlier prepared for such an eventuality.

He pulled a sheet of paper from a folder and began some calculations, probably trying to pull the wool over our eyes by sketching some imaginary arithmetic, having no doubt decided from the outset what he was willing to offer us.

This went on for ages. But we had agreed to the rules of this particular game. If anything, our centuries isolated on the Island had turned us into very patient creatures.

The silence lingered. We stood there watching him fret, our expressions neutral.

Finally, he straightened his back and looked us straight in the eyes and quoted a sum.

Unfortunately, it meant little to us, unaccustomed as we were in the new ways of the world, but we were prepared for the moment, had meticulously rehearsed how this should play out.

'That's nowhere near its true value,' I pointed out.

'Absolutely,' Katerina agreed.

The pawnbroker grinned. He had evidently played this game many times before.

We looked at each other.

'Half as much,' I stated. 'And a little non-pecuniary extra …'

His grin broadened. He knew he was close to a deal.

'Such as?'

'Documents, identity papers.'

We had previously mapped out in detail how we were going to proceed.

'That's a big ask. It's illegal.'

'We know, but when have you ever bothered with the parameters of the law, I wonder? Clocks, watches, cameras on this side of the store; might there also be weapons and such in your back room too? Not that we have any interest in any of those.'

He peered at the golden pipe again, as if assessing his options, the likely profit set off against the risks involved. We knew that a man like him would know the right people and sources to obtain the documents we would require to be able to move around freely.

Greed prevailed.

'It's a deal,' he stated. 'But it will take a few days …'

'We understand,' Katerina said. 'Oh, there's one more thing …'

He looked up at her, warily.

'We'll need a small sum to tide us by until you have all the money and the papers we desire. And, no, we will not leave the pipe with you until then. You will have to trust us. But surely you are a good judge of people, and know we will stick to the terms of our bargain.'

Had we pushed him too far?

He looked down at the floor, deep in thought, glanced one more time at the golden instrument and made up his mind.

'Agreed.' He stood and shook our hands on the deal.

His name was Magnus Christiansen.

He led us to the back room after locking the store's front door. It was a jumble of dusty properties left by their owners ages ago or long become unsaleable; he located a boxy Leica camera and took a series of photos of our faces for the false documents he would endeavour to procure. We didn't ask him how. Trust had to work both ways. Then, from a safe concealed behind a picture frame he handed us over a fistful of notes.

'That's all I have today,' he stated as he counted out the currency, in order to be able to deduct it from the principal when the final hand-over took place.

'It'll be fine,' I said. Anything was better than nothing and it was the first time we had been solvent since fleeing the colony and having to rely on petty thievery.

'I assume you don't have a telephone number where you can be contacted, so I can let you know when all will be ready?' he asked.

We didn't and, for a brief moment, I had to remind myself what a telephone even was.

It was midday by the time we left the pawnbroker's store and walked out into Hannover with a new energy in our steps.

We had already drawn up a list of priorities.

The first was to find a bed.

There was a pleasant, busy area behind the Bahnhof, albeit distant enough from it to avoid the hurly burly sounds of the trains coming and going from the station's platforms and we found a bed and breakfast establishment who were happy to provide us with a room and a roof with few questions asked. Had they demanded our documents, we had agreed to pretend they were in our luggage which had been delayed on our journey from wherever and would present them soonest. But there was no such request and we were led to a cosy, warm bedroom on the second floor at the back of the building, its window looking out on an alleyway where the opposite walls were awash with graffiti. Our landlord, a Frau Gerner, did eye us suspiciously so the first thing we did the following day after enjoying a peaceful night's sleep in an actual bed was to acquire some new, somewhat up to date clothing, to replace our outmoded peasant linen garb. At least our appearance would no longer raise eyebrows, although as we initially roamed the Hannover streets, I'd overheard some children calling us 'hippies' so we did fit in to some extent, if only as curiosities or weirdos!

Christiansen had said he would endeavour to procure the much-needed documents from a contact in Hamburg and we hadn't asked any further questions, but he had warned us that it would take at least a week to arrange. He was as eager to get his hands on the golden pipe as we were to see the colour of his money. Katerina carried it with her at all times, to avoid leaving it unprotected in our room at the B&B, in a large leather bag we had acquired from a charity store close to the train station, where we had also stocked up with other modern paraphernalia: sunglasses, some silk scarves for Katerina which she had taken an immediate liking to, baseball caps and a couple of extra pairs of jeans to vary our garb and allay curiosity about our lack of possessions.

With little else to do and not wishing to draw any undue attention to ourselves, we walked the city streets, drinking it all in, witnessing the wonders of the modern world which had only been hearsay until now, lingering in electronics stores and casting our eyes over the hitherto unimaginable objects everyone here took for granted, dragging my feet behind Katerina as she explored the busy clothing sections of department stores, her hands lingering over the many sensuous fabrics available and their rainbow of colours. Once we could afford it, she made me promise, we would buy her blouses made of silk. We had come from a drab world and this explosion of the senses was still uneasy to get accustomed to. We even visited a movie house. The film we saw was loud, full of car chases and explosions and actually rather silly, but we nonetheless stayed for two performances because of the sheer novelty of the experience. We took tea and coffee at the outside terraces of cafés or beer cellars, our taste buds slowly adapting to the new experiences so liberally available here. We even tried beer, which neither of us found in any way palatable and actually tasted quite unpleasant. There had been beer in Hamelin in distant days, but it was just something we saw our parents consume on rest days and hadn't given any particular thought to.

We had left matters with Magnus Christiansen that he would place a particular antique glass domed clock in his store window to indicate our documents had arrived, and once a day, hoping to appear as casual as we could, walked down his alley to check.

It took longer than we had expected and we daily had to refrain ourselves from entering the store to impatiently pursue the matter at hand. Aside from the fact the small amount of money he had advanced us was fast shrinking as we were learning about the cost of things in modern Germany. We were also beginning to realise that the sum we had initially agreed for the pipe with the pawnbroker would not stretch as far as we had hoped, even once we had it in our hands.

It was eleven days gone from our initial encounter and negotiation when the bric-a-brac in his shop window finally reconfigured to make place for the clock. We were both in a foul mood that morning, having argued into the small hours of night about the future and how best to survive it. Our views differed quite radically on the matter.

The pawnbroker still wore the same three-piece suit as if it were a second skin he never parted with and looked unwashed, unkempt and as unpleasant to lay eyes on as ever.

'My friends,' he said, as we walked in. Extended his hand to greet us but neither of us chose to shake it.

He glanced over at the large leather bag Katerina was holding and smiled.

'So?' I asked.

'All in good time,' Christiansen said and led us to his back room after locking the store's front door and switching round an Open/Closed sign attached to the glass. He switched the light on, a thin neon tube precariously hanging from the low ceiling, flickering initially as if had been asleep for a while and was only now getting accustomed to do its job.

Opening the wall safe, he pulled out a bulky dirt brown envelope and handed us a pair of identity cards and passports each.

We were now Rutger Rucker and Marta Ewers. We were from the Netherlands. Not that we spoke a word of Dutch and had no intention of doing so. We had taught ourselves to speak English back on the Island, almost as a game, to while away the hours, although we knew we probably still had strong accents. There is an abyss between the written page and the movements of the tongue and there had been no one to correct our no doubt many mistakes.

Neither of us were enamoured with our new identities, but we had little say in the matter. It was a necessary step to our survival here, and we both knew who we really were anyway.

The documents appeared genuine for all we knew, stamped with official-looking patterns in ink and with blurry, unflattering photographs of our own faces peering out of us from the opening pages.

'They're good. Professional standard,' Christiansen assured us. 'Good enough to cross borders with no questions asked.'

'If you say so.'

Until this very moment it had never crossed our thoughts that we might ever want to travel to another country. As it was Lower Saxony was now strange enough. But I could see on Katerina's face that the fact had registered as it had with me. The further we moved away, the better our chances of eluding possible pursuit by the Master, we believed. Our naivety equalled our ignorance.

'So?'

She dragged up the muslin bag in which she had been carrying the golden pipe, pulled the instrument out and handed it over to the pawnbroker. A wide grin swept across his features.

He cautiously held it in his palms, feeling its uncommon weight, rightly assessing we hadn't made a switch and it was the same golden object we had offered him in the first place.

'Excellent.'

It felt strange, as if a final link to our past was being sundered.

'I think I already have a client for it,' he continued.

'You have to pay us first.'

'Of course.'

While hanging around the city waiting for today's transaction to finally take place, we had already clearly established the fact that the sum we had agreed to take in exchange for the pipe was quite insufficient. We thought we had struck a good bargain, but it was far from the case. We now knew if would barely tide us over for four to six months, depending on our expenditure. Life was expensive. We would have to come up with another form of income stream down the line.

Magnus Christiansen handed over a couple of rolls of banknotes, held tight together with elastic bands. We didn't even bother to count them.

As we walked away from his store, it began to rain, a thin curtain of drops was spreading across the city as we moved away in the shadow of the massive cathedral towards our room at the bed and breakfast on Müllerstrasse.

Our first dilemma now that we were solvent was to decide whether to remain there or find a somewhat less spartan place to stay; maybe a hotel?

The rain quickened and we took temporary refuge inside a beer cellar that offered us a temporary harbour halfway to our destination. We sat sipping coffees, one of our new indulgences. Another was cigarettes, me more than Katerina. We had smoked herbs back in the colony but tobacco was so much more powerful and satisfying.

'What about moving to another country, as far away as we can manage?' Katerina asked. She still woke up several times every night in fear of the Piper tracking us down. I was less convinced that distance would make much of a difference.

'Why not?'

There was nothing to keep us back in Hannover, in what had now become Germany. When you are centuries old, almost immortal, there is no place for sentimentality.

We began our planning.

Even though we were unaware of it, at that very same moment a tall, thin if not cadaveric man was knocking at the door of the pawnbroker's shop.

'I think you now have it,' he told Christiansen.

'Indeed I have, and a beautiful object it is. Rightly deserves to be in a glass showcase in a museum, if you ask my opinion. The way the instrument has been carved out of the finest gold is a joy to behold.'

'I know,' the stranger said. 'It was mine. They stole it.'

The pawnbroker swallowed hard, worried his visitor was taking umbrage, might be about to blame him for the alleged theft, maybe pull away from the deal and not pay him the sum agreed.

The stranger noticed his discomfort and waved at him to dismiss his worried thoughts. He burrowed inside the pocket of his voluminous cape and pulled out a sack and slid it over the table to Christiansen.

'Just as agreed,' he said.

The pawnbroker heaved a sigh of relief. And pulled the sack to his side of the table, and passed over the golden pipe. He had a lot of questions, but knew they would not be answered. The contents of the sack were enough to make a large profit on the mysterious transaction and he would file the whole thing away to memory. In his occupation, you knew when to remain silent and curtail your curiosity.

There was an aura about the bearded stranger who was reclaiming the pipe, as if he wasn't quite there. It was difficult to pin down.

In the blink of an eye, he was gone, fading into the rain.

The pawnbroker locked the door to his store. It had been a most unusual day.

By then we had reached our room. The rain had been unceasing, buffeted by a rising wind from the east and we were soaked to the bone.

We undressed. I dried my hair and looked at my face in the mirror of the miniscule bathroom. I was the same as ever but then there was a difference, a weariness, something I couldn't pinpoint. Katerina was in the shower and through the plastic curtain, I could guess at the voluptuous contours of her body as she moved around. I thought she was growing more beautiful by the day since we had escaped from the Island. I peered again at my face. Was I growing older? Would we eventually be capable of dying on this side of the worlds? Once it had been something we could but dream of but maybe now that we were no longer in the clutches of the Piper's curse we had become mortal?

In which case, we still had a lot we wanted to do before fate caught up with us.

5

We boarded the aircraft in Berlin mid-morning. It was the first test for our false documents. The uniformed airline staff at check-in didn't bat an eyelid nor did the glass-eyed border control officials. There would be a further possible challenge on arrival in Paris, but we were gingerly taking matters one single step at a time.

We had a single piece of luggage each, nowhere near the weight limit we were allowed. They contained all our belongings. Mostly clothing we had acquired over the past months to make us fit in better into the world of 1984. A couple of slacks, some jeans, a handful of shirts, an assortment of spare underwear, toiletries for me. Katerina had more: silk blouses, pencil skirts – in which she looked just stunning, in the way her curves and angles espoused the fashion of the day – some dresses in colourful patterns, make-up, high heel shoes, a shapeless NYU sweatshirt she had taken a liking to and trainers, lingerie and a handful of cheap and cheerful clip-on earrings she had been accumulating.

I carried the rest of our money in the inside pocket of my denim jacket. I was nervous we might be searched at some point in the journey and would be unable to account precisely for its origins, even though there was now so much less of it than the sum we had extracted from the pawnbroker. It sort of melted away, not that we were spendthrift, just the cost of necessities in our new day to day existence having taken its toll. Hotels weren't cheap either, but renting an apartment had proven too much of a problem, as we had no proper references to show to prospective landlords or housing associations.

Katerina was nervous. So was I. The idea of flying miles high in the sky over the land was a frightening prospect, almost more than the magic we had lived through and experienced. It didn't feel normal.

She held my hand tight as we were seated. I relinquished my allocated aisle seat to her as she felt claustrophobic being squeezed in between the corpulent businessman who sat by the window and me. We swapped around and I was assaulted by the strong smell of his aftershave. He never spoke to me once during the journey, concentrating on his paperwork full of figures. Our hearts jumped as the aircraft took off and our throats went dry but we quickly accustomed ourselves to the odd sensation of flying. It wasn't a long journey and by the time we approached the Paris airport, Katerina's grip on my fingers was more relaxed.

We had prepared for this journey like studying for an exam, spending many hours in the Hannover Central Library researching ways of making money for the coming day when our cash would eventually run out, learning more about the modern world's particularities and arcane workings, taking copious notes and arguing endlessly at night in our room about the multitude of options that would present themselves to us.

The initial thing we had agreed on is that we would not remain in Germany. We needed a new start and it would have to elsewhere, as far as possible from that remote valley in Lower Saxony and its invisible portal that still in our minds connected us to the past. And the Master.

Almost every day as we walked outside the hotel, both of us still felt his presence, imagining he was following us, that his shadow would appear around the next corner at any moment, that he would suddenly sit himself at the next table when we were having our coffees. We felt his wrath. We feared it.

We had decided on the French capital. There was a touch of glamour about it, Katerina argued, which might serve us well. Since we were in the real world, she had come to the realisation that she was indeed beautiful. We saw other women and, true, many were attractive but Katerina had a form of otherness, of mystery. There was no mistaking it and the surreptitious looks of other men in the street as we walked by was unmistakable.

'I could model,' she suggested. 'It's reputed to be rather

lucrative.'

It would also increase our visibility, I pointed out, something we were trying to avoid. And I was becoming more and more uncomfortable at the way men looked at her, even though she did nothing to attract their attention in her regular attire of jeans and T-shirts. It was the way she walked, unprovocative but hard to ignore, her hips undulating in a gentle swivel with every step, her head held high, her eyes alight with the fire of our secrets.

Paris, she convinced me, would offer all the right opportunities.

I reluctantly agreed, unable to offer any better alternative.

I had read about New Orleans across the ocean in America and there was something about that city that drew me to it in odd ways, but it would have been a longer and much more expensive journey.

We retrieved our two pieces of matching luggage from the arrival's carrousel. Passed through immigration with no questions asked and opted to travel to the city by public transport rather than a taxi, having sensibly agreed to ration our remaining cash as much as we could until we found out how expensive the city would prove to be.

The hotel we had booked in advance had only three stars and was situated on the Left Bank on a narrow street that rose from the Boulevard Saint Germain and climbed in a semi-straight line all the way to the Jardin du Luxembourg. Rue Monsieur le Prince. The hotel's lift was barely large enough to accommodate the two of us if we held the suitcases between our legs. The room was small and its only window looked across the tiled roofs of the surrounding buildings and dark wooden beams crisscrossed its ceiling. It was half the size of our room at the B&B back in Germany.

'For what they are charging, I expected something larger,' I remarked.

Katerina sighed.

'And breakfast is not even included …'

We had somehow hoped that we could stuff ourselves at a

morning breakfast buffet and save on midday meals.

'We'll have to find some work.'

'I'm sure I could wait tables or something of the sort.'

Manual work was all I could aspire to. I had no qualifications or technical knowledge.

For a brief moment, I regretted our journey from the Island. But then so many questions would have remained unanswered and gnawed away at our brain. All the countless what ifs. But, surely, there must be another way? There should be more to life, regardless of where we were.

She was right. She was offered a job waitressing at the first place she visited with a 'for hire' sign displayed in its window. It was an old-fashioned but popular brasserie situated halfway between St Germain and Montparnasse. She had the right looks. She was different from most of the French women. Exotic, long-legged, unfathomable in an enigmatic way.

I was less successful. I had no practical experience when they asked about my previous work and there was no point in lying as I would be easily found out on the first day of any job.

But her wages and tips barely covered the daily cost of our hotel room, while I spent my days wandering through the city, familiarising myself with its quirks and how each different *quartier* seemed to have a personality of its own. I rationed myself to no more than two coffees a day at random café terraces and whiled away the hours, frustrated by the fact that we were standing still, not achieving anything. Coming to the realisation that the lack of currency on the Island had its virtues, something we had taken for granted.

Katerina returned most days in a foul mood, angry at the rudeness of some customers and the unceasing sexual advances she was the object of.

'They just see my body,' she said. 'That's all. Just a potential fuck. Some of them disgust me. Never in a cluster of centuries would I sleep with any of them. Even if they paid …'

'Have any of them actually offered money?' I asked, out of curiosity.

'Not openly. But there have certainly been heavy hints.'

'Bastards.'

'Swine. Maybe I should make you pay for it, Tristan,' she suggested with a broad, mischievous smile.

'That would be highly problematic as I'm the one with no earning power …'

'Hmm …'

That brief exchange planted a seed in her mind.

The following morning, she broached the subject. I was taken aback.

'If they're willing to pay for my body, maybe I should oblige …'

'Whore yourself?'

'Not technically.'

'What do you mean, not technically? Either you sleep with them or you don't.'

The idea revolted me. It took a sledgehammer to my feelings. How could she even think of it? The grin on her face as she calmly evoked the possibility aggravated my growing unease.

'Don't you see?'

'What?' My anger was rising, how could she even think this, bring it up in my presence?

'I could take the money but not sleep with them.'

'How?'

'Let's think of ways …'

This was a side of Katerina I never knew had existed. Or was the new world changing her? Helping her to see that all was not black and white, but could be painted in various shades of grey.

Over a croissant and café au lait, we began to consider the situation, the realistic prospects.

'It can't be with men who frequent the brasserie. They would know where to find you later.'

'I agree. So where do I meet them? It's not as if I can put an ad in the newspaper, and I'm not standing on a street corner in Rue St Denis or the Halles like a common prostitute, advertising my wares in all sorts of weather.'

'Somewhere social where you can attract them like bees to honey,' I suggested.

We occasionally visited some of the jazz cellars around the rue de la Huchette, around from the Saint Séverin church. It wasn't so much the music that attracted us but the smoky, shady atmosphere and the warming camaraderie of the small crowds packing the low-ceilinged clubs.

Yes, that might prove a worthwhile hunting ground.

Not without trepidation, the following Saturday night when Katerina had her first full week-end off from work, we journeyed towards the Seine and the cluster of small streets just a stone's throw from the river where packed couscous restaurants and kebab joints disgorged smells of food and aromatic spices and the jazz clubs and experimental theatres coexisted side by side.

It was still early evening, and easy to find an empty table in the dimly-lit cellar. We ordered a round of drinks and rehearsed once more how we hoped our plan might pan out. The clink of glasses was louder than the distant music being piped through the speakers dotting the walls. Apart from a piano and a few music stands, the stage was empty. The musicians never began their first set until well past ten.

Soon the place began to fill up and before it did so, I left Katerina alone at a low circular table and installed myself on a high stool at the bar, from which vantage point I could observe her.

Cigarette smoke rose slowly like a low-flying cloud towards the cellar's red brick ceiling as the customers puffed away as if there was no tomorrow and the sound of their voices blanketed the enclosed space. A couple of men approached Katerina's table and asked if they could join her. She politely declined. There was no way we could handle more than one. Two would have proven enormously risky on all fronts. They shrugged and stepped away to one of the stone alcoves carved into the walls of the club.

There weren't many free seats left by the time the band trooped onto the stage, first the youthful-looking pianist, a black trumpet player and a hirsute stand-up bass player with red hair, dragging his voluminous instrument along.

Just as the pianist lowered his fingers to the keyboard with an exaggerated flourish to get the set underway, a slender man in his forties, wearing a black suit and an open-necked white button-down shirt made his way down the stairs and rapidly glanced around and spotted the available seat next to Katerina. He decisively moved towards it and over the opening arpeggios said something to her. She nodded back and he sat himself down.

The trumpet joined in while the double bass punctuated the rhythm and I could no longer hear anything but the music, although I saw by now that Katerina and the man were engaged in a full-blown conversation. Her smile was patently insincere but the stranger appeared to ignore the tell. He waved at the barman and a bottle of champagne was brought to their table and they began drinking while continuing their sotto voce dialogue.

By the end of the first set by the jazz combo whose retreads of familiar tunes had sounded much too discordant and hurried to me, the thin man's fingers had already ventured across her knees, encouraged by the fact she had not rebuffed him.

Even though the music had temporarily ended, the tumult of conversations in the enclosed space of the cellar was louder than ever and I was unable to catch any snippets of their exchanges. They both were leaning across the table in a semblance of intimacy, casually sipping from heir tall-stemmed glasses. He'd been hooked.

We had nervously rehearsed all this for days.

Time ticked away ever so slowly for me, as my stomach tightened at the prospect of what might occur next.

It was around midnight when the musicians returned to the stage. Just as they manoeuvred their way through the narrow gap between the club's tables and customers, Katerina and her suitor rose. I swiftly moved away from the bar and made a beeline for the stairs and was waiting outside on the Rue de la Huchette, just ten or so metres away from the cellar's exit onto the cobbled street, in a prime position to observe them. And then follow them. They were deep in conversation. Katerina shook her head quite vehemently on several occasions, as the man pleaded with her, his hands moving to her shoulder by way of encouragement.

He was either suggesting she follow him to his apartment or suggesting they visit a hotel, I guessed. Neither of which opportunity would suit the plan we had set out.

Finally, by the time they reached the open space of the Place Saint Michel, he shrugged, took her hand into his and they crossed the road leading to the Quai and the Seine.

I followed, fifty metres away. It was a warm night even though the moon was partly obscured by low banks of clouds.

They reached the Pont Neuf and he pulled her towards him and kissed her. She allowed it. I swallowed hard, watching them embrace from a short distance, bodies pressed tight against each other. It was necessary. He had to agree to take the steps down to the Ile de la Cité, whose western promontory ended below, beyond the small garden and its shelter of trees.

Did his lips taste different from mine, I wondered? How was she feeling right now?

It felt like ages, but they soon parted as she indicated the stone stairs leading below. Still holding hands they ventured down. My heart skipped a beat and I rushed forward to follow them.

The darkness was the colour of ink and I could barely make out their silhouettes further down towards the tip of the peninsula-like extremity of the Ile de la Cité, just Katerina's long pale hair fluttering down her back like a fading light in the nearby distance. Water lapped against the stone slabs of the embankment.

The couple reached the triangular trip of the thin strip of land. There was a wooden bench where they sat down. His hands were now all over her. Slipping inside her dress, another pulling her hair back.

Was it a struggle or an embrace? Now was not the time to speculate.

I tiptoed towards them. The moon suddenly peered out from behind a cloud, and I saw the older man had his back to me, his arms busily attempting to part her from her top, her face was buried in his shoulders, looking towards me, her eyes cloudy with tears, begging me to intervene urgently.

I reached them. Even though I was treading lightly, he heard my steps and looked up in surprise.

'Fuck off, man. Just mind your own business,' he shouted out, in English, warning me away. Just another tourist, like us. Led astray. The blind leading the blind!

I stood still, not moving an inch.

I pulled out the kitchen knife we had bought together a week ago at the local Monoprix on the corner of Boulevard Raspail from my coat pocket.

The moment he saw the weapon he pulled himself away from Katerina, defensive, visibly scared.

Katerina, now free, moved behind him and placed the tip of the pen knife she had been concealing in her handbag, against the back of his neck.

'Fuck!' he repeated himself. 'What do you want? I haven't done anything to her, man …'

Yet.

'Just your money,' she whispered in his ear as I stood menacingly brandishing the knife in his face.

He looked deflated, offered no resistance, and promptly handed over his wallet.

I heaved a massive sigh of relief. I had never fought anyone in my whole, rather lengthy life and had dreaded the prospect.

We ordered him to sit, and tied his hands together with a length of string we had brought along. Ordered him not to move for at least ten minutes and fled the scene flushed with excitement at having pulled it off.

We lost ourselves in the labyrinth of narrow, dark streets surrounding the Ecole des Beaux Arts, constantly checking if we were being followed and in a roundabout way finally reached our hotel.

Out of breath from climbing the stairs, as the elevator was

once again out of order, we locked ourselves inside our room, sat on the bed, allowed ourselves a nervous laugh and opened the American's wallet.

He'd carried so little cash. Barely a thousand francs and sixty six dollars. The credit cards, we knew, were of no use to us.

The whole farrago had not been worth the damn risk. It appeared that criminality was not our forte. In addition, the whole St Michel and Saint Séverin area would now have to be avoided in the near future, in case our American victim had reported the event to the police. The area's sported an attractive plethora of cheap eateries, so we hadn't done ourselves any favours. There had to be another way.

Katerina stayed on at her waitressing job at the brasserie and I began enquiring about some form of employment where, like her, I wouldn't be subject to too many questions, due to our foreign status in France and lack of genuine documentation.

The money we had left from the sale of the Master's pipe was about to run out, putting us on the street, with no means to afford our hotel room or anything much else, when luck fell our way.

An elegant woman dining at the brasserie one evening was struck by Katerina's looks and bone structure and happened to be a genuine model agency booker and, on the spot, offered her a photo-shoot the following week. Her name was Christiane and she was the booker for a model agency with lavish offices by the Bastille. Not only did Katerina enjoy the day, but both the photographer and stylist at the studio, also fell in love with her potential and she was offered a slew of other shoots. She was paid every hour what previously took up a fortnight of waitressing, including tips, and we were saved from destitution.

It put me in an awkward position as the half of our couple who wasn't earning any money, but the situation didn't faze Katerina in the slightest. I kept on looking and, finally, was offered a menial post in a financial agency near the Bourse, where my work mostly consisted of checking long columns of profit and loss figures with a handheld calculator and much filing of folders, papers, files and documents.

Within three months, as our way of life hadn't changed much despite our now earning decent wages, we had saved enough money to leave our three-star hotel and rent a tiny furnished studio near Censier-Daubenton, a stone's throw away from the Latin Quarter.

Having lived so long on the Island, patience was certainly one of the virtues we possessed in abundance and we began looking forward to what life in this brand-new world had in store for us.

6

She was somewhat reluctant to accept the gig.

I disagreed.

'It's such an opportunity,' I argued. 'And the pay is incredible. Your most lucrative booking ever …'

'But it's in Germany,' Katerina protested.

'So what?'

'I don't want to go back.'

'You have a Dutch passport, another name altogether. It must surely be safe by now.'

'But what if he …?'

'The chances of his coming across you are infinitesimal,' I insisted. 'Anyway,' I continued, 'I have no doubt that if he genuinely was seeking us, he would know exactly where we are. He has the power, we both know that. Look, it's been almost a year since we fled, and have we seen any sign of him? We're nothing to him.'

'We stole his magic pipe,' Katerina added. 'We must have mightily angered him. Christiane and the agency won't mind if I don't take the job; I can just pretext I am unwell that week.'

Would we ever be allowed to forget our past?

We debated for days on end and, somehow, I convinced Katerina it would be good for her to go to Cologne and participate in the catwalk show the Parisian design house was organising to present their winter collection for German chainstore buyers. It wasn't a high-profile event, so unlikely to attract undue attention outside the small circle of prêt-à-porter fashionistas.

She flew out, with her agent Christiane, and half a dozen other models signed up to the same agency.

For the first time since our escape, I was going to be alone for a handful of days. It was a strange sensation, being adrift in a foreign city, although I reasoned every place we had been since that fateful day when she had brought the pipe to her lips had been alien to us in so many ways, as we were to the world we presently inhabited and probably didn't belong to.

I paced across our sparsely furnished room, with just a sofa bed which unrolled at night, a small commode, a desk, and a scattering of bookshelves in which I was rapidly accumulating random volumes I was finding in the boxes of the *bouquinistes* on the *quais* by the river, an art-deco lamp which barely illuminated the chiaroscuro of the studio, with its one window looking out onto an inside garden which was more full of pebbles than grass.

I couldn't seem to concentrate on anything. Thinking of Katerina sharing some lavish hotel suite with three or four other willowy models at the Cologne Sheraton, wondering what she in turn might be thinking. Of me? Possibly not, as she was likely in thrall to her first evening of being apart from me in ages. I was restless. And frustrated.

At work that afternoon, I had come across various investment folders outlining opportunities when stocks of certain companies had recently gone public. When I came across a reference to an American tech company called Apple, it had rung a bell. I remembered that in years to come the people there would develop computers and other technologies which would have a major influence on tomorrow's world. I also recalled reading about the coming 2020 Covid 19 pandemic. Then there was another American company called Amazon which would come to revolutionise retail, the deaths of a number of well-known people, a deadly tsunami in Asia and countless wars and localised conflicts dotted across the whole globe. I knew well in advance of the rise to power of all too many politicians who were right now still relatively unknown. Placing bets on some of these blips of history still to come but known to me through the capricious winds of time that had landed us in 1984 might generate some capital, but on the other hand it might also attract unwanted attention. I still didn't fully understand how the stock market and shares worked, but reasoned that acquiring some shares in one of these technology companies might reap favourable dividends in the future, although when to cash in might prove problematic. I resolved to do so, although I was also aware that it would be some years before they could be sold again at a good profit. But time was on our side, I reckoned.

I did so the following day, to the surprise of my French colleagues in the financial agency who harboured serious doubts about the sanity of the investment in the belief that IBM would forever continue to dominate the market. Another company who would soon make their mark on the evolving world was in Seattle in the USA, called Microsoft, but right now there was no evidence their stock was even available. It would be in two years, I subsequently found out.

I was kept awake at night trying to recall the exact shade of Katerina's eyes, the subtle, elegant geometry of her cheekbones, the precise sound of her orgasms, the way she often pursed her lips when she was annoyed, the unmistakeable accent she couldn't hide when she spoke French to others in my presence; people always guessed it must be Russian, rather than German or Dutch, a confusion that made us smile.

A silent movie unspooling at the back of my mind of the tangling of our limbs between the sheets, the searing heat of moving inside her, the silences we shared that were worth a thousand words.

Damn, one night apart and I missed her so much.

So, was this what love meant?

As the years had slowly gone by back on the Island, us children, whether we were growing older or not, had grown accustomed to an indifferent form of casualness in our relationships. But on this side of the fence, everything just felt stronger, more vital, urgent.

I could no longer think of life without her, however many days, years, possibly centuries life now might mean. I wanted to explore that hopefully glorious future with Katerina at my side, to the extent that my stomach tied itself up in knots at the thought.

We spoke daily on the phone, but somehow our tongues were tied, unaccustomed as we were to communicating in this manner.

'By the time I get back to the hotel, I am exhausted. You wouldn't think modelling clothes would be so tiring, but somehow it's always a rush, having our make-up done, the garments adjusted before we parade down the catwalk and then back again to change and again ...'

I told her about my idea of investing in the American company's shares.

'But it will be years, I guess, until the value increases enough for us to benefit from them.'

'It's a good idea,' she readily agreed.

It was the next morning as I walked to my place of work on the Right Bank, crossing the Seine and emerging on the Place du Chatelet that I experienced the feeling I was being followed or closely watched.

Passing the Palladian facade of the theatre and its white arcades, I swiftly turned my head but the sparse crowd appeared no different than usual. No one stood out. I continued forward, opting to journey down the wide sidewalks of the Boulevard de Sébastopol, rather than through the Halles, which was my normal itinerary.

On a number of occasions, I took the opportunity to glance behind me but couldn't spot anything out of the norm.

But still that menacing sensation lingered all the way to the suite of offices where I worked.

My immediate thought was, naturally, that the Piper, our Master, had finally caught up with us and the first thing that came to mind was an urgent impulse to somehow contact Katerina in Cologne to warn her and suggest she not return. If someone had to pay for our transgressions, I'd rather it was me and Katerina was spared.

The day unfolded slowly, fuelled by my anxiety and a lack of attention to the intricacies of the reams of paperwork I was processing.

I ate at my desk, having asked one of our prim middle-aged secretaries to fetch me a sandwich from one of the many stalls and cafés in the immediate vicinity. I forgot to ask her to get me a beverage, so had to content myself with water from the bathroom tap. I hated water; it just had no taste. Ironic, considering the fact that we had all survived on the Island on just water; no coffees, tea, juices or soft drinks. In this respect, the modern world presented such a wonderful embarrassment of available drinks. How easily we are spoilt!

On the journey back home, the feeling had evaporated, although the crowds on the Paris streets were now larger and pinpointing a specific, interested onlooker would have proven even more problematic.

I arrived back at our studio apartment and knew within seconds that someone had been there in my absence. Nothing was visibly missing, nor was the equilibrium of the place disturbed or vandalised in any way. Nor was there a sign of a break-in.

But a book had been left on our small circular table that had not been there previously. A volume that had not been part of our growing collection.

An encyclopedia of mermaids.

Past the shock of the intrusion, I experienced a prolonged period of puzzlement. Left the book siting there, nervous about even picking it up at this stage.

What sort of message was this? Or a threat?

I gingerly picked the volume up. The book was not new, its spine cracked in places, its pages yellowed by prolonged exposure to light. I hastily leafed through it, checking for any inserts, messages, annotations. There were none. Just a common second-hand volume.

Was there a clue in the content?

I fixed myself some toast and coffee and began leafing through the book's pages.

Legends, myths, sailor's tales, fairy tales, a flourish of fascinating illustrations going back to the years of early antiquity through to the present, mermaids in art and, later, the movies, speculations, a dash of actual history, it was all here and the book didn't restrict itself to actual mermaids, encompassing in scholarly ways mermen -which I had never read about before – and all varieties of other bizarre sea creatures.

All in all, it was fascinating and I immersed myself in the pages with an open mind and not a touch of curiosity, but still couldn't fathom why it had been left in our studio apartment and by who?

It just made no sense.

I was briefly of a mind to contact Katerina in Germany, but decided against it; felt no need to worry her unnecessarily.

And, inevitably, that night in bed, I dreamed repeatedly of the sea and the mysteries of its faraway depths until I was drowning in an avalanche of questions.

The following day, I somehow completed my work at the office in a daze, worried, nervous and unable to concentrate fully on my tasks. Katerina was due back in 48 hours and it occurred to me that she hadn't called me the previous evening, as she had done on earlier nights apart. I'd been too busy racing through the book of mermaids to register the fact.

I would phone her as soon as I was back home.

It was rainy, grey skies gliding silently across the Paris roofs like a movie in slow motion. I was soaked by the time I reached our door on the second floor of the building.

A quick glance at the room showed no signs of change, or further enigmatic books.

I slipped out of my wet coat and kicked off my shoes.

Dialled the number for the hotel in Cologne.

Asked for the room she was staying in.

A voice with a pronounced Italian accent picked up. 'Giulia speaking.'

'It's Rutger, Marta's partner. Can I speak to her, please? I'm calling from Paris.'

'She not here.'

'Is she out?'

'Yes, don't you know?'

'What do you mean?'

'Two hours ago, after the final show, you come to pick her up and go special dinner.'

'What?'

'She spend evening with you.'

'You must be confused.'

'No, no, *e vero* ...'

It made no sense. I asked the Italian model if I could speak to Christiane, the agency booker. We'd met briefly on a couple of occasions. She was staying in another room, but it was on the same floor at the Sheraton and Giulia agreed to fetch her.

'*Bonsoir* Rutger. Is there a problem?'

'I wanted to speak to Marta. Something important.'

'Where are you?'

'Back in Paris, of course.'

'You must be joking, no?'

'Not at all, why?'

'We saw you earlier today. You came to fetch Marta at the studio where we were doing the shoot. I was surprised you even knew where we were working, as the location had changed at the last minute. Said you wanted it to be a surprise and swept Marta away for some celebratory dinner. I thought it was so cute. Romantic and all that ...'

I was speechless.

'Rutger, are you alright? Is Marta OK?'

My throat was dry with a mounting wave of apprehension rising up from my stomach, tightening my chest, paralysing my limbs.

'I don't know,' was all I could mutter. 'You're certain it was me?' I asked. 'You've only come across me so casually. Maybe you confused me with someone else?' Who?

'Not at all, Rutger. I know what you look like; actually, you have striking looks. You and Marta make a lovely couple and I've often thought of pairing the both of you up if the right sort of work came along. Anyway, Marta knew it was you. She was so pleased to see you.'

If I kept on asking more questions, she would think I had gone mad. I mumbled some apologies and put the phone down.

I was unable to sleep that night, tossing and turning between the bed covers, a touch feverish as my imagination turned uglier and uglier by the minute. First thing in the morning, I rang the Cologne Sheraton again and asked for the models' room. Again, it was Giulia who picked up.

'She not come back.'

'It's impossible,' I protested.

'I not understand,' the Italian girl said. 'Why you phoning as Marta with you.'

I knew all too well that I had been in Paris the previous day and night and not been anywhere near Cologne, let alone taken Katerina out for dinner.

Something bad was afoot, and I was totally helpless to do anything about it.

Katerina never returned to the room where she had been staying with other models. The team returned to Paris without her the following day. Christiane and I spoke on a couple of occasions that week, but there was a definite hint of suspicion in her voice. She was familiar with the often capricious nature of models and was more annoyed than angry at Katerina's –or Marta as she knew her – disappearance. Chalked the experience off to some possible lover's quarrel and had no intention of delving into it further. On the final occasion we spoke, she reminded me that Katerina's fee for the Cologne shoots was still owed to her and whether I wished to receive it, but I turned the opportunity down.

Our studio apartment felt like an immense desert of emptiness and absence for the months that followed. I worked at the financial agency like an automaton, pouring through my memory for every single word Katerina had said in all the days since we had escaped the clutches of the Piper's Island, hoping for a clue, some form of explanation, but it felt as if my thoughts were stumbling through a dark and foggy labyrinth with no port of call in sight.

A year went by.

I held on as best I could to my memories of her, treasured all those remembered moments when we were still Tristan and Katerina as if I were in mourning.

But I never heard from her again. No letter, phone call, hint. Why was she punishing me in this cruel way? What had I done wrong?

There were days of pain when I imagined she was back on the Island, walking naked along the beach, the orbs of her regal arse in perfect harmony with her languid movement through the sand, her long hair pouring down her back like a stream of silk, catching the rays of the sun, feeding from their sensuous warmth.

But I knew I couldn't return there. I no longer had the pipe.

On impulse, one day, I rang Hannover, having found the telephone number of Magnus, the pawnbroker's store, but the number had been disconnected. I doubted anyway he still had it, remembered him mentioning he had the perfect client lined up.

I now felt like a stowaway in a strange land. Lost without my anchor.

Time passed.

Memory turned to absence. Absence turned to memory.

Although I knew I had little in common with the people I worked with or occasionally met, I made an effort to fit, socialised a little, adapted. Did I have any other choice?

I read a lot, accumulated books, borrowed assiduously from my local *bibliothèque municipale*, browsed at leisure through second-hand stalls. Reading had long been my favourite activity anyway, aside from my worship of Katerina's body and similarly inquisitive mind.

It was a weekend in the summer of 1986 and I was sitting in mid-afternoon at the terrace of a café facing the Pompidou Centre. Paris had emptied of residents and tourists were swarming across the city. My sickly-sweet grenadine syrup and lemonade shone scarlet in my half full glass and I was reading F Scott Fitzgerald's *Tender is the Night* in a used Penguin paperback edition I had picked up in an English-language bookstore near Odéon.

'Wow, that's a great novel, really is!'

I looked around at the young woman sitting at the next table who had just taken notice of the book I was reading. She was in her mid-20s, wearing a Grateful Dead T-shirt and skin-tight jeans, her nose was perky, her hair auburn and cut pageboy style, she was freckled and her lips displayed a muted scarlet hue that had no need for added lipstick. Our eyes met. Hers were a striking shade of hazelnut brown.

She smiled as I acknowledged her presence.

'Have you read his other novels?' she continued. '*Gatsby*, *This Side Of Paradise* ... I've read every single one several times. I was born in Saint Paul, the same as he was, so I sort of identify with him, you know ...'

I introduced myself. As Tristan. What was the point of lying to an attractive stranger?

'Are you also visiting?'

'No, I've now been in Paris for a few years. Now working here. Although I'm thinking of moving somewhere else soon.' Which was true, but I hadn't made up my mind as to a possible destination.

'Really, that's wonderful. If only I could I would live here forever. It's such a beautiful and exciting place. But I only have four weeks left before I have to return to the States.'

She was an art student in Paris on a summer internship at the Musée d'Orsay.

We fell into conversation. It was a long time since I had interacted in any significant way with anyone, aside from my work colleagues, so being able to dialogue at length with someone else was a pleasant experience. Her name was April Dawn, and despite her Minnesota roots she now lived in New Orleans. Which triggered my curiosity.

My answers and questions were initially a touch abbreviated but I quickly got into the rhythm of the dialogue. April Dawn was voluble enough for two anyway. I hadn't read any of

Fitzgerald's other books, so she made it her duty to describe them in detail. I loved her infectious enthusiasm. It made me want to read them as soon as I had the opportunity.

Evening happened much too quickly. Reluctant to go our own ways, we agreed to prolong our encounter by eating together. I introduced her to Polidor on Rue Monsieur Le Prince, an old-fashioned working man's restaurant which only accepted cash and specialised in traditional country dishes among its extensive menu. She was determined to try snails, dripping in garlic and parsley. I was not as adventurous.

I walked her back close to midnight to the Ecole des Beaux-Arts dormitory where she was lodging and she pecked me on the cheek, French-style, a custom I had hitherto studiously avoided since I'd been in Paris, finding it too intimate despite its outward casualness. We agreed to meet the following day, Sunday; somehow the subject of the Vincennes Zoo had come up in our conversation and though I had no sympathy whatsoever for pets and animals, I agreed we should visit together.

In a clearing in the forest that bordered the zoo, on Sunday night, she moved closer to me, took a firm grip of my hand, raised herself on her toes and kissed me. Her breath smelled of mint.

PART TWO

Katerina in the Underground

'Beautiful women are easier to follow, as a rule, because they
expect to be watched. Men's eyes are sunlight on their skin.'
Leo Benedictus, *Consent*

7

'Marta, you're needed on set now …' one of the runners cried out, his face peering through the half open door to the starkly lit and crowded side room where we changed our outfits and had our make-up done.

I hated the name. Couldn't relate to it. Missed being called by my real name. Unless, it was Tristan, of course. My partner in crime.

Strange to think that we had known each other since we were children. And now we were lovers.

Or, as he called himself now, Rutger. Another stupid name.

Maybe we could legally change back to our old names? I'd heard it was possible. And inexpensive.

I adjusted the thin leather belt of the beige linen trousers I was modelling one extra notch, and instinctively smoothed down the matching shirt it was assorted with. For the past couple of days, the other two girls and I had been working on the fall collection for a top of the range Italian chain store. It had begun with the filming of a fake catwalk presentation which after careful editing would be cut into a television ad and now we were finally coming to the end of the actual photography for the retailer's catalogue. I was still wearing the uncomfortable high heels which had come with my earlier outfit, an evening dress which had felt like a second skin and was reminded to change into a pair of flat and shiny ballet shoes whose colour-coded sticker matched them up with my present casual wear.

I pushed the door fully open and moved into the actual studio, where the overhead lighting bathed the set in a curtain of shimmering heat.

'You look wonderful, dear. That suits you so well,' the photographer said, as one of his assistants held a light meter up to me with an air of concern. He said the same to all of us and reacted likewise to every single outfit we wore. His way of gaining our confidence maybe.

I was directed to the unfurled white background sheet against which I was to be photographed and he began clicking away, as we played out the slow motion ballet we had danced so many times already, he barking instructions, directing my movements as he stepped like a running dervish from foot to foot, juggling cameras, angling for the best view or composition.

My mind switched off as I redirected myself to automatic pilot. Other photographers I'd worked with back in Paris had often used music on their set, which was more inspiring, while Hans preferred silence and the sound of his own, insincere words. To be fair, Hans was generally undemanding and seldom got angry if I or any of my model companions from Christiane's agency mistook his stream of instructions and spoiled the ideal shot he had in mind. Others had been more temperamental and insulting, so I reckon it was a compromise between the ease and fluency of modelling to music or the risk of being treated like cattle.

I was trying to remember the tune I had improvised on the pipe which had enabled us to escape the Master's Island and couldn't quite pinpoint its shifting melody and I was miles away, my limbs moving to the rhythm of the camera's gaze when the spell broke.

'Great. That's a wrap. Thank you, Marta, and all you other ladies. We're done.'

The overhead lights were switched off by one of his assistants and the temperature in the studio dropped a few degrees in an instant.

My train to Paris departed around noon the following day. Christiane and the other models were flying out from Köln-Wahn airport, but I had elected to travel back by train. I still hadn't come to terms with planes and that awkward feeling they triggered in me. Flying was for the birds.

Giulia and Christiane were still lingering in the changing room as I hung my final outfit up on the rail, waiting for me to put my street clothes on again. We had earlier planned to share a taxi together back to the Sheraton.

They were both smoking and glancing through the pages of well-thumbed fashion magazines as they waited for me when one of Hans's assistants put his nose through the door and said 'There's someone here for Marta ...' Then 'Oops ... sorry ...' as he'd caught me in a partial state of undress, pulling my grey sweatshirt over my head, my bottom half fully exposed. I gulped. I was sensitive to the fact that unlike the other models I still had abundant pubic hair, although Christiane had long encouraged me to depilate as they did, arguing that it would become necessary if lingerie shoots were offered. At any rate, the assistant had probably seen it all in his work at the studio, and his eyes didn't linger on me or my thatch any longer than necessary.

I quickly slipped my knickers on as Christiane asked 'Were you expecting anyone?'

'No.'

She imperiously walked out into the studio.

And returned to the changing room an instant later with Tristan.

'Your boyfriend,' she said, with a broad smile.

'What are you doing here?' I asked him. He was wearing a dark suit, with a white open-collared shirt. An outfit I had never seen him in before.

'A surprise,' he said.

I was glued to the spot. This was so unusual. So unlike Tristan.

'How lovely!' Christiane and Giulia were beaming. 'I guess we'll leave you lovebirds alone, then and get that taxi. Breakfast together in the morning?' Christiane suggested. She winked 'And you can tell us all about your night ...' They made for the door.

Tristan was grinning. It felt false, forced.

'When did you arrive?' I asked him.

'Just now.'

'Did you fly or take the train?'

'Flew.'

He was lying. There had been no air connection between Paris and Cologne today. I knew this because Christiane and the rest of the team had mentioned the fact of the lack of incoming flights on which they could hop on to return to France, rather than spend another night here.

'OK.'

'I thought we might go out and have a meal. Suits you?'

I acquiesced, although it all felt odd to me. He could have said that he missed me. But he just stood there with that fixed grin as if it was all a joke.

He had a cab waiting outside the studio. An extravagance which was so unlike him.

'It's a Russian restaurant called the Dostoyevski, a mile and a half away from the cathedral, away from the crowds. I've made a reservation.'

There were no other customers around that evening and we had the whole place to ourselves, among the shelves full of books in all languages of the Russian author, the memorabilia and prints of St Petersburg in its czarist heyday. The waitress wore a peasant costume and had her hair in braids. The food was good, lentil and barley soup, thick slices of tongue with horseradish, glutinous potato dishes that melted in your mouth, garnished with heavy, aromatic sauces, but somehow, I found it difficult to concentrate on the meal. Tristan was, unusually, also less than voluble, and felt like a stranger, ignoring my random questions, swatting them away like flies as we ate in almost silence. Outside it began to rain and cars raced across the intersection, honking their horns in their rush to beat the weather and head to dryer parts before the pregnant heavens opened up.

The same cab was waiting for us outside. I couldn't see the face of the driver, who wore a felt cab and never turned round towards us.

We drove to a hotel, whose neon lights flickered in and out of service and I was unable to decipher its name. Tristan had already checked in earlier and fetched a heavy key from his jacket pocket, as we bypassed the empty reception desk and took an elevator to the fourth and last floor.

The suite was more lavish than I expected, all dark red velvet and flocked wallpaper repeating gothic Prussian imperial patterns like a fortress around the bed and low flung sofas. How had he found this place?

I dropped my handbag to the earth-coloured shag carpet and shook some droplets of rain from my hair, having rushed from cab to door to avoid the worst of the downpour. Tristan smiled, gazed at me, drew his fingers through his own dark blond hair in a familiar gesture and I realised how much I had missed him in the few days we had been apart.

My doubts evaporated.

I stepped closer to him and sought the shelter of his body, searching blindly for his warmth, that particular smell of his skin when he was aroused and wanted me, something I knew I triggered uncontrollably, like atoms being drawn to each other, ever since that faraway day on the beach when we had realised the time had come for us to mate.

His chin grazing my shoulder, he nibbled at my ear lobe with uncommon delicacy, while one of his hands travelled across my back with tenderness, quiet gestures that took me by surprise as I couldn't recall him ever having proceeded that way before.

But I liked it, felt ready to abandon myself to his touch.

'Did you miss me?'

'I did. More than I expected.'

My heartbeat quickened as we adjusted our stance and our faces met, lips blindly coming together. I closed my eyes.

I knew every step of the sublime dance we were about to repeat, even though every single time we performed it there were new variations, different breaths and sighs punctuating our movements, deforming our words at moments we could never predict, our bodies taking charge, our brains just a combined mass of joy and wonderment, following the instructions of our mutual desire.

The light in the room dimmed.

His tongue slipped through my half open lips, grazed my

teeth which I opened wide. I had never known it to be this hard and hot as it wrapped itself around mine with studied elegance and lingering negligence, every papillae mapping the texture of my mouth like an explorer of the New World. I shivered.

Heard the call of my lust rising uncontrollably from both my brain and my insides, an orb of fiery light taking root in my lower stomach and travelling at the speed of infinity but somehow also contradictingly slow along my nerves, my muscles, my skin, still light years away from the explosion my whole soul begged for.

In the part of my mind that hadn't yet fully closed down and abandoned all pretence of will I knew this was going to be a fuck like never before. Something different and memorable that would mark me forever.

The silence that surrounded us was louder than a symphony in full swing as Tristan's hands roamed along my body, with the dexterity of an octopus, one moment at my waist, then tiptoeing across my nipples, then again lingering insistently along my lower stomach, one finger tracing my private lips, readying me, wetting my nub from both the inside and the outside, or yet another hand tracing the valley between my arse cheeks and another finger testing my other, tighter sexual door. How many hands and fingers did he have?

Finally, he undressed me.

A choreographed ceremony of desire. Lifting my sweatshirt above my head, my nose catching briefly on its collar, unbuckling the belt of my jeans, and pulling them down, unveiling my intimacy, every step in my undressing an agreed ritual. I kicked my shoes off, my toes dipping into the jungle warmth of the carpet. And I was nude.

As he wanted me. As I wished to be, bare as the day I was born, available, his for the taking.

I was wearing a necklace of black Polynesian pearls. As if hearing my silent plea, he unhooked and removed it.

Had I not already washed away the make-up I had to wear during the photo shoot, I would have asked him to wipe it off too, as I wanted my nudity in his presence to be purer than pure, unsullied.

I lowered my eyes, my gaze moving to my naked body. My pale skin dotted with the red and green flicker of the hotel's neon sign just outside our window, the growing hardness of my nipples reacting to the ambient cold, the downward curve of my breasts, the small garden of my pubis. I tried to imagine how I looked to him, the still life he was witnessing, how his own inner chemistry was beginning to react to my unveiling. Of course, it was far from the first time he was seeing me nude, but this time it felt different. Though I couldn't quite pinpoint how as a torrent of thoughts swirled through my head, inducing dizziness, even anxiety.

Tristan stood there, facing me, as we stood just a few inches apart, his breath a regular cadence, his eyes searing dark, peering into mine, somehow undressing me even further, exploring what was under my own skin, seeking out a second degree of nudity.

'You ...' he whispered, his voice a stream of velvet baritone.

I stepped towards him and, in turn, began to undress him.

His shirt falling to the floor, revealing his chest, the subtle patterns of his ribs beneath the skin, the dark hair surrounding his own nipples, the crevice of his navel and the slim stream of lighter-coloured hairs leading down, arrow-like, towards his waist.

I kneeled and undid the laces of his shoes. He wasn't wearing socks.

Had never done since we had left the Island, a piece of apparel he had never grown accustomed to.

His toe nails were long and overgrown, reminding me of some of the beasts of prey we once saw at the zoo. Likewise, the nails on his fingers which, though carefully trimmed and exquisitely shaped, he wore much longer than most other men. Something vulpine about him, I realised.

His penis was already hard, standing at attention as I gently pulled it out of his tight-fitting underwear. I was as much in love with it as I was of him. Long and thick (not that I'd much basis for comparison as on the Island we all took each other's genitalia for granted and not worthy of much examination, since we had grown from the state of children to adults, at any rate some of us, and it was all part of the unremarkable spectacle of each day). A gentle pattern of veins travelled across its stem and I wondered whether I had similar subtle inverted canals inside of my intimacy that fitted against those veins like a completed jigsaw puzzle and made us whole when we made love.

A faint but noticeable tremor flashed through his heavy ball sack, his wrinkled skin ebbing to and from like miniature waves, possibly sap rising in expectation of me. I drew my eyes away.

'You're quite beautiful,' Tristan said.

Someone had switched off the hotel's outside sign and the room now stood in semi-darkness, his silhouette outlined against the window. It had stopped raining and the sky beyond was like a painting. He turned and drew the heavy damask curtains.

I was fixed to the spot, following his movements in the chiaroscuro of the hotel room.

'So are you …' I muttered.

'Come to bed.' He moved towards me, the heat of his body as he approached already wrapping itself around me in streaming, unseen tendrils.

First it was his warmth, then his hands, then his fingers and finally Tristan's body and mine made full contact and the electricity of desire caught us in its web and all thoughts faded into oblivion so all that remained was just us, our skin, our feelings, our lust and we willingly became instruments of basic animality and abandoned ourselves to pleasure.

He was soon inside me, and it felt I was inside him too in an impossible way.

The sweat we generated between the crisp white sheets of the hotel bed was like glue as our limbs danced in unison and our free will melted.

But, all the time, an ash of doubt resonated at the back of my mind, alerting me to the fact that even though the mechanics, the hydraulics of our sex were identical to the hundreds of other occasions we had mated, there appeared to be a new element I couldn't quite pinpoint.

As the ley lines of desires sputtered out of control inside our flesh, every square inch of our skin on fire, literally begging to be annihilated in some devastating apocalypse, it came to me.

I was the same.

Open to him, available in every possible way, obscene or bizarre, willing prey to his lustful assault, but his taking of me seemed different.

More powerful.

All consuming in ways I had never experienced. A new Tristan.

But, quickly, his thrusts varying in speed and intensity as he played me, the thought moved away and I couldn't avoid but surrender to the power of the moment and the way it made me feel so terribly alive, even though I also seemed to the skirting the very frontiers of death itself in the intensity of the pleasure we generated together.

I orgasmed.

My consciousness briefly waned and I harboured the deep-seated desire to never emerge from its abominable depths, to remain there in that abyss forever, praying that the burst of lust that had torn my whole being into a million pieces until I was just dust floating in an empty void would hold me forever in its sway.

I was no longer in the world.

In space.

Marooned.

Blissful. In agonising pain of already wanting this moment to never fade and last forever.

Which a single grey cell hidden far below the folds of my cortex knew was unrealistic, whispering to me in the night of a thousand galaxies of the void, that I would wake, open my eyes and find myself once again in a hotel room, crucified under Tristan, both begging for more and also resentful that the experience couldn't last longer.

I delayed the moment as much as I could until he finally moved out of me, my moistness flooding across the soiled sheets.

I opened my eyes.

Accustomed myself to the darkness.

He turned over on the bed, his damp back to me.

I raised myself on my elbows to peer at his face, wishing to thank him or translate in some way the complex emotions I now felt.

Just a kiss was all I wanted, a way of expressing my thanks, of strengthening that bond we had cemented anew.

A ray of moonlight pierced the night darkness and illuminated Tristan's head.

I leaned over, drinking in his familiar smell.

He adjusted his angle of repose so that our lips might meet, guessing at my intentions.

Looked up at me.

My heart dropped in freefall as if gravity had been cancelled at the stroke of an unseen lever.

It was no longer Tristan's face.

I held my breath, my stomach knitting itself into the most painful of configurations.

The face gazing at me, the eyes drilling into my soul belonged to the Piper, our erstwhile Master.

A sickening feeling invaded me.

I'd been a fool, taken in by his terrible magic, violated not just in the most private part of my body, but lured into a dreadful betrayal.

I fell silent.

The whole room shimmered as I lay there naked, hypnotised by the prone shape of the man alongside me. His whole body shifted imperceptibly and within seconds he no longer displayed Tristan's silken hair, or his shape, even his resting cock had metamorphosed into something longer, reptilian, nonetheless seductive in its dangerous appeal, so much so I had to make an effort to draw my eyes away from it.

I shuddered at the thought of how it had invaded me, and I

had welcomed it, used it for my pleasure.

He smiled, purred like a sly cat as he noted my obvious disarray.

'You?' was all I could muster, drawing the sheets towards me to conceal my nudity, although I reckoned it mattered little to him, likely capable as he was of seeing clearly through the thin material.

I knew not how to address him.

As if reading my mind, he said 'You can call me Becker. It's always been my name down here.'

8

'Is this the way I am to be punished for escaping?'

Becker peered at me, with a wry look spreading across his craggy features. For the first time, I realised how much he resembled images of sundry devils I had seen in prints, books and popular imagery. How could we have not realised earlier?

'Do you deserve to be punished?' he asked.

The anger inside me rose. 'Wasn't being torn away from Hamelin punishment enough? Us children were innocent. It was our elders who transgressed.'

'Taking you from them wasn't meant to be interpreted in such a way,' Becker answered. 'It was to protect you from the world.'

'Did we really need to be protected so badly? Kept for centuries, isolated, with even the memories of our families and loved ones unable to survive the weight of the years?'

He gravely considered the question.

'I shielded you from sin ...'

'Did you really?'

'Well, I tried, but some of you were alas already tainted ...'

'How so?'

'Ah, well, theology and the arcane, often contradictory currents of good and evil are a complicated subject. Maybe we can discuss all this on a future occasion ...'

He stood there in his dark pinstriped three-piece suit (when had he dressed? I'd never taken my eyes off him!), the buttons of his waistcoat like shining gold coins. He looked like a lawyer preparing for trial.

'What now?' I asked.

'You are not to be punished,' he stated. 'But you owe me.'

'For stealing the golden pipe?'

'No, it's safely back in my hands. That was never a problem.'

'So?'

'You will bring me three souls.'

'Souls?'

'Souls,' he reiterated.

'And how do I do that?'

'You are enterprising. I'm confident, you will find a way.'

I was flummoxed.

'And Tristan is mine,' Becker continued. 'You will steer well clear of him; is that understood? Mine and mine alone.'

'What will you do to him?'

'That will depend,' Becker said, thoughtfully as if he was right now considering the matter for the very first time. 'Maybe his soul, but even that might prove insufficient. He is marked by sin and must be made to repent properly.'

I shuddered.

I'd always felt much affection for Tristan, and intense attraction, but realised his ceaseless curiosity might have affected me from an early stage and, in strange ways, brought me to this fateful point. I missed him already, realising it was unlikely I was to ever see him again. Unless in the treacherous guise of Becker, as had happened last night. But I couldn't afford to feel sorry for him. I sighed. Felt terribly deflated, in the certain knowledge I would be betraying him in everything I did from this point forward.

'Will I ever be allowed to return to the Island?'

'Maybe. But penance and compensation must come first. Sin will have to be purged. Severely.'

I had lost all sense of time.

'Come,' he ordered.

I docilely followed him out of the hotel once I had hurriedly made myself decent and dressed. I hadn't had the opportunity to wash or shower and felt dirty. Outside and inside. My shame reminded me I probably still carried his seed. I felt sick.

We caught a cab to the airport where he handed me a ticket and a wad of cash together with a large envelope.

'I own you now, Katerina. You will become my collector of souls. This is the first one.'

'And how do I go about collecting souls, Sir,' I asked him.

'You offer them what they desire most in this world or any other, until they will surrender anything in their desperation to obtain it. Money, power, minor miracles, you … I am sure you will prove persuasive.'

I took the orange envelope in hand, it was thin, bore no name or address. By the time I looked up again, he was gone and I was standing alone in the midst of a swirling crowd in the airport departure check-in area, businessmen and tourists navigating around me pulling cases on wheels and carrying bags across their shoulders.

I found a place to sit and opened the envelope. There was an itinerary, a ticket to New York in the USA, my passport which he had seemingly retrieved from my Sheraton hotel room, and a left luggage key. There was also a sheet of paper with a name typed out, an address and a blurry photo that must have been taken in a failing photo booth. A man with melancholy pouring from his eyes, good-looking but distant, his dark, curling hair like a wreath of darkness against the blank background of the cabin where the photo had been taken. My initial target. I was feeling nauseous already at the idea of such a long flight to a place that until now had just been a name to me, some modern mirage of modernity I could barely fathom. I asked an official for directions to the left luggage area. It was on a lower floor. The key fitted snuggly into the small lock and I found a Samsonite travelling case. Inside it was the majority of my clothing; not just what I had brought along to Cologne for the shoot, but also some of my more precious belongings that I had left in Paris. Becker was certainly good at planning, as if omniscient. Which was no surprise, all things considered.

The flight was still three hours away. I made a beeline for a public bathroom and washed the smell of sex away from my body, applied a smidgeon of make-up and changed into more appropriate travelling clothes.

Fourteen hours later, I found myself sitting on a bench in

Washington Square Park in New York, watching squirrels parade impishly on the thin grass and climbing the ancient trees with matchless agility in a curious but inspiring dance of life.

The Lebanese cab driver who'd picked me up at the airport terminal had brought me here. I'd asked him to take me to what he felt would be a nice area of the city to stay in. During the course of our journey through Queens and the Midtown Tunnel, he kept on telling me of a possible apocalypse from a nuclear reactor that had exploded in Ukraine, but I couldn't quite understand what he was on about. Surely Becker would not have sent me here if the end of the world was nearing. He knew everything, our demonic master of space and time. There was a small hotel on the north west corner of the park and they had vacancies, but my room wouldn't be available until three in the afternoon.

The sun was weak still, an early spring light trying to break through as I moved my gaze from the gallivanting squirrels to a procession of darker-skinned nannies pushing baby carriages down the alleys of the park. In the distance, its famous arches stood triumphantly, like a magnet and the sounds of a solitary piano echoed along a soothing breeze.

Once the room was free, I crashed down on the bed over which a hand-coloured print of the actress Ingrid Bergman hung on the pink brown wall and slept for an eternity, waking up in the middle of the night on a few occasions but easily finding sleep again. I had been awake throughout the transatlantic flight, a tight bundle of nerves, not just from the flying but also the aftershock of all the events of the past days which were only now beginning to register properly in all their sheer horror. I realised I had had no further thoughts of Tristan and guilt assailed me in unceasing waves.

I had missed breakfast by the time I was fully awake again and ventured into the nearby park where, yesterday, I had noticed a variety of small trailers offering food, drinks and ice-cream and got myself a pretzel that tasted better than any I had ever eaten in Germany, which came as a surprise. I washed it down with lemonade, sitting on the rocky edge of the central fountain where I had an unbroken view of the canyon of 5th Avenue through the arches. A diminutive Asian-looking nanny walked by, hectoring a small blond boy and his smaller sister as they ran merrily towards the enclosed swings area. Down here, the city had a distinct charm, not at all like the warren of skyscrapers I had been expecting.

As if released by a starter's gun, crowds began to pour into the park and I realised it must be lunch hour, and workers from nearby offices and the university buildings had been set free, craving for the open spaces and the fresh air. I checked my watch and realised I hadn't adjusted the time difference from Europe.

I could see single men eyeing me with curiosity. Did I look that different from American women, or was I perhaps wearing the wrong kind of clothes? No, lots of others were sporting jeans and sweatshirts too. Now was not the time to stand out.

I pulled the sheet of paper with the man's address from my pocket, walked back to the hotel, and asked the Lithuanian woman on duty in reception for a map, and she helped me navigate it. He actually lived within walking distance on Hester Street. She heartily recommended the salt beef sandwiches from an allegedly famous diner close by to there, but my mind was not on food.

It was a four-storey building in dire need of upkeep and there was no access to the building unless you knew the code. The pavement outside was cracked, tendrils of grass peeping through the gaps in the concrete slabs. I installed myself at the outside table of a café on the other side of the street, with a lemon-lime Kool-Aid to sip, which allowed me a full view of the door and began my vigil. The man I was seeking did not make an appearance, and then it got dark. I had confirmation he still lived there from the intercom listing. Maybe he worked from home? I resolved to return early the next morning.

I was in situ at the break of the dawn, a thin curtain of spit-like drizzle breaking through as soon as I was a few blocks on my way, coating me as I walked south through the streets of Greenwich Village to my destination. The café was not yet open so I had to seek shelter under the nearby awning of a kosher meat and sausage store. I should have borrowed an umbrella from the rack in the hotel lobby.

Growing crowds of commuters swelled and went by as the rush hour traffic roared along the busy streets and still the door to the building opposite remained locked, with not a single person exiting the house. The rain cleared just as the kosher butcher's pulled its shutters up and I would have stood out like a square peg, so I installed myself again outside the convenient café. And waited. Did I have any choice?

The woman behind the café counter was giving me strange looks as the hours passed by and I ordered cookies and further drinks to justify my presence. I could see she was dying to ask me questions but maybe something in my unsmiling attitude prevented her from doing so.

It was mid-afternoon when the door across Hester Street yawned open and I caught a sight of the man I was seeking. He was wearing a dark navy baseball cap and a puffed-up sleeveless waistcoat over his T-shirt. I was certain it was the right person. He headed west. I stood, left the café and followed him until he crossed the road at the second set of traffic lights and moved toward Houston. He was just a stone's throw away and we were now on the same pavement. He didn't appear to be in any particular hurry. Or had any inkling I was following him.

Finally, he turned on La Guardia, walked north, entered a supermarket on the corner of Bleecker Street and exited half an hour later with two bags full of goods and made his way back to his apartment. At least I knew he was in town.

His name was Conrad.

It took me another week of lurking in his vicinity and following him until I got the opportunity to finally make some form of contact by deliberately brushing against him and profusely apologising for my clumsiness in forcing him to drop what he was carrying. By then, I knew which bar on Sullivan Street he would occasionally go to on odd evenings and arranged to seat myself close to his stall a few nights later.

I'd consciously worn a low-cut blouse and my shortest skirt in an attempt to appeal to him, which also drew unwanted attention from several other customers.

'Don't I know you?' I asked, as he ordered his customary glass of bourbon.

He looked round at me quizzically, hunting for recognition.

'I'm ... not sure. We've met before?'

I briefly feigned ignorance then beamed.

'Yes, yes, I remember now. We bumped into each other just two days ago outside the Katz deli at Houston and Ludlow ... I made you drop your bag ... I'm so clumsy sometimes ...' I exclaimed.

He recalled the incident and beamed at me.

'So it was. You ...'

'Such a coincidence. There are so many bars in the Village and we bump into each other here! I'm Kate,' I introduced himself, unsure whether I should shake his hand or not.

'Conrad Kurtz.'

'Is this your regular bar?' I asked. 'I'm visiting the city. Just walked by and felt it might have a nice atmosphere.'

'Not so much regular than I'd be here every night,' he answered. 'I'm not much of a drinker. Maybe once or at most twice a week. I work from home, so it's nice to be out in public.'

'What are you drinking?'

'Bourbon. Four Roses.'

'I'm not keen on alcohol,' I stated, which was the truth. 'It's not a principle, just taste. Just a soda and tons of coffee sort of girl ...'

'No harm in that. So where do you come from? I hear a faint accent.'

'Holland.'

'I've never been there. Tulips, hey?'

I'd never been there either. Maybe I should be lying more intelligently?

'So what do you do? At home, I mean, you said you work from there.'

'Nothing glamorous,' Conrad said. 'I'm a copy editor and

proof-reader.' He hesitated. 'Hmm ... I'm also trying to write a book. I hope that doesn't sound pretentious?'

'Not at all. What is it about?'

'I'm sure you wouldn't find it very interesting. It's non fiction, a study of how the devil actually became the devil, you know falling angel and all that. Been researching a lot of theology and legends. Sounds silly, but it's a truly fascinating subject. Although I don't think many people would hold the same fascination for it as I do ... I hope that doesn't disappoint you. Would have been so much more romantic if I'd said I was writing a novel, no?'

'Maybe. I have a soft spot for romance.'

'Don't all women?'

The pieces of the puzzle were coming together. The reason why Becker, as he now called himself, was fishing for his soul.

A blanket of silence briefly moved between us amongst the growing hubbub of the bar, as if our conversation had run out of fuel. I'd become pensive, idly wondering if the fruits of his research might enlighten me about my own fate and what sort of pawn I had become in Becker's game.

Conrad was the one to break the ice.

'So where are you staying in New York?'

'Oh, not far from here, the Washington Square Hotel.'

'Nice. I've walked by many times. It's a splendid location.'

'Yes,' I agreed. Just that morning, I'd come to realise that the funds Becker had supplied me with back at the airport were about to run out and that I'd no longer afford to stay at the hotel, let alone feed myself. But, as I'd walked past reception, the Assistant Manager had called out to me and advised me that my 'father' had called and left his credit card details to cover the indefinite rest of my stay. There was no escaping the unseen grasp of Becker; he knew everything, shadowed me, turning me into his willing puppet. So why then couldn't the bastard catch his own souls, if he was so powerful?

The gaps in our bar side conversation grew wider as both of us struggled for further subjects to talk about, Conrad was visibly as inexperienced as I was in the art of seduction or social niceties. Both absolute beginners. I didn't know what to ask him next and he seemingly had no interest in quizzing me about Holland, which was actually a relief! Tonight, he wore blue button-down shirt and khaki slacks and there was an underlying beach of sadness in his eyes, witness, I guessed, to countless past disappointments. I already hated what I would have to do to him, even as I knew I hadn't a clue as to how I would go about it.

He recognised the fact that our dialogue was faltering and elegantly tried to bow out.

'Oh well,' he said, emptying his glass. 'I always make it a rule to never get a second bourbon on the same evening. I should maybe run along. Still fifty pages of proofs to check for one of the publishers I freelance for. Due in 48 hours and I do pride myself in never missing a deadline.' He reluctantly rose from his stall.

I struggled for words.

'Oh … Well, it was lovely to talk …'

'It was, Kate …'

'Actually it's Katerina.'

'Nice. I thought Kate wasn't a very Dutch name.'

'But more common here …' I mumbled, stretching the conversation. 'Listen … I only have a week or so left in the city: would you be willing to show me around maybe? It's so much nicer having a real-life tour guide of sorts, an actual native, rather than facts and figures in a guide book …' Since I had arrived in New York I had seen nothing beyond my treks through Greenwich Village tailing Conrad. Not that I had any interest in sightseeing, monuments or museums.

His eyes opened wide as his smile transformed his pale features.

'I'd love to.'

The heavily-tattooed barmaid picked up our glasses and winked at me in complicity, not having missed a single word of our conversation.

'That's great. Tomorrow or the day after?'

'Tomorrow is fine. I have some research I'd planned to

complete at the New York Public Library uptown in the morning. We could meet midday in Bryant Park? It's close by.'

'I'll find it. Sure.'

I didn't want to make it too obvious and wanted Conrad to feel he was the one seducing me, so it took ten days of regular dates, drinks and meals and countless chats that stretched the powers of my imagination to find something intelligent to say and not betray my murky background when confronted by all his well-meaning questions.

Finally, sitting in an almost deserted sushi joint on Thompson Street late one evening, Conrad finishing his last sip of sake and me a Diet Coke, my tongue still tingling from the wasabi I'd liberally coated my thin slices of salmon with, I saw that glint of unrequited desire light up his eyes. He was ripe. In a state of want. His fingers had grazed mine repeatedly across the table, had earlier as if on automatic pilot at the bar placed his hands on my knees in a gesture of both tenderness and understanding.

I looked straight at him, held his gaze and asked 'You want me, don't you?'

In the warm penumbra of the restaurant, I thought I caught the hint of a blush spreading across his cheeks. He gulped.

'Hmm ... Yes, I do. A lot, actually, Kate. I'm sure you're aware of the fact. You're a beautiful woman. You're different.'

'I'll be yours.'

'Really?'

'Tonight, even.'

He moved his hand forward to touch me, pushing aside the ceramic plate on which only a clump of ginger and thin strands of horseradish remained either side of his chopsticks.

'You're certain?'

'Absolutely.'

He caught his breath.

'Where?'

'Well, not here, for certain,' I joked.

'You can come back to mine, if you wish?'

I was now playing with him. Hook, line and sinker.

'Or would you want to come back to my hotel on the Square, maybe. Don't they always say there's something exciting about sex in hotel rooms?'

'Whatever you prefer ...'

'There is one condition, though ...' I added.

'Yes?' Conrad probably assumed I was about to demand we use protection.

'You must sign your soul away to me first.'

There was a look of surprise on his face, followed by a broad smile.

'That's so funny, Kate.'

'It's not a joke. I want to be Marguerite to your Faust ...' He was nonplussed. 'Surely, you know about the practice since you study the devil and his works?'

I could see he couldn't quite decide how serious I was, or whether he was the object of derision.

'And how would I do that in real life?' he finally asked me.

In fact, I was unsure how to go about it in any proper manner myself.

'We could ask the waiter for a piece of paper. Just a few lines, and you sign.'

'This is so weird,' Conrad pointed out. 'Never happened to me before.'

'And never will again.'

'You're such a strange girl, Kate, but in a curious way, it's all part of your attraction.' He called the waitress over and asked for a blank piece of paper. It took him twice to explain to her.

He pulled his silver Parker pen from his jacket pocket and surmised the lined yellow sheet torn from a legal pad.

'Can you help me with the wording?'

I improvised.

'I hereby ... surrender my soul if Kate offers herself to me,' I suggested.

'No mention of the devil?' he jested.

'I don't think it's required.' I knew he was no longer taking this seriously; thought I was playing games with him and was just happy to oblige.

He signed with a flourish.

'There, it's done.'

I picked up the scrap of paper and dropped it into my handbag.

9

I made love with Conrad Kurtz under the fixed gaze of Ingrid Bergman.

He was gentle.

A man of few words but tender gestures, unhurried, slow but methodical.

But to my everlasting shame throughout our coupling, all I could remember was the terrible ardour that had taken hold of me when Becker, masquerading so slyly as Tristan, had taken me.

Every sinew of my body, every aroused cell in my mind, harked back to that occasion, craved in abominable ways for those sensations to return. I had been spoiled, transported to a level that, it appeared, no other normal man would ever be able to return me to. Even as quiet waves of lust travelled through me and I was aware of the staccato breaths of this pleasant man, Conrad, taking his pleasure and kindly teasing with mine, silent howls of frustration roared inside me.

I pretended to respond. Faked my desire.

Our limbs disentangled, Conrad caught his breath, kissed then nibbled gently at the lobe of my right ear, brushed my damp fringe away from my forehead, sought reassurance in my eyes.

I tentatively smiled back in return, unable to come up with any suitable words.

'That was so good,' he whispered.

I just nodded.

There was the sound of two other hotel guests laughing in the corridor outside as they exited the elevator, then silence again as their door locked across the corridor from ours.

We lay in silence. Pensive, neither of us wishing to interrupt the sense of repose enveloping us first.

Conrad adjusted his position, leaning forward on his elbows.

'So where do I deliver my soul?' he asked with a grin.

'I don't know.' I was as much in the dark as he was, even though only I knew that it was anything but a joke.

'That was so funny, you know, asking me that, Kate.'

I remained silent.

'Well,' Conrad finally said, 'call of nature …' as he raised himself, slipped out of bed and counted the few steps to the bathroom door.

I lay there waiting.

Ten minutes later he hadn't returned. There was no sound emerging from behind the door.

I left the bed and, nervously, opened the bathroom door. It was empty. Conrad had gone. Taken. His clothes were still scattered across my hotel bedroom floor as a stark reminder of my predicament, my guilt.

I breathed a heavy sigh of relief.

I didn't get out of bed for the rest of that day, deep in thought, anxious and relieved at the same time, apprehensive about what Becker might demand of me next and in no hurry to find out.

A few days later, as I searched through my sole handbag for a tissue, I realised the small piece of paper with which Conrad had bargained his soul away had also disappeared. I disposed of his abandoned clothes by stuffing them in a plastic hotel laundry bag which I, later that day, left on a subway platform.

My body hankered for some fresh air and as dusk fell onto Washington Square, I resolved to leave my room and wander through the park, if only to settle my mind.

An envelope had been left for me at reception. It was identical to the one I had been handed by Becker at the airport back in Germany, in what felt ages ago. There was a single sheet of paper inside the envelope, with a name. And a small passport-size photograph. Of a young woman.

Her name was Cornelia St John and she lived off Gramercy Park.

I peered at her face in the photo, somehow seeking some answer as to why she had become a target and her soul was so coveted by Becker, the Piper. Trying to establish a pattern.

A surge of anger coursed through me and I resolved to act in no hurry. There was no rush to contact her. What difference did a few weeks more make to Becker's unholy plan?

I spent whole days in my room at the hotel, not going out, even as late spring bloomed outside and the leaves of the trees in the park changed colours in a swirling panorama I spied from my street-facing window. I relied on takeaway food, which I called in from nearby Chinese and Japanese restaurants, which I settled with my ever-dwindling dollars. Unless Becker came to my financial rescue again, I would soon have to make changes to my way of life. The room was paid for but that was all. Back when we were all on the Island, the notion of money was something exotic and unheard of. Life in this world was expensive, a drip drip of petty demands. I knew I must somehow be under his constant observation; he wouldn't allow me to starve, would he?

The face looking back at me in the mirror on the bathroom door was drawn, a hint of darkness emerging under my eyes, my hair tangled, uncombed and unwashed, my lips dry and pursed. I was aware it was not just the ageing I was subject to here, but also a general lassitude, a worm that was gnawing away at my soul. Why hadn't he just taken mine? I wouldn't have resisted.

What happens when your soul is snatched? Do you just fade into darkness, a state of non-being? Is it painful? Is it like death? I imagined my body sprawled out on a bed, my eyes glazed, peering blindly at the ceiling, my limbs akimbo, lifeless, and my skin drying then rotting as the hours race by. Would there be anything left of me by the time I was found? Who would bury or cremate me?

Cornelia's photo lay on the bedside shelf, next to the telephone.

I determined to find out why Becker had chosen her.

From the moment I actually met Cornelia I took a strong liking to her. She was earnest, an open book, warm and friendly. I contrived to bump into her into the pizza parlour where she normally grabbed a bite during the break she had between lectures at NYU, where she studied, and we then shared a table where we ate and exchanged confidences. She was in her third year as a biochemistry undergraduate. She came from Louisiana and, like me, was finding life in the Big Apple more expensive than she had expected. I pretexted that I had arrived in town with a few months to spare and explore until my own classes – I lied, pretending I was about to study literature – began in the fall.

'It's a struggle,' she admitted. 'But my parents are already stretched financially subsidising my rent that I can't rely on them for more.' Her student loan was woefully insufficient and had long run out before the end of the school year, still a couple of months ahead. 'I've been looking for something I could do in the evening to earn some cash and …' She hesitated, as if embarrassed to disclose more.

'Where?' I queried her. 'I'm in the same boat. I wouldn't mind finding some part-time work too.'

'Well,' Cornelia admitted. 'It's not very savoury, if you know what I mean, but I think I've run out of alternatives. Waitressing or bar work would bite into my class hours and I don't want to jeopardise my studies.'

I was intrigued.

'Doing what?' I asked her, as we both shovelled up the remaining crumbs of hardened dough from our paper plates.

'Dancing.'

'That sounds sort of fun.'

'But it's … not just dancing …' she blushed slightly.

'What else?'

'Naked. Stripping.' Her eyes avoided mine.

'Oh …'

'It's a club down in Alphabet City. I know another girl who used to do the occasional shift there before she moved on to California for her postgrad work. She said the customers are not too overly shifty, or dangerous. You just dance, that's all; nothing else is expected of you. No funny business involved.'

She was petite, with dark flowing hair that fell all the way down her back and curvy in all the right places under her loose sweatshirt and baggy jeans. I could see that men would like watching her.

'And it pays well?' An idea was forming in my mind.

'Better than waitressing once you factor in the tips and, to a certain extent, you can choose your own hours.'

'Interesting,' I concluded. 'So have you made your mind up?'

'Not quite yet,' Cornelia said. She glanced at her watch. 'Time for me to go. My next class is just a couple of blocks away in the sciences building.

'I'll see you around,' I bid farewell to her with a wave of the hand. 'Maybe you'll let me know if the dancing works out?'

'If I go ahead with it. Still unsure.'

'Good luck.'

I waited a couple of days then arranged to come across her again at the same cheap pizza slices place on the corner of Greenwich and Sixth. She was wearing a similar outfit, her version of a student's uniform but her hair was tied in a bunch at the back, and she wore a pair of large square sunglasses balanced on her forehead

'Hey!'

'Oh, hi!'

'Join you?'

'Sure.'

We munched away. The pizza wasn't great but it was inexpensive and copious.

'Tried the dancing yet?'

'No. Need some Dutch courage to take the first step, I reckon.'

'Well, I happen to be Dutch,' I said, grinning at her in complicity, despite the familiar lie. 'Listen, I also need a bit of cash. What if we went there together and offered to dance? Provide each other with moral support?'

Her eyes opened wide, surprised by my proposal.

I could see her thinking. Then nodding her head.

'Why not?' she said, looking me over, no doubt reassured that I had the right looks too.

'Great. Do you know who we have to see to get the gig?'

'Yes, my friend gave me the booker's name before she left for the West Coast.'

'Well, no time like the present. When is your last lecture for the day?'

'I should be free around five,' Cornelia said. 'But the club doesn't open until eight in the evening. We'd have time to change into something more suitable.' She looked me over. My crumpled grey blouse hadn't seen an iron in ages and my denim skirt was full of irregular patches.

We met up by the Tower Books store on the corner of East 4th and Lafayette.

She was wearing a low-cut floral print dress with thin straps that reached the top of her knees and flat shoes. A country girl outfit. I had slipped on the skin-tight little black dress I had worn for my evening with Conrad, and a pair of high heels I'd found at a bargain price in a local Goodwill.

We walked south, passing CBGB on the Bowery.

'Have you ever been there?' Cornelia asked me. 'Best rock'n roll in town. Just amazing.'

I hadn't. As a matter of fact, the only other live music I had experienced was the seductive sound of the pipe in Hamelin and the often cacophonous jazz from the smoke-ridden cellar Tristan and I had visited on the Paris Left Bank.

From the outside, the Mermaids Club was just a hole in the wall, stuck between a Korean all hours convenience store and a Ukrainian bakery on Avenue C, with a metal door that looked as if had been kicked in on repeated occasions. But once past the door, the standards rose rapidly, a narrow corridor lined with incongruous old black and white prints of sea creatures and monsters from the deep leading to a surprisingly cavernous space, dominated by a circular stage facing a bar area. Not all the lights had yet been switched on and the stage stood in darkness while just a couple of middle-aged businessmen in pinstripe suits sat at the bar nursing drinks and deep in hushed conversation.

The barman, shaven-headed and lip-pierced indicated a door on the right-hand side of the unlit stage to us, where the manager had an office. His name was Bertram and he looked like an accountant on a furlough, anonymously middle-aged, wearing glasses, his hair parted with military precision on the side, white shirt and scarlet red tie, sitting behind an untypically tidy desk. Cornelia had called in advance.

'What's this. two for the price of one?' he asked.

'My friend Kate was also interested.'

He looked us over in a matter-of-fact way, assessing our looks and our determination. We held his gaze.

'You know what's involved?'

'Of course.'

'Students?'

'Yes, both of us.'

'OK, we run a strict no touching policy and dancers are not allowed to advertise any extra service, and if we find out any of you are hustling or arranging for contacts outside the club with any of the punters, you're out with no recourse. No fraternisation. Understood?'

'We do,' I said. 'That's why we came here. Our friend told us this was all above board. We're not whores, just want to dance and make some cash.'

'Good to know that's crystal clear.'

He paused, kept on watching us as we nervously shuffled from foot to foot under his examination.

'So what do you have?' he finally asked.

For a brief moment, I was unsure what he expected of us, but Cornelia was more savvy. She unzipped her floral print dress on the side and pulled it over her head, standing there in just her matching blue silk underwear. I followed suit, slipping out of my tight back dress.

His eyes never left us, and again we stood in silence as he detailed our bodies.

'Looks good enough,' he remarked. 'Let's see more.'

Standing side by side in the claustrophobic back office, we

must have presented a contrasting spectacle, compounded by the fact Cornelia wore flats and I had chosen high heels in addition to my extra height. Her hourglass figure was all curves and her skin a pale landscape of whiteness, while I was more angular, large-boned and smaller-breasted.

'You'll have to trim a little,' Bertram said, addressing himself to me. 'It's not the 1960s anymore.'

I looked down at my pubic thatch, comparing it to Cornelia's which was just a thin landing strip, neatly shaped and vertical, like a dark arrow pointing to her sex.

'You'll each have to bring your own mix tape,' he said. 'Enough for two five-minute sets. And let me know what you have chosen beforehand. Can't have the same tune played over and over and I know you girls have a lot of similar tastes. Nothing too fancy either. And definitely no classical stuff.'

I nodded, along with Cornelia, although I had no clue what Bertram was asking for. Later, she explained that we would both have to prepare a music tape which we would be dancing to. When I confessed to my total ignorance of current music, she promised she would help me chose. 'We can even rehearse a little together,' she suggested. 'Devise some moves.'

It was all a new language for me. I hoped my dancing could pass muster and I wouldn't look like a giraffe plodding across that tiny stage, my limbs tripping over each other, my naked body all clumsy and anything but elegant, let alone seductive.

We agreed on the hours and what we would be paid. It wasn't a fortune, but Cornelia had told me it would be substantially boosted by the tips we would get, which the club would have no claim on. Drinks would be on the house, but alcohol was not part of the deal. Which was fine by me.

Following the unusual interview, we were heading back to the Village, deep in thought.

'Cornelia?'

'Yes?'

'There's something I have to tell you.'

'What?'

'I've never danced,' I revealed. Which was the truth.

'Never?'
'Never.'
She burst out in laughter.
'Wow!'
'It's a problem, isn't it?'
'I'll teach you, Kate. Anyway, with a body like yours, they won't be that interested in the way you move ...' She giggled like a schoolgirl who's pulled off a successful prank.

A week of mirth and merriness ensued, as we practiced in the gym of her student dorm after hours, sharing headphones in close proximity, as she drilled me in the art of exotic dancing or, at any rate, instructing the absolute beginner I was how to move with a modicum of sensuality, avoiding anything that smacked of vulgarity, let alone avoid tripping over myself when I finally began to connect with the beat and launched into improvisations inspired by the music and its steady, insistent rhythms.

Even though I could never quite banish the reason I was fraternising with her from the back of my mind, we became steadfast friends, hardy accomplices as we bonded over dance, music and our coming work at the Mermaids Club, speculating as to how we would be greeted once we trooped out onto that exiguous stage. Catcalls or boos. Winks or applause.

Jesting that the men who wouldn't appreciate Cornelia's charms would have no choice but to fall back on me, and that between the two of us we would be catering to all possible masculine tastes.

The day we were to make our separate debuts was nearing. We'd thrown the dice and it was decided that Cornelia would take the stage first. All we had to do now was take a final decision about what music we would respectively dance to. Cornelia had settled for a for a song from a classic musical, *My Fair Lady*'s 'I Could Have Danced All Night' and I had gone more contemporary and opted for David Bowie's 'Let's Dance'.

I'd tried out quite a few other tunes, but this one spoke to me in invisible ways, setting my body in eternal motion like a puppeteer controlling its wooden creature.

Cornelia had selected what we would initially wear and later gradually shed as we disrobed. There was a charity store on West 10th Street, with rows and rows of used clothing and we had spent two hours there picking from the endless rails, trying things on and complaining all too often that it was never quite the right size, until we finally settled for our outfits.

To top it all off we found glitzy underwear in a head shop on Americas which also doubled as a sex store, where shelves of porn videos and toys were openly displayed in all their explicit wonder, something of a new experience for me.

We carried our acquisitions back to my room at the hotel on Washington Square, stimulated by a strong drink in her case and a triple espresso at the bar downstairs first, and in turn showered. Then Cornelia helped me with my make-up, our war paint as she called it, applying party glitter across my cheeks, my cleavage and my stomach. 'We'll shine,' she insisted.

'Like stars in the night sky.'

Cornelia danced first. It was still relatively early in the evening and a weekday, so the attendance was initially sparse. With her button nose, all too candid smile even as she tried to look sexy, and overall clean-cut demeanour, there was something of a disconnect between the movements of her delightful body and the seductiveness of her dancing, as if she was studiously going through the motions by numbers, ticking off with assiduity every progression in her disrobing. 'Don't show too much too fast,' we had agreed, at Bertram's recommendation, but somehow her timing to the big musical number was out of sync, and she found herself fully naked in the spotlight a few verses away from the end of the song, surprised like a deer in headlights, not quite knowing what extra movements to launch to keep the mood going. There was just a thin harvest of tips on stage when she ended her set. I was sitting waiting in the changing room watching her on close circuit TV and felt my heart drop for her.

Finally, as the music faded, she fumbled off the stage,

picking up her scattered clothing in a rush to shield her private parts, even though the spotlight picking her out was no longer so harsh. On the way, she gathered up a couple of low denomination green bank notes customers had thrown onto the stage as tips.

Otis Redding's '(Sittin' On) The Dock of the Bay' played through the speakers, a soothing, necessary pause until the next act was to take over the stage.

Me.

10

'Let's dance. Put on your red shoes and dance the blues ...'

Bowie's voice emerged from the darkness as I took my position on the stage. The spotlight's glare swam across my skin, almost blinding me momentarily, cutting me off from the audience that was became invisible.

I was alone in my own world.

A world of sensations, music, the pulsing smells of cigarette smoke and alcohol fumes swirling around me, as I triggered my arms and legs and set them in motion, attempting as I had so carefully rehearsed to communicate with the very essence of the music, allowing its words and rhythm to take over my body, to be one with the beat, the emotion.

My flesh was here on Avenue C in this somewhat sordid cave of darkness and light but my mind was elsewhere, transported back to that day, so long ago, when the notes emerging from Becker's magic pipe had taken hold of us, catching a crowd of helpless children in its inexorable spider's web and led us away, entranced, in its footsteps, eliminating all volition, thought, past ties and affections.

I stretched my right leg to its full extension, like all the dainty ballerinas always dressed in white I had so admired in photos, so full of suppleness and dexterity, my foot tapping a beat against the floor to the rhythm of the bass guitar that formed the backbone of the song. Extending my arms in an offering, my fingers fluttering like the wings of a bird, flying across the spine of the song. Counting down one move at a time towards the algebra of desire as seen in men's eyes.

I was one with the bass, part of it, a willing slave to its heartbeat.

I gently pulled on the velcro fastening and allowed my pink, flouncy skirt to float to the ground where it spread across the dance floor like an unfolding water-lily. My long legs were revealed. I'd always been told they were my best asset, that they went on forever, happened to be shapely and elegant. It had never occurred to me before; for me they were just a pair of legs.

The music ran through my veins like blood, coexisting with it, magically blending with it in harmonious alchemy. Bowie's voice briefly faded allowing just the instruments, the music in all its glory to dominate, surge, move like water, swirl, dance, until his mellifluous baritone returned and grabbed the melody by the throat and delivered an uncommon form of peace and tranquillity to the unstoppable flow of the music. I pulled my top off. I was not wearing a bra.

Shimmied in the hot spot in just my G-string and my bargain high heel shoes. I had decided not to wear stockings. On one hand I had thought I would look vulgar with them and on the other had feared the perils of a clumsy balancing act involved in pulling them off while continuing to dance.

The final verse of the song rushed through the speakers on either side of the stage and, on cue, I tore off my final piece of minimal underwear and stood there fully nude, punctuating the action with a modest bump and grind to coincide with the fading notes of the song and in unison with the spotlight racing across the stage before being switched off as my intimacy was revealed. I had reluctantly trimmed myself earlier, and was sorely self-conscious of the fact that my slit was now fully visible through the faint and pale curls that remained. On the Island we had walked along in the nude quite freely, with nothing to hide from each other, but this felt different and the eyes fixed on me in the audience were those of unknown men, maybe predators and a wave of discomfort ran through me.

There was a scattering of applause.

Cornelia was standing by the side of the stage, waiting for me. I was about to ask her how she thought my set had gone but she quickly reminded me to step back and pick up the tips which had been dropped by some of the punters on the now empty stage. Half a dozen notes, not that I was interested right now in checking their actual denominations, too busy that I was holding my discarded clothing against my breasts and bottom half as we were still in full view of the watching audience which had alarmingly grown since we had arrived at the club.

'Wow, you were so good, Kate. Amazing. A natural. Look at all those tips …'

Later, Bertram even complimented me. 'That was pretty sexy, girl. For a beginner. If you can sustain that style, I'd be happy for you gals to work on week-end nights, if you wanted.' Friday and Saturday evenings were the most sought-after slots for the club. Larger and more generous audiences. 'You looked as if you were the only person in the room,' he added. 'Next time just try to acknowledge the audience a little more, the guys looking at you. Connect. Give them a sense you're not completely out of reach, if you don't mind me suggesting.'

Did this mean that, in the pursuit of Cornelia's soul, I had become a sex worker?

She was giddy with excitement, having now banished all her earlier reservations, and we returned to my hotel room to celebrate with coffees and ice cream from the Duane Read all-night pharmacy on the corner of Americas and Waverly Place.

Even though I had earned more tips than her, we agreed to split that extra income down the middle, on the pretext that I had taken to the stage after her and that she might well have favourably warmed up the paying audience for me.

We confided in each other. My stories mostly a pack of lies about what I knew of Holland and girlhood memories garnered from books I hoped she had never read. She with elaborate tales of past found and lost love, high school in Louisiana, forbidden excursions through the sin-filled streets of the nearby metropolis of New Orleans with its echoes of voodoo and forbidden booze, and the petty jealousies of the other students she shared the NYU dorm with. I cherished her innocence, the open-hearted way she looked at life, already scared by the knowledge I would soon have to betray her in some deceitful manner so that Becker could fish for her soul.

Why her?

Could it be he coveted her because her soul was unsullied,

an open book?

She was involved in an on and off relationship with another student at NYU who was studying history and military affairs at postgraduate level, what she called a friend with benefits and was curious I was not involved with anyone.

'Aren't you into men?' she hesitantly asked me.

'Of course,' I said. 'There was actually someone, he was called Tristan, some time ago in Europe, but I don't think I'm ready for someone else right now.'

'Is he the reason you came to New York?'

'Yes.' For once I could be truthful.

She queried me more about him, but I made it clear the subject was closed and out of bounds. She reluctantly accepted my reticence.

'I'm not so much into gossip,' I tried to apologize.

She beamed at me. 'We should try to double date, no?'

I couldn't think of anything worse to do.

Summer came, and we settled into a routine. Bertram was right, Friday nights were the most productive when it came to the amount and size of tips from the men in the audience. Wall Street traders in thousand dollar suits, businessmen smelling of money seeking to let steam off after a hard week's hedge funding. We soon began to spot the regulars. Cornelia veered away from classic musical tunes, went full rock n' roll in her choice of music, and began to move more freely on stage as her inhibitions gradually melted away and her deceitfully innocent features took on a more knowing appearance in tune with the fluidity and provocation of her dance moves. Very quickly, she was matching me for tips. As for me, I added a few other songs with a strong backbeat to my repertoire, allying myself in all cases with the heart-like rhythm of the bass punctuating the melody, driving it and my limbs along. I went on automatic pilot, losing myself in the music, eyes often closed, my mind miles and centuries away, but no one noticed or complained. I'd finally moved out of the Washington Square Hotel and had found myself a small sublet on Carmine Street which Cornelia agreed to share with me, after her university term ended. It wasn't fancy or large, and we had an arrangement whereby one week I had use of the bedroom while she slept on the living room sofa, and we swapped around every seven days.

As I'd been such a regular at the hotel and been on good terms with the staff as such a long-term resident, I had arranged a deal with the manager to draw a couple of thousand dollars against Becker's credit card which had been paying for my room, so I now had some cash reserves in addition to what I was earning from the dancing. I knew it wouldn't last, but my needs were modest. My only fear was that it would draw him out and he would come to confront me about the transaction and hurry me into collecting Cornelia's soul. But he didn't manifest himself. Surely, he had not forgotten about me?

The late, humid August heat spread across the city like a shroud of discomfort. I had never experienced this sort of weather before. Long ago in Germany, we had navigated the ups and downs of the seasons with few extremes and on the Island we had accustomed ourselves to an invariable gentle and soothing form of constant sun which seldom even raised a sweat. This was altogether different, clothes sticking to the skin, wetness pearling down your back if you stayed out too long on the streets. Cornelia introduced me to sun cream as my pallor absorbed every single ray of sun with greed and my skin turned pink and itchy under its assault.

As most of the moneyed men who visited the club disappeared to the Hamptons and Long Island, the audiences became sparse and our income faltered. Bertram suggested we take a few weeks off. The suggestion was welcome.

Cornelia hinted we might travel down to New Orleans for a well-earned break. An aunt of hers owned an empty apartment there since she had retired to Florida and would willingly put it at our disposal for a fortnight.

'I hate flying,' I protested. 'I really do.' I still shuddered at the memory of my flight from Europe.

'No problem,' Cornelia said. 'We can take the bus. It will be an adventure. And cheaper.'

We had barely any luggage between the two of us when we emerged from the subway at 42nd Street and searched for the exit that led to the Port Authority Bus Terminal one block from Times Square, dragging our rucksacks along the peep show parlours, sex shops and theatres to the labyrinthine block where the buses were parked underground. Pimps and countless loitering individuals with a host of bad intentions eyed us greedily as we rushed by. Cornelia had warned me it was not a savoury place, but that we would be safe once we had found our bus and driven off.

We had to change Greyhound buses several times along the journey in cities that until now had just been enigmatic names on the map for me, passing through sleepy towns, endless plains and hills, the landscape receding alongside us as we moved forward in a constant state of somnolence. By the time we reached Baton Rouge and within sight of New Orleans, I was already wishing that I had agreed to travel by plane. Maybe we would, I considered, for our return to Manhattan. For someone who had lived for centuries. I was developing a strange sense of impatience.

Even though I'd dozed on and off for most of the journey, I took to my bed upon arriving at Cornelia's aunt's apartment on Burgundy Street and slept for a further 24 hours, despite Cornelia urging me enthusiastically to take my first dip into the fragrant madness of the French Quarter. We had hardly set down our bags that she was on the phone to old school friends and diverse acquaintances and arranging to meet in one bar or another. She was much too chirpy today, excited by our return to her home ground, and I blanked her out as I lay my head on the pillow and sought respite.

By the time I was back in the land of the living and ready to face the Crescent City, Cornelia already had one too many hurricanes under her belt but insisted we visit Bourbon Street. Night was falling and the air carried a curious fragrance of rotten flowers and stale beer as we walked towards the noisy hubbub of the Quarter's principal artery. Clubs, restaurants and bars were already full, snatches of music filtering through onto the busy pavement where folk of all kinds and ages journeyed along carrying tall glasses holding a variety of cocktails in every colour of the rainbow, bottles of beer and necklaces of equally multi-coloured shining beads. The music rose, skirting along the bougainvillae-clad balconies and roofs of Bourbon, snatches of rock battling with zydeco harmonies, incoherent jazz, and every rhythm under the sun or, in this case, a pockmarked full moon rising over Canal Street.

She pointed out some of the many strip joints as we passed them advertising bottomless activities and bargain prices for drinks. Through half open door, I caught sight of a small stage spread out from a central metal pole on which a lithe mulatto woman was performing acrobatics with her strong legs wide open and revealing the shocking pinkness of her intimacy to all and sundry to the sound of 'Big Spender'. We didn't loiter and walked on.

'These are cheap and dirty places. I would never wish to work here,' Cornelia remarked.

'The girls who work here are die hard professionals,' I pointed out, defending our own somewhat more sophisticated New York dalliances. 'Unlike us, I suspect they don't have much choice. We have.'

From the look on her face, I could see Cornelia was not convinced by my argument and was visibly troubled, beginning to both identify with the women who toiled here and feel the germ of a seditious attraction to their more sordid exploits.

Was this a pathway as to how she might sell her soul, I wondered, still puzzled how I could nudge her in that direction? Not that I wished to, far from it. She had become my friend and I felt the urge to protect her. From herself. From me. From Becker.

We ended up at The Pearl, on the other side of Canal, where she introduced me to the fine art of slurping oysters in a single gulp. A first for me but something I grew to enjoy past the first couple of mouthfuls. The taste reminded me of the sea off our erstwhile Island and brought back mixed memories.

The Piper's Dance

Later, sharing beignets at the Café du Monde, caster sugar spilling all over my black tee-shirt, dipping the sweet dough into my coffee, musicians playing gold time trad jazz on the nearby sidewalk, I finally began to acclimate to the New Orleans zeitgeist Cornelia had been joyfully advertising ever since we had met. I began to relax, allowing my mind to drift aimlessly, drinking in the fragrances and the ever-present echoes of all styles of music coming at us from every direction in town. Just a stone's throw away the wide Mississippi river's waters lapped against its banks.

I was beginning to understand why Cornelia had become so attached to this unique place. It was so different, a blend of implied sensuality and risk blanketing the general atmosphere, a dangerous combination of invisible elements ever swirling through the air.

Maybe what we had done in New York, our decision to work at the Mermaids Club, had changed her. She was no longer the same timid student who had left the Big Easy with her innocence intact; she was now more tempted, vulnerable, having crossed over to some other fuzzy side, no doubt encouraged by my moral support.

'We should try it?'

'Have you ever before?'

'No. But I think it could be fun. Only live once and all that, eh?'

She'd heard talk of a clandestine voodoo ceremonial taking place on a nearby bayou a few days later and urged me to come along, on the understanding we would not become personally involved, just remain spectators. Warren, a high school friend of hers knew the location and we hopped into his Ford Bronco SUV in late afternoon; there was another couple already onboard.

'I'm Lucy. This is Mark,' they introduced themselves as we fitted ourselves onto the backseat, and the car took the direction of the Louis Armstrong Airport, flashing by the Superdome on our way.

It was dark by the time we reached the clearing by the muddy river where a dozen of other cars were already congregating, their headlights illuminating a central wood fire burning bright, surrounded by folk. I had half expected most of them to be of colour, but the majority were white, like me. I found that reassuring, proof that what might ensue would just be a case of mild exotic tourism and would not actually skirt the supernatural.

'So what happens now,' I asked Mark, as we sat down in a circle around the blazing fire.

'We await the Grand Priest,' he said.

In the meantime, a bottle of rum was being passed around. It burned my throat and left a bitter aftertaste. Cornelia, sitting on my right, partook several times and was soon visibly inebriated which she had never been previously in my presence.

'Do you think they'll sacrifice a rooster, slit its throat?' she whispered in my ear.

I hoped not.

The priest who arrived shortly after was a stooped old man with long white braided hair spilling from his black bowler hat and sunken eyes. He supported himself with a cane carved out of wood, and carried an assortment of random small heteroclit objects hanging from his wide, worn leather belt. A couple of rusty knives, bazaar knick-knacks, beads, pieces of string and a discoloured purse. I noticed something else, dangling on his side, between one of the knives and a necklace of white beads. I narrowed my eyes and focused on the object.

It was a pipe.

Unlike Becker's it was not made of gold, but seemed moulded out of clay. Otherwise, it was identical in shape in length to the one Tristan and I had stolen to gain entry to the real world.

I shuddered.

I knew deep inside it was a sign, and the shadows surrounding me were closing in.

The priest in a resonant patois blending English and French

ordered us to switch off all the vehicles' headlights, so that we were left in a circle of darkness, the raging fire in the centre the only source of light in this night without stars where the moon was obscured by a permanent wall of low-lying clouds.

He straightened his body, slowly rising to his full height and began to intone a droning melody. Cornelia took a nervous grip of my hand as we sat there watching and listening to the old man.

Then, as I had feared all along, he snatched the pipe from his ragged belt and began playing it. I felt a brief surge of relief as its sounds in no way resembled the hypnotic golden tones of Becker's golden pipe, but all too soon the remote melody took shape and like a snake in slow motion began circulating around the circle, passing from head to head, ear to ear, and I felt a growing sense of drowsiness assault me. Cornelia's grip on my fingers loosened.

I did not wish to get involved further, be taken in by the illusion, and I tried to place myself in the position of just an observer but it was difficult to detach myself from the situation.

There was movement to my left as, somehow, the sounds of the roughly-carved instrument superposed themselves with a torrent of words spilling at the same time from the mouth of the priest, an unholy prayer rising towards the sky, punctuated by the unearthly sound of the pipe and Lucy rose, her eyes glazed and shed her clothing and began to dance. It was nothing like the dances we knew, just a slow, almost painful shaking of her limbs as her feet appeared to be nailed to the sandy ground, and tremors in waves uncontrollably traversed her epileptic body.

Soon, all the others had thrown their clothes off and stood naked, swaying, puppets to the priest's ju-ju. I grabbed Cornelia by the waist as she began to rise.

'No, don't do it. Please.'

She shrugged me off and joined the circle of oblivious dancers, trampling her skirt in the dirt, tearing off her blouse and casting it off asunder with wild abandon

I was the only one left sitting.

11

Had I at this point expected a bacchanalia? If so. it was a disappointment, with all the gyrating participants twisting their limbs in a parody of trance around the fire as the voodoo priest's undulating melody controlled them and directed their movements in slow motion, shadows eclipsing each other in the light of the flickering brasier, silhouettes hopscotching against the background of the dark night sky and its procession of thick clouds.

Cornelia was no more animated than any of her friends, barely breaking a sweat. I thought for a moment she was faking it, just tagging along for the sake of propriety, until I caught a fleeting sight of her eyes. They were glazed, empty of feeling, as if she was miles away and someone else was pulling her mental strings.

What should I do? Participate in some way to avoid breaking the spell the priest was attempting to cast? Or keep on sitting, remain a mere observer of the bizarre and half-hearted ritual?

In the near distance, the waters of the bayou casually lapped against the muddy shore, dragging flotsam in their wake, the muted sound of the river's tributary combining with the sparks from the fire as they crackled away, a mural of sound as background to the constant hum of the priest's clay pipe.

The voodoo man's voice rose and fell and rose again.

The central wood fire slowly began to wane as no one was any longer feeding it and its warmth lessened. I shivered, pulling the cardigan I was wearing tight against my body. The active participants in the ceremonial were still naked, but the creeping cold didn't appear to be affecting them.

Still they all gesticulated.

My mind wandered. A surge of drowsiness washed over

me. I briefly closed my eyes. Distanced myself.

Did I doze off? I was awakened by a sharp detonation, something in the fire, a branch, a random piece of wood in its final throes combusting loudly.

The priest was gone.

Cornelia's friends were scattered across the ground, holding each other, now seeking warmth and comfort, their movements halting and shy, as if victims of a terrible hangover. I half smiled.

Then realised I couldn't see Cornelia. I turned round, peered in every direction. She was nowhere to be seen. My stomach tightened, expecting the worse.

I walked to the car just in case she had taken shelter there, but there was no one inside it. I returned to the camp fire area and looked out across the stagnant surface of the bayou but not a ripple disturbed its surface.

I stepped over to Mark and Lucy who sat, cuddled against each other on a tattered blanket shielding them from the ground's cold and humid reach.

They both looked lost, their movements tentative, their focus distant.

'Have you seen Cornelia?'

They looked up at me as if they didn't even recognize me, puzzled by my appearance.

'Who's Cornelia?'

'Who are you? How did you get here?'

I tried Warren who was stretched out a few meters closer to the bayou's edge and he was equally surprised by my appearance and non-plussed by my questions.

None of them remembered either me or Cornelia. All professed having journeyed here without us, had no memory of the two of us joining them.

I breathed a deep sigh, my heart in free fall.

Cornelia had been taken.

A wave of guilt coursed through me. Had she not been with me, none of this would have happened. I'd given her moral support to take up stripping. I'd agreed to visit New Orleans.

All along I had unwittingly approved each and every step that had led us to this desolate bayou. Even though I hadn't always been aware of the fact, I had been doing Becker's subtle work.

And now he had collected her soul.

Two gone. One to go in our unholy pact.

I wanted to cry, but knew it would be out of self-pity, which I didn't deserve.

Even though I had now become a stranger to them, Cornelia's friends agreed to drive me back to the city. I didn't even have the keys to her aunt's apartment, and had to discreetly break in, if only to pick up my belongings and head to the bus station to find a Greyhound bus which would return me to New York. Again, it was a slow and tortuous journey, full of night stops in desolate towns but two days later, unwashed and famished, I arrived at the Port Authority Terminal where I was immediately accosted by a couple of pimps who had mistaken me for yet another country girl visiting the Big Apple in search of fame and glory and promising me riches and celebrity in short order. I loudly swore at them in German and they quickly decamped. Why didn't the Piper harvest the souls of men like them?

I reached the small Gramercy apartment we had shared, wondering whether if all Cornelia's belongings would also have vanished, as if her existence had been in a single stroke expunged from reality, but they were still all present, clothes, books, documents, toiletries, even the flowery scent of her cheap perfume still lingered, a sharp reminder of my guilt.

I felt aimless and disenchanted. Waiting indifferently for what might happen next. Should I return to the Mermaids Club. It wasn't as if we had been a double act and I was confident Bertram would have me back. But that chapter of my life was now so inextricably connected to Cornelia that I couldn't muster any enthusiasm. I had danced because of her, to get closer to her, and it wasn't as if I had ever taken great pleasure from it. I could easily live without it, I knew, even though the sensations of losing myself in the music under the hot glare of the spotlight and the invisible gaze of a male audience had proven bizarrely powerful and compelling.

I was still pondering what to do next when, inevitably, another of those identical envelopes made an appearance two days later in my mail slot in the building's exiguous lobby.

Back on the sofa, which I now always slept on, the bed holding too many memories of Cornelia, I opened it, pulled the customary sheet of paper out, gazed at the page and immediately dropped it to the floor, and ran to the bathroom where I was violently sick.

A name.

An address.

A photograph.

Of a child.

A young boy, around ten years old.

Blond haired, wide-eyed, wearing a red soccer shirt.

A terrible coldness ran down my spine.

Surely not? Why in hell could Becker require a child's soul? It was just inhuman. Uncalled for. Grown men and women, I could barely understand as it was, but this was just going too far. It was unacceptable.

No way could he justify it, nor could I take a single step towards condoning it, have anything to do with this new set of instructions.

I dragged my feet back into the room and picked up the slightly crumpled piece of paper from the wooden floor, peered at it again, hoping against hope I had misjudged matters.

The photo was the same as before.

Bile still coated the insides of my mouth, its bitterness tracing a way through my veins and my nerves to both my heart and my brain.

I tried to steady myself, slowed my breath and deliberately folded the sheet of paper with the child's details and placed it back inside the orange envelope, opened the apartment's door and took the stairs down to the shabby lobby of our building.

Here I slid the envelope back into my mail slot, stuffing it between the familiar crowd of assorted junk mail and free coupons I had little use for and returned upstairs.

This was my answer to Becker.

I knew he would understand the meaning of my gesture.

But could not at this early stage foresee his response. How his wrath might turn against me.

He allowed my anger to stew for a whole week until he finally made an appearance.

I was considering returning to work at the club as the need to raise some cash was becoming more pressing and I still felt it was a better alternative than waitressing or bar work. I was sitting in a falafel joint on Sullivan Street making my coffee last and doing mental sums, calculating how many more days I could make my remaining dollars last if I budgeted with care.

I was lost in dark thoughts, concentrating on the ripples moving to and from the rim on the surface of my half full coffee cup every time my knees made contact with the table's legs, negligently trying to discern patterns, some sort of meaning in them. And concluding it was a form of geometry that eluded me.

I vaguely noticed someone seating himself on the opposite chair and his gaze landing on me. I looked up. It was Becker.

Rage welled up inside me.

'You look rather beautiful when you are angry, my dear,' Becker said.

He wore a three piece elegantly-cut dark beige suit, a pale pink shirt and no tie and a pair of expensive sunglasses sat perched across his nose. As ever he fitted right in, adapting like a chameleon to every environment or country. The slope of his nose as sharp as his prominent cut glass cheekbones, his beard carefully trimmed and sculpted.

'You …'

'I gather you wanted to see me.'

'Yes, I did.'

'So,' a slim Middle-Eastern teenager deposited a plate of sickly-sweet patisseries on our table. Becker nodded his approval. 'Did you not get my information sheet? I know you've seen it, so don't embarrass me by pretending you haven't.'

'I did.'

'And?'

'Why?'

'Why a child?'

Becker smiled enigmatically, a rictus that broadened his features as if his skin was made of rubber and he could change its configuration at will.

He took his Raybans off and the endless well of his eyes confronted me in full.

I shuddered. I had forgotten how hypnotic those eyes of his were, its depths as unfathomable as his thoughts. He literally lived in another dimension, had no doubt seen things I never could imagine or would ever wish to contemplate.

'Does it concern you?' he asked.

'Yes, it does. A lot.'

'It shouldn't. I own you, Katerina. You do what I command. You have to pay the price of your betrayal.'

'But a child, come on ... You always give us heavy, melodramatic hints about the sins we carry. A boy that young hasn't sinned. Surely not? So why do you wish to steal his soul? It doesn't make sense.'

'Much in these worlds we journey through doesn't make sense, my dear. It's not for you to reason why, though.'

I slammed my now empty cup of coffee down on the formica table top.

'And what if I don't go along with it?'

'You will.'

'And suppose I reluctantly accept, how the fuck do I seduce a ten-year-old kid?'

'That's for you to puzzle out. There are so many ways to sway the guilty or the innocent, Katerina; or would you rather I called you Marta now? I'm confident you will find a way.'

I couldn't imagine how in my wildest dreams.

He took a bite of a square-shaped piece of baklava, his teeth sinking into the dough, a few chopped nuts dropping to the table. The fragrant odour of cinnamon wafted across towards me.

'Have one, they're delicious,' he pointed to the overflowing plate.

I'd never had much of a sweet tooth and declined.

'You don't know what you're missing.' He wiped his lips clean.

Back in Paris when Tristan and I had lived together, we had often speculated whether we would be able to conceive children. On the Island, where the laws of nature were in effect suspended and the majority of us never aged one iota, we were safe in the knowledge it would not have proven possible. But having moved to the other side, crossed through the mirror separating the worlds, we had noted that we could at last age properly and had wondered whether we could procreate too. When mating, we had never taken any precautions but I had not fallen pregnant. You always hanker for what you can't have, and this seeming impossibility to have a child had for months triggered a profound feeling of emptiness in my heart.

So the suggestion I might be party to desecrating one was unthinkable to me. I would not be able to live with myself should I become involved in this next stage of Becker's plan.

'I won't do it, Becker.'

'That is a pity, dear Katerina.'

'Never.'

'You're repeating yourself. It's tiresome.'

'So what do you plan to do about it, then?'

'I don't think the problem is mine, young lady.'

He appeared quite unperturbed by my apparent rebellion. He looked at me with what appeared to be genuine sympathy, pity even.

'I'll give you time, Katerina. Reflect, consider. I am in no rush.'

Time was on his side. Why should I be grateful for the reprieve? I recalled he had somehow impersonated Tristan, taken over his body by way of magic and my anger welled up again, like a kettle about to come to the boil. I pushed back my chair, stood up, seized my tote bag and rushed out of the café without looking back at him or saying a single word.

I guessed he watched my fitful departure with that infuriating smile, as ever curling his lips, entertained by my rush of temper.

Over the following few weeks, my mind a veritable jumble of conflicting, agonising thoughts, I was obliged to return to the club as my money was fast running out and rent and food became an urgent preoccupation.

I agreed to three evenings a week. Two sets a night, one early and one around midnight. Bertram asked me, 'Try and connect a bit more, Marta. Sometimes the punters complain you're too aloof, lost in your own world. Acknowledge their presence a little at least. I know it doesn't come naturally to you, but make an effort. It will pay off, you'll see.'

To break up the monotony and not feel like a dancing automaton straight out of a bad science fiction movie, I would sometimes appropriate some of Cornelia's tapes, to vary the sound, the rhythm of the dance and the way it affected my movements, tried in vain to make myself more desirable in the eyes of the customers in an attempt to garner better tips. I began, despite the glare of the spotlight in my eyes, to recognise some regulars out there, assessing me, weighing the suppleness of my gyrating flesh, speculating about my fuckability, my availability, my willingness to accept a drink in private and maybe more, even though it was against the rules. But it was a line I wouldn't cross. As it was I did not overly like myself these days, and saw no point in retreating further into personal abjection.

On a day off from the Mermaids, out of infuriating curiosity, I travelled uptown to the address Becker had provided for the child and watched, one early morning, as his nanny walked him and his slightly older sister to a nearby private school from where she picked both of them up later in the day.

He seemed unremarkable, just transparently normal and I

couldn't for the life of me determine why he was a target of Becker's. Or were his parents the final target, to be punished for sins unknown by proxy?

'You're a strange but beautiful woman, Marta,' Bertram walked into the changing room after my final set on a Friday evening. I was still dressing, not that he hadn't seen all my attributes time and time again as I exhibited myself on stage. I suppose we were just part of the furniture for him, little, large, tall, short, skinny or voluptuous, a gallery of familiar feminine shapes and faces spanning the spectrum of sex.

'You could have knocked, 'I remarked, slipping my leggings on, not even looking up at him.

'Spare me the modesty.'

He stood there observing me.

'Since your friend Cornelia walked away, Marta, you appear distracted, dare I say unhappy.'

'I'm OK, just earning a living the best way I can.'

'Hmm … There's something about you I don't get. You say you're from the Netherlands, your ID confirms it, but my gut feeling tells me the accent is wrong. I just can't place it. A girl with secrets, no?'

'Maybe. But does it affect the way I dance? You still have a full house most occasions I'm on stage, don't you?'

He looked at me quizzically. 'We do. You're certainly a popular dancer. That air of mystery and remoteness that invariably surrounds you, I think it attracts them. OK, Marta, subject closed. Join us for a drink at the bar when you're ready and we've closed up. It's June Ann's birthday.' She was one of the older dancers, but we'd seldom spoken to each other.

I knew I had to fit in better and agreed to join the small celebration.

Even indulged in a few glasses of wine.

You'd think that a late-night party in a strip club, with staff, dancers and a couple of regulars who were harmless enough to be allowed to join in, would prove interesting but, as it turned out, most of the ongoing conversations I joined centred on Bertram and June Ann's children. They were the same age and were seemingly going through similar growing pains. Not a subject I was quite ready to face right now, let alone knew anything about.

The next morning, I was posted across the street from the luxury apartment block on the Upper East Side where the boy and his family lived and witnessed him leaving for his soccer training by the Pier. As he was stepping into his father's car, he must have felt my distant gaze on him and turned his head. Our eyes briefly met. His were pale blue with echoes of grey. The sun was rising over Manhattan and my heart dipped into the deepest abyss.

I slowly walked away as the car sped south down the almost empty road and found a diner where I had breakfast. By the time the plate came, I'd already forgotten what I had ordered. I thought of Tristan, the children of Hamelin, Cornelia and so many things I had lost.

I took the decision.

Did I have any other choice?

How to contact Becker?

I decided I could wait. He would come to me. He always did.

I had two hundred and twenty dollars in my purse, the rent on the small apartment was paid up for another three weeks. I vowed not to return to the Mermaids.

I would sit it out and await Becker's next appearance.

It was dawn. It was going to be another beautiful day in Manhattan, not a cloud disturbing the immense blue sky draped over the countless skyscrapers or the slightest tremor of wind racing down the canyons of the Avenues. I had been up all night, reading a book of legends and fairy tales I had picked up from a street stool on Americas. It even included a much romanticised retelling of the Piped Piper of Hamelin's story, as well as the story of the Little Mermaid, which I had never come across before and which caught my attention because of the strip club's name and its corridor full of prints of sea denizens.

Later, I was thinking of jogging down Fifth to spend some hours in Washington Square, communing with the unruly army of squirrels and dipping my toes in the fountain. Pretending I was a true a New Yorker.

The air shimmered behind me. And there he was. Becker.

His familiar, unreliable smile. his aquiline nose and dark as coal eyes.

Dressed casually in a white shirt and jeans, with an uncommon tan replacing his customary pallor. Like a man on a holiday.

'Katerina.'

'Becker.'

'You wished to see me?' As if he could read my mind at a distance.

'I did.'

'So you will provide me with my third soul, as ordered?'

'I will.'

'Good.'

I swallowed hard.

'But not the boy?'

'Why?'

'I just can't.'

'I'm in no mood to make deals, Katerina. So what have you to offer me instead?'

'My soul. In exchange for the child's.'

I'd said it; there was no going back. But would he accept?

'So be it.'

12

I was swimming.

Something at the back of my mind told me it must be an inland sea, although there was no shore to be seen under the moonless but starry sky, a thousand and one lights shining down and casting a sheet of silver on the waters.

I didn't know how long I had been here; my memory didn't reach that far back.

My limbs wearily dictated my movements, my muscles hard, stiff, tiring further with every stroke forward and getting me nowhere for lack of any precise destination. But a voice inside me told me I had to keep on moving, couldn't afford to stay in place or I would succumb and be dragged down to the depths into the darkness that lay below. Soon, I knew, I would spasm and become incapable of swimming any longer as all my energy reserves would run out and there was a limit as to how long I could just remain in place in a floating position. Was this limbo, the first circle of hell? In which case, I would still have a further eight circles to confront before my purgatory was complete, or had I, too many years back, read Dante incorrectly?

Or had I become Eurydice and Tristan would come to the rescue on some mythical white stallion? I wished I had taken a better notice of the stories in those dusty pages in the Great Library on the Island now. How did they all end?

The increasing pain spreading along my nerves and now reaching my extremities was exponential as were the questions running through my fevered mind.

I was desperately trying to breathe through my nose as I swam, but I was faltering more and more, my lips parting involuntarily, allowing water to invade my mouth. The water was cold, tasteless. I tried hard not to swallow it, spitting out as much as I could with every breath.

How much longer could I last before my body gave up?

Minutes. An hour at least.

I was swimming in place, not moving forward at all, nailed to a spot, still striving unsuccessfully to reach an impossible destination. For all I knew, I could be moving backwards.

A torrent of conflicting emotions raced along the screen of my eyes, images of the first time us children of Hamelin had encountered the sea shortly after our arrival at the colony, and how we had rushed noisily through the wet sand and immersed ourselves in the warm sea, a joyful communion with this amazing new world we had been transported to; of making love under water with Tristan once we had hooked up and our leisurely mornings on the beach, watching the immutable horizon, taken in by its beauty but also hearing the seeds of discontent it slowly began to evoke, those questions which had brought me here and lost him to me along the way.

Out of nowhere a wave appeared and I was unable to duck in time and my head went under, acrid salt water seeping into my nose. I gasped. My movements lost their coordination and I had to quickly straighten my legs to rise back to the surface where I could breathe freely again.

The wave made no sense. There were no conceivable tides in this sea. It did not taste of salt. Had I not known there were no rules in the worlds, no fixed laws of nature, and everything was quite arbitrary? It was as if a puppet master (Becker?) was pulling distant strings to make me squirm or suffer more.

I kept on swimming.

Towards nowhere.

Finally, the rest of my strength ebbed and I came to a total halt.

I felt the pull of the deep streaming into my exhausted legs and arms. My heart dropped as I realised the time had come, and I could not force it back any further.

My chin dipped under the water, then my mouth and my nose and within seconds my eyes.

The view from under the sea was a brief thing of beauty: the fluttering roof of the water's surface shone eerily as if lit by a non-existent moon or a mighty spotlight, like a sheet made of electricity dividing the land of the dead from the domain of the living.

I let go and allowed myself to float down towards the sea's floor, holding on for dear life to the last bubbles of air in my lungs until I felt like bursting.

My mouth involuntarily opened and the final vestiges of air abandoned my body. I exploded, my lungs and chest ripped apart in one mighty conflagration, the searing pain tearing at my heart and then my brain. If I could, I would have cried out in sheer agony but I was incapable of sound, of anything resembling life.

I closed my eyes. Imagined for a moment I was now a mermaid and could roam the seas with total freedom and abandon.

Vaguely felt the sea floor greeting me as I floated down in a foetal position onto its soft bed and then everything drifted away and my consciousness faded.

Centuries passed. Time enough for stars to die and faraway galaxies to form anew.

It took a terrible effort and force of will to get my eyes to open. They were caked, gritty dust or sand cementing my eyelids to my skin, but I raised my hand and swept it across my face to clean and free myself.

The glare of the sun blinded me.

I was naked, sitting in a plain of ice. Whiteness surrounded me. Even the cloudless sky was losing a battle against the encroachment of sheer blinding white devastating its once blue bed.

My initial instinct was to shiver, but then I realised I wasn't actually cold.

In the distance, a snow-peaked mountain range sat like a throne over the horizon, the plain of ice like a flow of pale lava extending its tendrils towards it. The last thing I remembered was the agonising pain of drowning then things went blank and

I found myself here.

A new circle for my personal hell?

Behind me the immensity of the ice plain, around me that uninterrupted bed of permafrost stretching to what appeared infinity. Ahead of me the faraway mountains. Instinct whispered in my ear that should become my destination. I knew it would take me forever to reach those craggy peaks. Days and nights. If even there were nights here, or was I held captive in a problematic land of midnight sun where the darkness was never allowed to fall and offer some form of relief and my eyes would burn out first in the constant glare reflecting from land and sky. Or I went mad from the relentless exposure? But was I not mad already?

I began my trek towards the heights.

Under my bare feet the ice was slippery and treacherous, not as even as I had initially thought: here and there cracks appeared, gaps in the surface running geometric patterns through the plain, this solid sea of whiteness.

My progress was slow, carefully avoiding the sometimes treacherous and many times often invisible to the naked eye irregularities in the surface for fear of stubbing a toe or twisting an ankle if I tried to hasten my pace. Feelings intermittently began to return to my body, first a tightness in my muscles as if the engine controlling them had been switched on after being shred to pieces and stalling in my previous underwater descent. Then the sensation of heat and cold brushing against the tip of my nose, my ears, my lips and then moving through my sore anatomy to my fingers and toes. Or rather just cold.

I had no clothes, no protection against the elements surrounding me for miles and miles. No hope of finding the slightest protection. How long would I last in these stark conditions?

I had been walking for what felt hours towards the initially gentle hills acting as a first rampart before the mountains actually rose out of the frozen earth when the cold began to bite in earnest. Seeping through my skin, insinuating itself in seditious ways through my pores and injecting itself into my sinews and veins, an increasing sensation of numbness invading me like an army on the march.

And still the foothills appeared as distant as ever, as if I had made not an inch of progress since I had begun my journey in their direction.

Would I reach them before my toes and other parts of my body froze to the point where I might become a statue of ice in the heart of this stark immensity, a monument to futility? 'Here stands Katerina who dared disobey the Piper'.

Or would my extremities turn black, fall off, and I would just become another Venus De Milo of the ice plain, limbless, a thing of legend, a warning to others. But then who would ever visit this desolate place? It was not a museum and open to tourists.

The pain steadily spreading through me began to affect my already halting progress. My brain slowed down, memories fading in and out, thoughts never quite reaching conclusions and racing back to their point of departure and beginning again with little hope of any conclusion.

I no longer harboured any concept of time, of how long I had been here. Through the mental fog I realised hunger had not raised its head, confirming again the fact this realm was not of the real world, merely a construct in which I had been dropped by Becker to purge my sins, suffer until I had reached a point of no return when my soul had been totally obliterated.

'My name is Katerina,' I cried out in vain. There was no one to hear me, no one to help, never would be any more.

Was this what it meant to be damned?

I stumbled on. No longer feeling the tips of my toes, the soles of my feet burning as if I were journeying over hot coals, my fingers just useless digits with seemingly no connection with the rest of me. Thin shards of ice stuck to my hair, brushed against my forehead, my eyes could barely stay open, my lashes captive in the cotton threads of snow flakes, my breath halting, gasping for air, registering the flow of coldness circulating through my nose and down my throat all the way to my faltering lungs. My heart beat in slow motion.

I stopped.

Fell down to my knees, grazing the skin against a sharp knife of solid ice protruding from the plain's uneven surface at an angle. Blood began to well under the torn skin and, transfixed, I watched it rise to the surface and a couple of miniscule drops fell onto the white soil. Where they were quickly absorbed, spreading outwards in a concentric circle like a growing stain until their progress came to a halt as my knee was already cauterising and the minute flow of blood ceased.

Ruby red flowers on the ice. Like a flower opening.

Tiny droplets of colour punctuating the unfailingly white curtain of the landscape in whose centre I was now kneeling. Helpless. Exhausted. Motionless.

'You win, Becker …' I whispered, convinced he must be somewhere watching me, behind the wall of the sky, lurking maliciously beneath the frozen earth, floating invisibly in the air, laughing at me maybe. 'You already own my soul … What more do you want? Just take me. All of me. Let this end … Please.'

There was no answer.

I tried to move, raise myself to my feet again, but was unable to do so. The skin of my soles adhered to the ice and I could not tear it away. I attempted to gain some traction by pushing my right hand down against the ground in an effort to move my body, but it also stuck to the ice.

My first teardrop froze before it reached my cheekbone. Turned to crystal.

Then life went into slow motion. If this was actually life.

The mountain tops in that forever distance shimmered.

My eyes filled, tears turning immediately into ice. My vision blurred.

The shape of the mountain range fading until it was one blank, white and uniform canvas.

The cold took a firm grip of my body. Wrested control from me.

It felt like being stabbed by a thousand simultaneous sharp daggers and accompanying arrows, my flesh offering no resistance, pierced, penetrated until I had fully transformed into a crucified pin cushion of hurt.

I struggled for a final breath of freezing air, in the hope it would revive my rapidly fading consciousness, but just opening my mouth, forcing my lips apart to suck in vital air was too painful.

I gasped one final time.

I capitulated and let go. Abandoned myself to the ocean of pain rushing across my wounded body as it transmuted into the pure, unassailable beauty of crystal. Becoming a million snowflakes, melting into the uniformity of the landscape.

I became earth. I became sky. Every atom of me split apart and merging with the Northern Stars

An eternity passed.

I was falling through the sky.

The heat of the planet spread out below me reached out to embrace my flesh as I surged through the canopy of clouds and shifting currents, a warm wind buffeting me as I plunged.

The closer I moved towards the ground the hotter it became. I turned my head in flight and glanced down at the planet below and the surface was a sea of flames, a wash of burning red and yellow in constant motion, spitting deadly saliva upwards and in all directions in a boiling ferment of rage.

Water. Ice. And now fire.

My next circle of hell.

I closed my eyes, waiting for my descent to come to its final conclusion and to be immolated in the furnace below, engulfed in its fiery and hungry mouth, turned to ashes, to nothingness.

By now, I was broken and unable to resist my inevitable fate. I welcomed it, if this was to my liberation from Becker's spell.

Drown me. Freeze me. Burn Me.

Would there be any further ordeals until I was fully broken and my soul sundered from me?

'No,' I heard his voice, out of nowhere, surrounding my senses.

Already, as I approached the roar of the flames, I could feel my skin blistering, my blood coming to the boil inside me, my halting breath like tongues of hot coal eating away at my insides.

'What?'

'It's done.'

I was back in New York, sitting at a rickety outside table by one of the food vans surrounding the pond; behind us stood the Loab Boathouse. It was sunny. I wore a floral print summer dress which I recalled as one of my favourite garments, fitting me like a familiar second skin and which I had found in a charity store in the Village. Becker sat across from me.

A second ago I was about to be engulfed by the sea of fire, immolated like an Indian widow on the banks of the Ganges and now I was back where I had begun the dreadful journey he had sent me on.

Two plastic glasses of freshly-pressed lemonade sat on the table, begging to be drunk. I seized mine and gulped it down in one go, my parched throat still halfway between the world of flames I had been in extremis snatched away from and the more prosaic reality of Central Park on a pleasant Spring day.

The cold drink was like an elixir of life and brought me back to my senses.

'What is done?' I blurted out.

'I have taken possession of your soul,' the Piper said, in a tone that was neither triumphant nor judgemental. Just quietly matter of fact.

'Is that it, then?'

'Yes, easy, wasn't it?'

'Maybe, but far from painless,' I pointed out, remembering the ordeals by water, ice and fire my mind and body had just gone through. I knew I would never forget those moments and they would be carved in my mind and body forever, keeping me wide awake at night as the stuff of nightmares.

'I know,' Becker said, as if he could read my mind. 'But it's all part of the process. I wasn't born bad, and I bear you and others no malice. It's just the way things are. I'm not the devil, nor even an angel, fallen at that. We all have a role to play in this absurd game we live through. Collecting souls and making temptation real is mine. Like you, I'm just a pawn. You assume I'm in control, but I'm not. There are rules, laws, traditions and all I do is serve. Some call this game a nightmare and they might well be right but none of us have any choice, do we?'

There was even a hint of sadness in his words. Or was I imagining it.

'So where is my soul now?' I asked him. I felt the same as before, despite the indelible memories, even though according to him a part of me was missing.

'It's out there. With all the others.'

Even though he spoke in riddles, I had lost all curiosity.

'So, what now?'

I looked into his eyes, in their charcoal depths was an abyss of arcane knowledge I would never have access to, and I was content with that. I had been broken on his rack and would have to live with that knowledge.

Again, he read my mind. 'You will no longer live forever, Katerina,' he informed me. Was there a hint of regret in his voice? 'Your days are now finite. It won't be tomorrow or the week or even the year after, but death will come. Maybe you will even see it as a relief.'

I could hear the sound of children's voices and turned my gaze to the pond where a gaggle of five-year-olds were gathered, following the progress of a model boat on the water as it skirted the central fountain.

And realised we were no longer in New York's Central Park, but in the Jardin du Luxembourg in Paris. Nothing surprised me any longer.

'I can leave you here,' he offered. 'If you prefer, or have you back in New York, or anywhere really. Your choice.'

'I'm sure this will do as well as anywhere.'

'You will not find Tristan,' he informed me. 'He is gone, and you will never see him again.'

'What has happened to him?'

'The plans have been made and his soul will be collected too in some manner still to be determined. I can't allow you to know more.'

I sighed, my heavy heart slowing under the weight of memories and past affection.

'You were both beautiful as children, you know. When I took you from Hamelin, the two of you stood out. You had an aura. Such a shame you rebelled.'

'I'll never forget him,' I insisted in petty response to his all-knowing arrogance.

'You will, Katerina, because I can provide you with a choice.'

'Between living with the pain of the memories, good as well as bad, or the grace of forgetfulness.'

'When can I decide?'

'Now,' the Piper said.

I was no longer drinking lemonade, but from a tall glass of sweet grenadine.

It didn't take me long to reach a decision. Retaining all those memories would be like a daily torture, I realised, every single shard reminding me of the joy of the past. The Island where we had been happy for centuries, Tristan, the becalmed sea surrounding the colony, the excitement of our escape, the nights spent in each other's arms in Hannover, Paris and elsewhere, the hapless Konrad, Cornelia and her simple version of happiness, they would all haunt me forever in their unavailability. And I also knew that the pain of my drowning, my virtual death on the ice and my fiery immolation in the flames would forever stain my days and nights and quickly contaminate all the good things that remained.

'Do it,' I said.

Becker rose to his feet, his silhouette briefly obscuring the sun and walked round the wooden bench we were sitting on side by side. He looked inhumanly tall as he bent over me, took my hair in his hands, caressed it, then nonchalantly moved his long, bony fingers to the bared skin of my shoulders and grazed it with awkward tenderness.

He looked down at me with both love and pity and his lips came level with my forehead as he leaned forward and kissed me. And all my memories faded.

I was a woman in Paris. I couldn't remember my name. I no longer had a past. All I knew, when I stole the opportunity to look at myself in a mirror, was that I was beautiful.

That would keep me alive until the days of my death finally came.

PART THREE

The Mermaid's Necklace

'Though the love song comes in many guises – songs of exultation and praise, rage and despair, erotic songs, songs of abandonment and loss – they all address God. For it is the haunted premises of longing that the true love song inhabits.'
Nick Cave, 1998.

13

The day Liv Lisa met the man she came to know as Dr Becker, she had no idea he would one day turn her into a mermaid.

She'd been drifting for what felt like ages, from place to place, from man to man, never quite knowing what she wanted. Adrift. With no overall grand plan.

A couple of years back she had met a pleasant man named Conrad at the Jazz Festival and enjoyed a brief relationship. They'd bonded over the band playing while sitting close to each other on the grass in Jackson Square. She had visited him twice in New York where he worked as a freelance editor, had felt at ease with him which raised hope in her heart that it might evolve into something more permanent. He was easy going, had no qualms about her past life and accepted her for what she was, in all her contradictions. It had been lust at first sight and fiery sex in his room at the Prince Conti Hotel had ensued, following more than a drink too many at the Bombay Club downstairs on the first day they met. Then he had vanished out of sight, his phone going unanswered, and later her letters returned with 'person no longer lives at this address' rubberstamped on the back of the envelope next to her return address. She'd been puzzled and saddened but after melancholy reflection had just put it down to bad luck.

She'd been totally honest with him from the outset about her short-lived career in pornography when she so desperately needed the money to supplement her student loan before she had finally graduated and found a position as a biochemistry researcher in a Tulane University laboratory unit. Conrad had found the news more titillating than shocking, and maybe felt a sense of masculine pride that he was enjoying sex with an actual porn star. She'd filmed just under a dozen clips, and after the initial shoots in an exiguous studio in Baton Rouge and several hotel rooms rented for the day with partners whose names she never learned, she had voluntarily signed a six-month contract with a California company who specialised in BDSM segments. She knew there was a strong submissive streak lurking inside her and though she found the latex, rubber, straps and spanking part of the job a tad ridiculous, but all the accoutrements involved made her feel less degraded than the straight sex with its dirty hydraulics, painful anal sex, monotonous double penetrations and vulgar dialogue which turned her off more often than on. Throughout the filmed sex and its implausible scenarios she had only ever come once and it had been with a black stud who advertised himself as Brandon Longwood on the occasion of her one and only interracial shoot. She had felt deeply ashamed by her participation and the fact she had been unable to repress her pleasure at being taken by him. She was a girl of the South and still marked by lingering prejudices. She had never used her own name, adopting a porn pseudonym for the occasion, and the clips could be hunted down on the Internet if you knew it. But Conrad had never asked.

She had never pegged him as someone who might cruise the web for porn but maybe he had negligently stumbled across some of the clips by accident and that was why he had disappeared from her life, unable to live with their reality and the stain of her past life, the things she had blithely allowed to be done to her, with her? But Liv Lisa knew there was no point in speculating. She had a fatalistic attitude to life, and had never expected eternal bliss and being happy ever after from it.

She had attended a Sunday morning gospel brunch at The House of Blues on Decatur Street with a bunch of co-workers from the lab, one of whom was celebrating a birthday, and still on the revitalising wings of song, they were reluctantly filing out of the building onto the street as the club emptied. It was more of a tourist attraction for visitors to the Crescent City but she had never been before. She had to be persuaded, but was not disappointed, having thoroughly enjoyed the uplifting experience as well as the abundant food.

Their group was breaking up on the sidewalk, hugging each other and air kissing when Liv Lisa glanced across the street and noticed a tall man, dressed all in black, standing in front of the window of Beckham's Bookshop, watching them, standing immobile like the living statues by Jackson Square.

As her friends were beginning to disperse, some ambling off towards Canal Street and others in the direction the Jackson Brewery, Liv Lisa realised his gaze had not left her. She was the one being watched.

She stared back at him but he didn't flinch, the ghost of a smile bending his lips.

She didn't recognise the stranger.

Some pervert who had somehow identified her as Calabria Lira, her porn name? Unlikely, she thought, those few years back her hair had been a different colour, she now wore if differently and she had lost a lot of weight. Not that her face had been the most prominent part of her anatomy on constant display.

She wondered whether she should walk over and confront the man, but prudently decided against it. There was no need to provoke an unnecessary affray.

But, annoyed by his interfering presence, she stood her ground and held his piercing stare. She was now alone, her friends all gone, albeit still surrounded by stragglers leaving the club. A large woman in a billowing dress stepped in front of her, making her way to the kerb, cutting off her sight of the opposing side of the street. Once the fat woman had moved on, Liv Lisa found the stranger had gone. She peered in both the directions he could have taken, but there was no sign of his black silhouette.

A few weeks passed following the incident, during which time she became incredibly busy, along with the team she was part of, working on a fascinating project at the university focusing on the possible isolation of a specific particle within certain pathogen cells, as part of a project to devise vaccine models against a possible new form of epidemic which could be transmitted through animals. Her work had become her passion and she often saw it as proper counterpart to the dark side of her previous life. It had been ages since she had sex last, a reaction to her brief porn career, and found some amount of peace in the knowledge she could resist its prurient call, although there were moments in the middle of the night when weak waves of lust called and she had to relieve herself by hand. She took pride in the fact that, when this happened, she relied on past memories of high school dates rather than the forgettable faces of the men she had encountered on her shoots.

The hurricane season was in full flow although this year the city had so far been spared the worst, just an accumulation of milder storms where the water pelted down and ran like a river down the streets and gutters only to evaporate within hours when the sun came out and washed it away. Professor Read had walked in to the lab where she was peering through one of her high-resolution electronic microscopes.

'Lisa,' he called out to her. He had never addressed her by her full first name. 'We will be having a visitor in the afternoon. His name is Dr Becker and he's from the English Porton Down research centre, here on a fact-finding jaunt. Feel free to answer any and all of his questions. He has full clearance.'

Absorbed by her work and complex calculations as she fed the data she was collecting into her computer, she skipped lunch and by three in the afternoon had completely forgotten about the visit.

'Miss Ritter, I presume?'

A deep baritone voice with an untraceable accent of European origin.

Liv Lisa looked up.

He wore a standard white lab coat and was extremely tall, his hair a darker shade of black and seemed ageless, at first glance middle-aged but with a depth to his eyes that evoked years of experience and toil.

It's when their eyes met that she recognised him. The stranger standing in front of Beckham's Bookshop on the other side of Decatur.

He extended his hand.

Liv Lisa hesitantly proffered hers and they shook. His grip was firm.

'I'm Dr Becker. Professor Read said you would be expecting me?'

'Indeed.'

He smiled, his lips moving in slow motion, his expression turning both cruel and sensual as a result.

Liv Lisa stood there, observing him, unable to speak for a moment.

Then, finding her resolve, 'Have we met before?'

Her mind was a jumble. Maybe it had been at a conference, a seminar, a lecture she had attended? Hence the troubling if puzzling sense of recognition.

'I don't think so,' the academic replied.

'You just looked familiar.'

'Unless you dined yesterday evening at The Gumbo Shop on St Peter Street, as I did, then this must be the first time we meet. I only flew into town yesterday mid-afternoon.'

'Oh ...'

'Professor Read has told me a bit about the nature of the research you've been undertaking and the progress made so far, but I'd love to hear more about it from you. Someone on the frontline, so to speak.'

'Gosh, it's hard to know where to begin,' she mumbled, troubled by his presence, the way his personality, his almost suffocating aura filled the small lab room.

He pulled a chair toward her bench and sat himself down next to her. His pristine, stark white lab coat brushed against hers. What struck her at first was the fact he had no scent, no trace of aftershave or fragrance, not even soap or distant perspiration. He was a blank slate to her senses.

'So start at the beginning, my dear ... With the sort of antibodies you're hoping to pinpoint. What makes you believe they might be present?'

She began a long-winded explanation of the analytical

principles she had adopted, the methodology she was pursuing in her initial research into the subject. She could still feel his eyes fixed on her, as if she were a target and should never be left out of sight. She felt uncomfortable with his undivided attention.

On occasions, he would nod, almost hum along to her monologue, a finger or two tapping against the surface of her crowded workbench, neither approving nor disapproving, blankly registering her words with no apparent reaction.

Liv Lisa paused, looked over to Dr Becker, seeking some confirmation he was still in the loop, only to find his questioning eyes fixed on her, an expression of mild amusement drawn across his sharp features.

'What is it?' she asked him.

'I was just comparing the way you appear in civilian life to those silly faces you used to pull in your amusing little movies, your version of pleasure unleashed, or did the producers specifically request you react that way?'

Liv Lisa blushed, a wave of heat racing through her body.

Now she knew why he gazed at her the way he did.

She had to take a hold of herself, hold on to her dignity. It was the first time she had come across someone aware of her previous activities.

'Oh,' she said, her voice strained. 'You know about it …'

Dr Becker smiled.

'I'm the only one in the know, Calabria,' he said, deliberately using her porn name. 'But I haven't said a word to Professor Read or anyone here, be assured. And have no intention of doing so, now or in the future. Our little secret, eh?'

Small mercies.

Was he enjoying her discomfort?

She tried to appear calm although she was boiling inside. She drew a shallow breath before talking to him again

'Are you here because of me or are you genuinely interested in the department's work, Dr Becker? Is it just coincidence you are aware of my past mistakes?'

'No coincidence, Miss Ritter. I just know things.'

'That didn't answer my question.'

'I suppose you could call me an observer of the human condition. I have a terrible fascination for the way humans act.'

'That still doesn't answer my question,' Liv Lisa remarked.

'Maybe there is no correct answer I could provide,' he replied.

Liv Lisa pushed her chair back, increasing the distance between them, as if repelled by this stranger invading her workspace. She switched her laptop to 'sleep' and the screen went blank.

Dr Becker remained motionless. Indifferent to her rising scorn.

'Look, whoever you truly are, I get the feeling you don't have a massive interest in vaccines or my scientific research. I have no intention of discussing my past with you, so maybe it's better if you left,' she suggested.

'I'm interested in you, Miss Ritter,' he said. 'See, when you peer down one of these clever microscopes, I'm sure you witness a whole fascinating world, invisible to the naked eye, a multitude of cells, particles of many origins and purposes, alive in a way only a scientist like you can fathom, but with no idea they are part of a larger equation, oblivious to what lies beyond the lens through which they are being observed, catalogued, defined.'

'I do,' Liv Lisa readily agreed, as Dr Becker uncannily put a finger on a thought she harboured repeatedly as part of her work. As if he could read her mind.

'Well,' he continued, 'Think of me as the person behind that big microscope in the sky and you are right now on that metaphorical slide and under careful observation, picked out at random from the mass of humanity and being studied.'

'And what if I have no wish to be pinned down like some butterfly on public display?'

'I'm not sure you have too much of a choice in the matter, my dear.'

'I'm not sure that makes me feel comfortable.'

She tore off her lab coat, hung it up by the door and flounced out of the room, wordlessly leaving the odd man behind. Her anger had reached boiling point and she rushed to the washroom and splashed cold water all over her face, then sat down in a cubicle to allow her mind to simmer down. How could he treat her this way?

Once she had sufficiently calmed down, she left the building and made her way to the car park and drove home to her minute apartment at the wrong end of North Ramparts, all the time trying to get the man out of her mind, worried that despite his assurances he might, faced by her rebuff, inform Professor Read or other colleagues of her past, dubious activities, which she knew all too well didn't sit comfortably with her position as a respected research chemist.

Once home, she couldn't get him and their conversation out of her mind. The man both repelled and fascinated her in equal ways. She felt hopelessly unable to determine why. She was a scientist, a rational person, but everything about him had a touch of unreality, and also of danger, a sentiment that enticingly recalled the way she felt all those years ago just before she presented herself for a shoot, nervous in anticipation, full of shame but also craving the experience, the expected as well as assumed degree of degradation. She had been so mixed up then and it was uncomfortable to be reminded of it now. There she was thinking she had turned a new leaf in her life, was more of a normal person by society's weird standards, but his appearance had revived all those complex feelings and the emptiness she had always known was at the centre of her soul but had tried to hide. Unsuccessfully, she now realised.

Liv Lisa had previously made plans to dine out with an elderly relative who had flown in from Minnesota and they were due to meet at the Café du Monde at 7, but she called her hotel pretexting a terrible migraine and rearranging for two days later before her distant family member flew back home. She was in no mood for socialising right now.

There was not much left in the refrigerator, just a half full carton of grapefruit juice, some cheese and crackers and assorted fare past its sell date. She nibbled away distractedly at the leftovers then, after darkness had fallen decided she craved some fresh air. Her air conditioning unit needed a service and would probably have to be upgraded before the full force of summer heat arrived. Already, the small apartment felt close and clammy, and it was only early May.

She aimlessly trudged down St Ann towards the river and the customary crowds, the nearby sounds of Bourbon Street and its music and revellers echoing across the roofs in her direction. She took a turn by the Faulkner House and emerged onto Jackson Square. There were still a few fortune tellers plying their trade, but none of them had customers at this time of night. She swept past one of the Pontalba buildings and crossed at Decatur. An overweight trombone player was playing in front of the café, hoping for tips from the tourists or sales of his CDs piled up in a battered cardboard suitcase left on the pavement by his tapping feet.

The Café du Monde was its usual bustle of tourists, die-hard residents and flotilla of ever unsmiling Vietnamese or Filipino waitresses manoeuvring their way between the tables balancing trays of beignets, coffee and orange juice.

Liv Lisa found herself a table at the far right corner, away from the music, and ordered.

Before her sullen waitress had even brought her plate and mug, she sensed him. An undefinable presence, the air parting in front of him as he approached, oblivious to his surroundings or the crowds he was navigating to reach her table.

'May I join you?'

It was Dr Becker. Who else? Was there no escaping him?

She declined to answer but he sat himself down at the table, facing her, regardless.

'I'm not getting rid of you that easily, am I?'

'Indeed.'

'So what do you want with me, then?'

'Maybe, Miss Ritter, it's a case of what you might want of me instead?'

'I don't understand.'

'As your Greeks once said, I come bearing gifts.'

'And we were taught at school to be wary of such gifts, lest they come with heavy conditions attached.'

'People interpret history in different ways …'

Their small plates of sugar-dusted beignets arrived, along with his coffee and Liv Lisa's glass of orange juice. He dropped a twenty-dollar bill on the sticky table and told the waitress to keep the change. He was wearing all black from head to toe: shirt, suit, socks, shoes. Not an ideal colour to consume beignets, the fine sugar likely to stain it within minutes however carefully he ate.

'And you're an expert in history? I thought you were also in scientific research, or pretended to be,' she said.

'Just a Jack of all Trades.'

Liv Lisa sneered back, still torn between her instinctive dislike of the man and a morbid fascination for the way he was visibly casting a net to snare her in. There was distinctly something of the night about him. A thought crossed her mind and she curled her lip in both amusement and caution.

'So are you planning to offer me untold riches in exchange for my soul? Or is it just my body you are after, which I suppose I should take as a compliment.'

'Your soul is of no interest to me,' he calmly replied.

'Really? Am I not worth it, because I've sinned too much already, or maybe it's a deal you only offer to men? I've read Faust, you know, listened to the operas …'

Dr Becker smiled. Evaded the question.

'Liv Lisa,' he said. 'I know you. How as a child you spent years in your imagination dreaming of all those fairy tales: Hansel and Gretel, Rapunzel, the Pied Piper of Hamelin, the Little Mermaid … How you sometimes believed in them so strongly, wished you could be a part of those stories, a heroine of fables … Something out of the ordinary.'

Her heart skipped a beat. How could he know that? She had never shared those deeply intimate and sometimes embarrassing thoughts with anyone, friends or parents. It sent a powerful chill down her spine. Her mouth dried up.

'How can you …?' she mumbled.

'It's my job to know.'

She tried to conceal her disarray. 'It was a long time ago,' she protested.

'But it haunts you still, does it not? Just a few weeks ago, did you not dream at night between the sheets that you were a mermaid and pictured yourself -rather obscenely, I daresay- seducing rugged pirates you had snared to the bottom of the ocean and ravaging them until they drew their last breath? It was most edifying, definitely more pornographic than those silly movies you were involved with in your needy student days, although I am sure those experiences helped the dream to appear so much more realistic.'

The man WAS the devil.

Being from a city where a sense of the supernatural was never more than a few blocks away and suffused the atmosphere, heady and tempting, seductive and taboo, Liv Lisa had always lived in her imagination, a place where everything was allowed, however impossible.

But being faced with the reality of it – or should it have been the unreality – was a profound shock.

It was as if her whole world was unravelling.

On the nearby sidewalk, outside the Café du Monde, the trombone player was now inevitably playing 'When the Saints Go Marching In' with increased gusto.

She tried to snap out of her frenzied mental paralysis and looked straight ahead into the man's eyes, losing herself in their pitch darkness, falling and falling like a bullet through its untold depths.

She knew she was now inexorably caught in his net. Even though he had not mentioned, to spare her the humiliation no doubt, that the pirate she had fucked in her dream had looked like Johnny Depp. But, for sure, he knew.

He allowed her thoughts to sink in, observing her with detachment.

'I could turn you into a mermaid ...' he whispered.

'Really?'

'Willingly.'

'And what would be the price to pay?'
'There would be no conditions.'
'So what do you personally get out of it?'
'The pleasure of watching you become a new person, a new creature. How you would react and it would affect your actions. I enjoy putting the jigsaw together, creating a new story.'

Liv Lisa's imagination was already running wild, blanking out the café, the sounds and smells of New Orleans at night, the illuminated clock at the top of the Jax Brewery tower. Trying to picture what it would feel like to roam the seas at random, luring men and boats to their rocky fate. What was holding her back, she wondered? A job so many others could do as well if not better, a tiny apartment with such a desperate modicum of possessions, none of them treasured in any way, the memory of men past so few of which had touched her the way she wished and had indeed hurt her, no immediate family.

As a mermaid she could wreak her revenge on the world, be someone, avenge the wrongs she had allowed men to subject her to.

The call of the unknown was already sweeping over any of her reservations.

Did she have any choice in the matter, anyway?

Dr Becker's eyes had, without her quite noticing, turned green, an eerie, disembodied gaze, like a firework exploding above the Mississippi.

Hook, line and sinker; all he had to do now was draw her in. She would not resist.

14

'I was human once, just like you.'

They had been travelling the world for near on a year now. Becker had insisted on it before he allowed her the freedom of the seas. 'You have to know the world better,' he had explained. Prior to meeting him, she had never set foot outside the United States, aside from a short trip to Tijuana in Mexico and another to Niagara Falls where she had glimpsed Canada through the mist. It wasn't that she had not often craved to see other lands, but it had been unaffordable, whether on the meagre proceeds of filmed sex or, later, as a relatively junior grade biochemist. She had to be fully aware of the world she inhabited before she was freed of it, he insisted.

'Are you trying to elicit my sympathy?'

'No, just saying. I'm not a fallen angel or a devil or any of that religious claptrap. Just another pawn, like you.' And never told her more.

Liv Lisa was anxious to ask him more but knew he was unlikely to respond.

Some of the places she had seen in movies or on TV, others she had read about, but the reality was overwhelming.

They drove along dusty highways, motorways, autobahns, dirt tracks seemingly leading to nowhere only to arrive at memorable landscapes, and encountering fields of ice, beauty and desolation.

They streamed down rivers and witnessed unending vistas of vineyards suspended on hills, gothic castles, and steadied their way through an infinity of locks along the way. They walked the steep steps of the Great Wall of China, visited the terracota warriors, and the great sprawl of Shanghai where a new skyscraper seemed to birth every week or so, and watched grandiose cities come to life at night as a wall of lights illuminated their splendour. They bathed in the mist rising from the falling torrents of the Iguazu Falls.

They flew a lot. Through her window at low altitude, she watched the shimmering roofs of the rain forests, a trembling splash of green floating in clouds; and later the dunes of the Sahara and other deserts, where the sand flowed like waves in a sea, ever restless, disturbed by the wind and constantly turning into a living entity always in perpetual motion.

On cruise and cargo ships, he demonstrated how so much of the planet's surface was just water, hinting at the joys and possibilities of what lay beneath the surface, a domain she would soon be able to call her own and explore at will.

Under his benevolent, if mischievous, gaze she stood on the shores of countless tropical islands and looked out at the infinity of the ocean and felt so terribly small, like an insignificant grain of sand in the grand map of the universe, uncertain about the role she played, or would play in it, according to Becker's whims and resigned herself to the fact she would never be given most of the answers.

She lounged on a remote strip of sand in an island in the Maldives that Becker informed her would no longer exist a year ahead as the ocean levels rose. In Mauritius she visited a village where she was shown a tortoise that was reputed to be nearly four hundred years old. It barely moved on its bed of mud and dust, weighed down by the years. 'I can't imagine ever living that long. I would get bored,' Liv Lisa remarked. Becker looked back at her with a questioning glint in his eye, as if finding her foolish, youthfully ignorant.

Fields of tulips in an explosion of bright primary colours as far as the eyes could see on a furlough from their Dutch canal river trip. Walking in the dead of night through dark and menacing Hong Kong alleyways, feeling the hostile gaze of a hundred male eyes measuring her up. Chuckling at the audacity of the squirrels in New York's Washington Square Park as they approached her and even tiptoed across her trainers as if she didn't exist and didn't look like a giant to them. Rambling through old cities of stone in Estonia and other cities of the Baltic and Eastern Europe. Navigating the Stockholm Archipelago and its cosy aggregate of picturesque islands. Trekking across dried lava flows at midnight in Iceland to catch the Northern Lights. Feeling trapped in the slums of Lagos or other African cities, starkly conscious of the whiteness of her skin and sensing centuries of hostility to her kind coursing through the air. Oh, the things they saw, the contradictions of the world.

Sometimes, Becker would disappear for a few days out of the blue on their journeys, leaving her stranded on the boat, a city, an island, but he always returned, secure in the knowledge she would be where he left her, had no intentions of escaping. On these occasions, Liv Lisa tried to socialise with fellow passengers, hotel resident or travellers, if only to present an appearance of normality. When anyone asked, they had always pretended to be father and daughter, although she could see in the faces of many of their interlocutors they didn't believe this, and guessed at a May-December relationship. She bedded a Dutch software salesman in Manila and a shaggy-haired Russian musician in Bangkok, but they were just one-night stands which meant nothing to her, a way to keep her body exercised, no more. When he was present, Becker shared a room or a cabin with her and slept – or did he actually sleep? He was always awake when she closed her eyes and likewise when she awoke – separately and never hinted at any sexual interest in her.

She was swimming off Kamala beach in Phuket in Thailand when a sudden wave she had not seen coming overpowered her, taking her by surprise, and, gasping for breath, she opened her eyes and realised she was underwater, gripped by a fierce undertow. Struggling to propel herself back to the surface, she thought for a brief moment she was about to die, but a hand took a grip of her hair and, painfully, pulled her back to the surface. It was Becker. Who had been absent for three days already, away on other mysterious errands he never gave a hint of, and had made a surprising, if timely reappearance.

'Well, well, Miss Ritter. If you are to become a pretty

mermaid, maybe you should be taught to swim better,' he smiled as she stumbled back to the shore, treading in the footsteps he was creating in the sand.

Liv Lisa was so relieved to have survived the accident that she ignored his sarcasm.

He evaded all questions about the practicalities of turning her into a mermaid. Would he wave a magic wand? Would she require corrective surgery? How would she find sustenance under water, food?

But, most of all, Liv Lisa agonised about why she had been chosen. Surely, she was not the only girl to have fostered such dreams in her callow youth. Because, in her heart, she knew Becker's intentions were never straightforward and there might be a terrible price to pay.

The year of travelling came to an end, and with it the ceaseless diorama of cities, landscapes and wonders. Their plane had landed at night in an airport that felt like any other airport, and submerged in tiredness, Liv Lisa had paid no attention to the pilot's announcements or any of the signs peppering the concourse they walked down. A black car was waiting for them outside the small terminal. Still fighting sleep, she threw her rucksack into the car's boot. Becker never travelled with luggage. Their driver looked Middle-Eastern and a necklace of prayer beads hung from his rear-view mirror. The inside of the vehicle smelled of incense and stale tobacco. The flickering lights of a nearby town shimmered in the distance as they drove towards it on a road littered with potholes, each of which made the car's suspension groan in protest as they speeded across it.

There was no one present in reception at the hotel they disembarked at and Becker slipped behind the counter and picked a room key from the panel on the wall. She hadn't caught sight of the hotel's name as its neon sign outside was switched off. The hotel itself felt as if was wrapped in mothballs and had not been modernised for decades, all heavy wood furniture, sepia-coloured velour drapes and dusty fittings.

Ignoring the elevator, they walked up to the first floor to their room. Becker switched the light on. It burned feebly, throwing a weak light from a single bulb, and all Liv Lisa could focus on was the large bed which occupied almost two thirds of the room. She had barely managed to close her eyes on the four-hour plane journey and her mind and body just begged for the immediate relief of sleep.

She kicked her trainers off and asked Becker 'Where are we?'

'Nowhere,' he replied.

It certainly felt that way.

She began to undress, unbothered by his presence which she was by now so used to as was his total lack of sexual interest in her.

'Well,' she remarked. 'This certainly ain't no palace or five stars lap of luxury, I must say.' She looked around the exiguous room as he stood at the foot of the bed watching her with his customary sense of detachment. A couple of solitary framed prints hung on the walls, depicting sea flora and fauna, etched in meticulous thin lines of black ink.

She could feel lazy tongues of somnolence reaching out for her and regretted turning down the coffee the air steward had offered her on the plane just a few hours back. Sleep beckoned.

She wearily dropped her head down to the pillow and closed her eyes. Faded into darkness.

The night raced by without a single dream to break up its desolate bleakness, heavy as coal, oppressive, disturbing in its singular emptiness.

And felt as if it lasted forever, stretching on and on, her consciousness trapped in quicksand, vaguely perceiving distant silhouettes, voices, motion but unable to act on it, paralysed in body and mind, just a helpless spectator on some operating table, knocked out by a powerful anaesthetic.

Like a night of a thousand hours.

A circle of light in the far distance. Just an elusive pinhole. Liv Lisa squinted, her eyes slow to react, struggling against the grip of some liquid form of quicksand, trying to focus on the white, circular spot looming over her personal horizon. Simultaneously, she experienced a sharp stab of sudden, excruciating pain racing out in concentric circles from her midriff, as if she was being sawed in two by a serrated metal blade, every inch of her skin being roughly torn apart inch by bloody inch. She screamed.

She slowly tried to control her breath in an instinctive attempt to mute the pain sweeping through her, calm her galloping heartbeat, gritting her teeth, biting the inside of her lip in the process.

She cried out again. No words, just barbaric, animal-like sounds generated by the all-conquering pain marching across her senses. It got worse before it got better. She felt herself losing control, urinating, the warm dampness spreading below.

'Becker? What is happening?'

There was no response.

Was he present and just cruelly watching? Or was he gone altogether?

Slowly the terrible pain began to ebb, in tiny increments, one small degree of agony at a time, so damn slow she could count to a hundred between each minor decrease in its searing intensity. Her breath finally got back to normal and, again, she tried to open her eyes wider, her vision still concentrating on that distant point of light on the horizon. Was it the white light she had so often read about? Was she in fact dying?

The end of all things? Becker's final betrayal? So why was she still conscious, pinned down at the very centre of things, acutely aware of the weighty burden of her body and senses?

It wasn't that the intense pain faded, but more a case of her becoming accustomed to it, navigating its highs and lows with new found knowledge and skill, as Liv Lisa regained a modicum of control over her heartbeat and slowed her breath.

She had briefly closed her eyes in a failed attempt to negate the agonising sensations flowing through her, but now slowly tried to open them again. That white circle of light was now nearer. She focused on it, allowing it to expand within her field of vision, until it grew large enough, like a target for her consciousness, for her senses to settle into some form of normality within the disturbed sphere of her hurting senses.

As her vision adapted to the blinding strength of the faraway light, her eyes opening wider, no longer squinting, she realised it wasn't, as she had first believed, some wondrous exit to a lengthy, dark corridor, but was actually the sun, blindingly fierce and distant. The spots of dust on the back screen of her vision began to float away, and with them the pain gripping her gut and limbs finally retreated.

She felt the sun's rays racing across her skin, soothing the fire inside with a kinder warmth, feeding her one tiny drop at a time with needed energy.

She was buried in soft dampness; assumed it was because under the effect of the pain she had lost control of her bladder, but the sensation was different. For the first time since she had awoken in the grip of those abominable sensations, she tried to move, put pressure on her spine, angled her elbow so she could turn and be at least half upright and realised she was sitting in sand. She turned her head around, her neck stiff and uncomfortable, her dry lips dragging through rough grains of sand as she shifted a degree or so. The blinding whiteness of the sun faded away and she had to focus again as her vision fully returned. The sand was golden and wet, and in her ears, as if magnified by the lack of wind and the silence of the day, nearby sounds of sea collapsing against shore, of waves breaking reached her. Without even touching it, still too weary to raise her arms, she felt her hair was matted and wild, weighed down by sand adhering to her scalp and knotting her curls together. She must look a proper mess, Liv Lisa thought.

A beach.

How did she get here?

She was lying on her side, her nose half buried in the wet, golden sand, the rhythm of her breath all staccato as it punctuated the gradual retreat of the pain that had held her body captive. Her legs felt numb. Her guts like a landscape after the battle, every inner organ haphazardly rearranged and still struggling to retrieve its right placement. Had she been mugged, kicked, stabbed?

She tried to relax, her skin now bathing in the beach's blissful and tender warmth and one section at a time, every part of her body calmed down, no longer screaming in protest as the tumult in her mind finally settled, her thoughts no longer jumbled and in an utter state of panic.

Having found her peace again she decided it was time to turn around and get up. She raised herself and stumbled, face down into the sand, tiny grains with a disagreeable taste of salt squeezing between her half-open lips before she spat them out.

Had she lost control of her motor functions? She looked down and her heart froze, while across her mind a veritable symphony of fear raced across her every cell of her brain.

JEEZUS ...

She had no legs.

Instead, was a tail, orange and shiny, scales catching the light of the sun in myriad refractions. Like a mermaid's!

It all came back: Becker's promise. Or had it been a threat? And the vague remembrance of her meek acceptance. And the fuzzy memory that she had never really believed him, believing he was playing along with her, what with his uncanny knowledge of her most secret dreams. Thinking it was all a game he was playing and this day would never come.

But it had.

Jesus fucking Christ, she sighed.

And from the still pulsing, retreating stabs of pain like pinpricks all over and inside her body, she knew it was not a dream she was now experiencing. This was real.

She rolled round, sand dripping from her skin and eerie metal-like scales like sweat, and managed to awkwardly sit and find some form of balance, unaccustomed as she was to the new configuration of her body.

She was naked all the way down to her ... tail.

Her breasts were unchanged, still firm, pale against the tanned skin of her shoulders and belly, her nipples blackcurrant pink and hard and with her familiar beauty spot – she called it a freckle – lodged in the shallow valley separating them. Their sensitive extremities caressed by the mild breeze fluttering around her. She peered further down to the area where skin and scales met, merged. She still had a vagina. But no surrounding pubic hair, her nude lower lips like a scar, an impudent coral slit where her legs had once begun, buried in the indistinct mass where flesh and fish combined. She did not recall from pictures and fairy tales whether mermaids had ever had genitalia. At any rate, she had.

Her throat was dry, the initial shock of the discovery retreating, becoming a new form of normal.

She knew there was no going back.

Was this truly what she had wished for, reward or punishment?

Liv Lisa rolled over and looked away from the ocean. The beach she was on was situated in a circular bay, surrounded by tall, rocky cliffs. At the top of the cliffs was an assembly of wooden buildings, fishermen's shacks, their wood burnished by wind and time. The sea facing her was calm, a picture postcard of monotony, not a boat in sight or bird swopping above the heavy waves and surf. She wondered where in the world she was. It wasn't hot enough for the Caribbean or the Indian Ocean she considered, where the pirates and mermaids of her distant memories roamed the waters. Or cold like the shores of Northern seas might be. No doubt she would find out soon enough.

She had so many other questions in mind. Would the sea, once she immersed herself, be cold; would she now be able breathe under water; what would she feed on for sustenance?

The only way to find out, she reckoned, was to drag herself down to the water line. She shifted her body, adjusted her angle of support so she could use her arms and elbows to pull herself along, almost like a baby crawling but, lacking legs, it felt more like the swaying, oscillating movements of an amputee crab. She felt so terribly clumsy at first but soon found a semblance of rhythm, equilibrium and began shifting her way forward in the damp sand, leaving the trail of her weight behind her like an undulating scar across the beach's hitherto immaculate surface.

Her coordination was improving with every pull and shuffle and she was halfway to the water when she heard heavy steps rushing towards her. She didn't have time to turn her head and look back when she heard it, 'woosh …', something flying in the air behind her and now above her. A net of rough meshes, reinforced lengths of rope sewn together, and held tight with rusty metal rings. The net hovered a brief moment over her body and fell across her back, trapping her momentarily as she struggled to escape it, throw it back from her body until a foot stamped roughly on her tail, pinning her down and halting any further progress in her attempt to reach the harbour of the sea.

'What have we here?' a sonorous male voice said. She couldn't place his accent. Or even the language he was speaking, although she could uncannily understand it.

Liv Lisa opened her mouth, hoping to plead her cause in some confused way, but words just wouldn't come, as if her throat was constricted at the base, her tongue disconnected from her lungs. Just muffled sounds seemed to be possible. Alongside her legs, she had lost the power of speech. Her heart skipped several beats on discovering this.

'Well, well, it's been ages since we've seen one of you lovely creatures in these parts,' the man remarked, taking his foot off her tail and tightening the net around her body until it felt like a cage. He then stepped forward and looked down at her, his prisoner.

He was enormous, well six and half feet tall, broad-shouldered, grey-bearded, looking partly Oriental, wearing a worn waterproof green windbreaker and matching plastic boots that reached up to his knees.

A heavy belt hung from his waist, from which knives in all shapes and sizes dangled, alongside a variety of hooks, knots and other fishing gear.

He looked down at her, a quizzical but meaningful look spreading across his rough features, thoroughly enjoying the situation and the fact she was totally helpless and at his mercy was so apparent in her reaction.

Liv Lisa's brain froze. She couldn't even plead her case. Would he gut her like a fish?

He leaned down and grabbed her hair and brought it to his nose.

'You stink,' he said.

He threw her head back and stepped back behind her so all she could hear were his sharp intake of breaths and muffled movements. The deadly arsenal hanging from his belt clinked as he moved. Then there was a pregnant silence before she felt the net imprisoning her loosen a little, enough for her to extend her cramping arms. But before she could adjust her prone position further, the fisherman had gripped her shoulders and roughly turned her around and forcibly positioned her on her back. His eyes were fixed on her midriff where her flesh merged with the scales and her vagina was impudently visible in all its rawness.

He smiled.

She wriggled around in the vain hope of exposing herself less to his leering gaze, but he kicked her in the ribs to express his disapproval.

'They say that whoever fucks three mermaids in a lifetime gains immortality,' he remarked. 'Pretty one, you will be my second. I shall allow you to live afterwards, although I know how dangerous you beasts can be. So you can tell your sisters of the power of my loins and invite another to visit this beach and get a similar taste of me. Don't want anyone to feel jealous, do we?'

He roared with laughter and unbuckled his belt, letting his trousers fall to the ground, exposing himself with unconcealed pride. He was already erect, thick and veiny.

He kneeled in front of her and inserted a finger inside her to verify her wetness and grinned with satisfaction, took his penis in his hand and pushed it into her in one brutal movement and began to pump away.

Liv Lisa closed her eyes, but couldn't prevent tears from breaking, pearling down her cheeks as the man mercilessly took his pleasure while she was totally helpless.

Time froze but he finally came and withdrew from her, a crooked rictus like a slash across his face confirming he was well sated and she had served her use.

He rose, his dripping cock now at half-mast, and pulled his trousers up. Before moving away, he kicked her again as a way of dismissing her as worthless and no longer of use to him. She listened to his steps fading in the distance as he walked back up the beach.

Liv Lisa found herself alone on the desolate strand of wet sand. The sky was now uniformly grey and dull, as if adjusting to her feelings. She looked down at her new body. Sighed. A distinct swell of rage rose inside her. One day a mermaid and already despoiled.

She resolved that one day he would pay for this dearly. As would any man.

Liv Lisa turned round and began her clumsy crawl toward the sea, dragging her weariness across the drying shore. The sounds of the waves neared, welcoming her back into her new world.

15

Several years had passed since Tristan had met April Dawn in Paris.

When he looked at himself in the mirror in the morning when shaving, he couldn't help but notice how the unstoppable passage of days was beginning to take its toll, his hair greying at the temples and no longer as lustrous, lines tightening under his eyes and his body settling into a comfortable form of lethargy, no longer as agile, slower.

But it didn't matter any longer.

He was resigned to the fact that by escaping the Piper's Island, he had forfeited his near immortality and his existence would now be ruled by the same laws all others here were also subject to.

After April Dawn's year at the Paris arts school had reached an end and she could no longer justify remaining in Paris, she had reluctantly returned to New Orleans where she had quickly found a job in one of the many art galleries on Royal Street, dealing in prints, militaria and vintage pop artefacts. They had desultorily corresponded, with the occasional phone call, but inevitably drifted apart. Although he had found himself exceptionally fond of her, initially transported by her earnest enthusiasms for certain books, authors and music, he had soon come to the conclusion they had little else in common outside of the bedroom where her boundless energy and youthful hunger for sex had soon grown tiring for him. He loved her body, the expressions that raced across her face when in the throes of pleasure but, ultimately, they were just two strangers finding comfort in each other in a foreign city neither of which belonged to, and he quickly realised that despite the gentle magic they created together, their bond was too tenuous to be a lasting one. The burden of the centuries he had lived on the Island and her exuberant youth could never properly connect.

But, most of all, she was not Katerina.

Would never grow into that kind of person. It wasn't her fault, of course, but he knew that in the long run he couldn't make her happy, let alone attain peace in his own mind while involved in such a disjointed relationship.

Soon, the American technology shares he had acquired earlier in his Paris days, informed by his memories of the future acquired in the Great Library, began to substantially increase in value, and he also enjoyed a significant windfall betting on the results of a couple of elections, both in France and abroad, aware as he had been of the outcome. Although regretful he had paid no attention to sporting results when racing through the textbooks and history manuals, as that knowledge would have been so much more lucrative. He sold a small percentage of the shares and found himself remarkably solvent on the proceeds, able to give up his job at the finance house and rent a small apartment near the Place Gambetta in the 20th arrondissement, in a street with a steep incline, where local kids would kick a ball around in late afternoons after school with boundless enthusiasm, despite regularly losing it to the slope and having to run breathlessly downhill to retrieve it every few minutes.

There was a spacious *bibliothèque* on Place Gambetta, behind all the bus stops for lines carrying commuters out to the nearby *banlieue*, and he became a regular there. If there was one thing that had rubbed off on him from April Dawn it was her love for fiction and he had years and years of literature to explore. Tristan was no longer interested in naked facts, finding more of a solace as well as a challenge in stories that informed him of the million contradictions of the human soul, of men and women and what made them act the way they did. He found it fascinating, although invariably struggled to compare himself to some of these fictional creations, never finding a proper match that would make total sense. He was a creature out of time, but now he craved for ordinariness.

It was through this love and fascination for books that he

came across Danielle, who worked in a minor cataloguing role at the *bibliothèque*. He'd been reading through the novels of Jules Verne in chronological order. A task which would take him almost two months. The library stocked them in a facsimile series reproducing the original books as published by Hetzel, with their intricate illustrations and lavish gold and red embossed covers. But for weeks he had been unable to find a copy of *The Mysterious Island*, although the cards in the filing system indicated it was in stock. He'd inquired and was directed over to Danielle's desk. She was in her late 20s, dark straight hair flowing down to her shoulders with a semblance of bob, and wore a grey cashmere cardigan adorned by a large spider broach.

She was puzzled by his request and they stepped over to the stacks where the book Tristan was seeking should have been but wasn't. After checking through the shelves situated above and under the proper location in case the volume had been replaced in the wrong sequence, she had to admit defeat and suggested he be patient and the book would likely reappear in due course.

'It's a pity,' Tristan remarked. 'I am trying to read through Monsieur Verne's books in sequence and hate the idea of skipping one.'

'You're studying him?'

'In a way.'

'Are you planning an article? Or a book? A thesis?'

'No. Nothing that important. Just for my own pleasure.'

She had a lovely smile.

'I understand. They are wonderful books and most of them just haven't aged, don't you think? Most people think all he did was to try and predict the future, but there is so much more to appreciate in his stories. Anyway, as happened, not many of his predictions turned out to be accurate.'

'You're right.'

He was about to step away, to check out the volumes he had already chosen.

'I think I have a copy of the book at home. I own it. You'd be welcome to borrow it. Or rather them, as it's a two volume *Bibliothèque Verte* reprint. It's quite a long book so they divided it in two. I've had them and others of Verne's since I was a teenager. I used to love them. They're more than just children's books. I'll just have to remember in which room of the house the books are.'

'You live in a house?'

'Yes, it's a small villa in Bagnolet. Used to be my parents, but it was left to me and my brother and he now lives in Panama. I used to collect books from the *Bibliothèque Verte* when I was younger. There must a whole shelf of them in my old childhood room. I don't wish to spoil your pleasure, but you are aware that Captain Nemo appears in *The Mysterious Island* again? Is that what draws you to it?'

'Actually, I didn't. It's just something personal. I love reading, learning about islands.'

'Have you been to any?' Danielle asked.

'Just one,' Tristan replied. 'But it was such a long time ago now.'

'Where was it?'

'I don't even recall the name. As I said ages ago …'

'Were you still a child then?'

'Yes,' Tristan half-lied.

Danielle agreed to search for her two-volume edition of the Verne novel and bring it in to the library the following day if she could find it.

A few weeks later, they met up for him to return the now yellow-spined books to her. He had read and enjoyed the novel, although the mysterious island in question that Verne had invented had little in common from the one he had known. He hadn't harboured much hope anyway. Danielle was about to take her lunch break when he arrived at Place Gambetta, and to thank her he invited her to a nearby Japanese restaurant by the Père Lachaise cemetery.

'That's kind of you, you know, but you don't have to. I'm just happy you were able to read the book. We still don't know where the library's copy has been misfiled.'

'It would be my pleasure. By way of thanks.'

'I've never eaten Japanese food before. I know it's becoming trendy, but also a touch expensive,' she remarked.

'No problem at all. I hope you like it. I was a bit hesitant myself the first time I tried, but have grown to really enjoy it. It's very healthy.'

Her first bite of the salmon sashimi slice was hesitant but once the thin portion of raw fish was inside her mouth, he noted how she carefully moved it around, tasting it, appreciating its texture, gauging its flavour as she carefully chewed it and then, after swallowing it, expressed her pleasure with a wide smile.

'That is actually very tasty,' she said. 'So delicate.'

'Glad you like it. I was worried for a moment that you might not appreciate it. Your French cuisine is so much more sophisticated, I feared you might scorn the simplicity of it.'

'Not at all,' Danielle said. 'And what is Dutch food like?' she asked. He had continued the pretence of being Dutch when he had initially introduced himself to her. That's what his ID documents identified him as for years now.

'Oh, a bit crude. We like cheeses, smoked fish, potato-based dishes, it's nothing special.'

'Sounds a bit like German food. I went to Germany on a school trip once and again for a month in the summer on a student exchange outside Hannover, and hated their food.'

Tristan half-smiled. Discreetly changed the subject of the conversation as far from keen to broach any further coincidences.

'So what sort of books do you like? You must have read so much, working in a library. Any favourite authors I might not be aware of?'

'My tastes are pretty diverse, broad-based. The classics never fail to satisfy of course, but also some modern people like Duras, Vailland, Drieu La Rochelle, Aragon or Romain Gary.' Danielle said. 'But you know what fascinates me most?'

'Tell me,' he sipped from his now lukewarm cup of miso soup.

'Books with maps.'

'Interesting.'

'Maps of the world as we knew it and as it is now; seeing how our human knowledge has expanded since the Middle-Ages and whole areas of the planet have been discovered and represented. How borders have constantly been moved, new countries created, names of places changed. But, most of all, I just am fixated, could spend hours on end examining maps of imaginary places, cities, lands, islands, domains that don't exist. Places from both the realm of legend but also the imagination: Atlantis, Shangri-La, Cockayne, Camelot, Hy-Brasil, Narnia, Eldorado, Arcadia, Middle-Earth, there's no end to them. I believe there are too many spoken of and written about that some must surely exist, lost somewhere, ready to be found again. Do you think I'm mad?'

'Not at all.'

A glint of light from the strip of neon crisscrossing the restaurant's ceiling bounced from her cheekbone, highlighting the razor-sharp lines of her angular features, shedding a whole new perspective on her uncommon beauty. Eyes dark as coal, skin inherited from Snow White and ruby-red lips stolen from the evil Queen in the eponymous tale in the Disney feature. The elements shouldn't have come together as a whole, but they did in an appealing way.

'How did you become a librarian? Had you always wanted to be one?' Tristan asked her, nervously seeking out further things they might have in common, all the time fearing she would say something wrong that would break the spell he was gradually coming under, the attraction growing with every word. A similar sense of intellectual quest, of a soul seeking for answers. A possible fellow traveller across undefined, unmapped territories.

'So did the Verne novel about the island meet your expectations?' Danielle asked, looking down at the two green volumes he had brought back for her.

'I'm not sure I had any expectations. I was just curious to read it,' he stated. Then, hesitantly 'I'm attracted by islands. There was one I remember being taken to by my parents on a vacation when I must have been only two or so and my memories of it are so vague. I've never been able to identify it.'

'Have you asked them?'

'My parents are long gone.'

'I'm sorry.'

'No need to be.'

They ordered coffees. It would soon be time for her to return to the *bibiliothèque*.

'Have you read *The Lord Of The Flies*?' she asked him.

'No,' he admitted.

'I seem to recall it's set on an island.'

'I'll look out for it.'

'I'll try and think of other books in which islands play a role; maybe I can find some you're not already aware of. Unfortunately, our cataloguing system is not thematic.'

He walked her back to the library on Place Gambetta, and she located the Golding novel, which he then borrowed.

Tristan read it that same evening. It had familiar echoes and a sinister streak that somehow brought back sharp memories of the Piper, although the children on his island had never gone to war against each other and had coexisted in blissful harmony.

He began seeing more of Danielle.

That late spring they became a couple after he moved in to her spacious Bagnolet *pavillon*. He was already spending most nights there anyway and Danielle argued there was no point him paying rent for a small apartment he seldom lived in any longer. He had now been living alone for a decade and thought at first he would find it awkward to share a space, however large, with another but Danielle was easy-going and accepted from the onset he was all too often a man of silences and needed his personal space. They were both voracious readers and would spend hours sitting on opposite chairs or sofas racing through pages, their attention rapt, oblivious to their surroundings. Within a few months they were already acting like a long-married couple, sharing the same space but at the same time orbiting each other like a dance of the planets, a familiar pattern of gentle consideration and distracted couplings when either of them felt the barriers of pleasure were ready to be breached anew. Despite her somewhat prim, reserved exterior, Danielle had a voracious sexual appetite and Tristan often thought he was not satisfying her fully, although she denied the fact. But he was aware that something was missing; the fire, the fact his mind was invariably too distant, divorced from his body while they made love, always under cover of darkness at her insistence.

In the summer, they deliberately opted to visit an island for their holidays and flew to Palermo in Sicily. They had found a small hotel a twenty-minute rickety bus ride away from the city, sitting in the rocky hills facing the sea. Tristan would have preferred travelling to the north, attracted by a documentary he had watched on TV about the clusters of Swedish archipelagos, but Danielle insisted she would rather lounge in the fiery sun of the south. Neither of them had sufficiently researched the matter and were unaware of the powerful sirocco winds that daily brushed across the Sicilian coast on their journey from the African continent and severely limited the time they could spent on the beach or the hotel pool that overlooked the tumultuous sea, parasols and deckchairs being inconsiderately blown away and tiny grains of sand scratching their skin in the wake of the wind.

They also hadn't realised when booking the hotel how isolated it was, with just a small pharmacy and grocery within walking distance as well as a restaurant specialising in cuisine from the Puglia region, featuring an abundance of appetising fish and seafood from the nearby ocean. They enjoyed the place so much, they returned every evening, preferring the open-air *trattoria* to their hotel restaurant where the menu was both sparse and unimaginative.

The waiter would guide them to a buffet table where all the catch of the day was laid out on a bed of ice for them to make their selection for their main dish, following some exquisite pasta.

'I've never eaten so much fish in my life,' Danielle remarked, a broad smile sketched across her tanned features. 'At this rate, I'll soon turn into a mermaid …'

Tristan looked at her quizzically, as if he didn't catch the joke, but then dismissed the idling thought her remark had triggered and pointed to his selection, an assortment of large grey shrimps which the chef in the kitchen would drop into boiling water and retrieve in all their orange splendour before the dish was served. The waiter heartily approved.

Danielle's brother was flying in from Panama City via Rome and joining them for the second week of their vacation. Danielle was excited at the prospect, not having seen him for a couple of years.

'I wonder if he'll bring a girlfriend along,' she said. 'He's very much a ladies' man!'

The hotel arranged for them to hire a local labourer who owned a car to pick Philippe up from Palermo airport, where they waited for him outside the arrivals hall. The flight from Fiumicino, where he had made his connection, was late and Tristan and Danielle were well over-caffeinated by the time her brother walked through the sliding doors pushing his luggage trolley. Two steps behind him was a slim, blond young girl, her eyes lowered as if in modesty, looking completely out of place and nervous.

Tristan's heart seized up. There was something oddly familiar about Danielle's brother's companion. The siblings met and embraced while the young woman remained a few steps behind. Tristan was introduced and took an instant dislike to Philippe. He didn't look like his sister at all, stocky, wearing torn jeans and a T-shirt that had seen better days, unshaven and over familiar as he took Tristan in and almost smirked. He wore deck shoes and no socks. The only thing they had in common were their prominent set of cheekbones, he reckoned. Tristan knew that Danielle, prior to him, had had a complicated sentimental life, and was aware that her brother was comparing him to some of his predecessors in her bed as he shook his hand.

'And who is this?' Danielle asked, turning to the young woman accompanying her brother, who just stood there in silence, observing their greetings with total blank indifference. She moved to embrace her but the frail beauty shuddered and took a step backwards, her eyes fixed on Tristan, turmoil swirling in their green depths.

Which is when he recognised her. Older, of course, but nonetheless familiar. Her mass of curling blonde hair like a Medusa's nest, uncombed, wild and so striking.

She was one of the children of Hamelin. He strained his memory to recall her name. She had been one of the youngest in their group of stolen kids and on the island he had never had much contact with her.

Sophie. Yes, that was her name.

Mute Sophie.

A thousand questions exploded in his mind.

How had she escaped? Would she know what had happened to his own sister Claudia? Or even Katerina?

She gazed at him silently amongst the hubbub of the airport crowds. There was no doubt she had recognised him too.

'Guys, this is Sofia,' Philippe introduced her.

'Welcome Sofia. It's lovely to meet you,' Danielle said.

'She doesn't speak,' Philippe added. 'I think she never has.'

'Wow,' Danielle exclaimed. 'So how did you two meet?'

'It's a long story,' Philippe said.

Meanwhile Tristan and Sophie kept on staring intently at each other.

'Did you two meet in Panama?' Danielle asked.

'It's a long story,' her brother repeated himself.

'With that blonde hair and those incredible curls, she just doesn't look South American at all,' Danielle remarked. Sofia's stare was still fixed on Tristan, all blood drained from her face.

Tristan experienced a moment of dark panic and swivelled around, seeking out another familiar face in the arrival area's crowd and dreading it. But the Piper was nowhere to be seen. Had it been just him finding Sophie familiar he might have put it down to coincidence, just a case of mistaken identity, but he could see from the young girl's reaction to his presence that she had the same certainty about where they had both come from. He took a deep breath as Philippe began, guided by Danielle, to wheel his luggage cart towards the exit to the airport's feed road, where their driver, Massimiliano, a local builder between jobs, had agreed to put his car at their disposal for half the cost a taxi would have charged them.

On the twisting road leading towards Palermo and their hotel, he kept on pointing out various areas of interest, bordering the rocky hills that washed down into the sea, highlighting the best *gelateria* in the region, particular bars, restaurants and places of pilgrimage as well as the sharp curve in the *autostrada* where, just a year ago, an anti-mafia criminal prosecutor's car had been blown up.

Tristan and Sofia sat glumly on the back seat, separated by her flimsy rucksack, while Danielle and her brother had joined Massimiliano at the front, squeezed together and lost in conversation.

This was neither the time nor the place to ask, but Tristan was wondering whether Sofia could actually understand what they were all saying, her muteness also a cover for deafness, in her total lack of affect, just her eyes a window to what she was thinking, or knew.

He vaguely remembered her as a very passive child, but now she seemed to have turned into an automaton, a pretty doll who followed her owner when he clicked his finger, which was just the way Philippe appeared to treat her, yet another reason for Tristan to intensely dislike the man in all his coarseness.

At the front of the car, brother and sister were chattering away in French to each other. By now, Tristan had a good grip on the language.

'You always had a strong taste for blondes, didn't you,' Danielle laughed. 'That's why I never understood what took you to Panama ...'

'The money trail, what else ...'

'Of course.'

'And was it there, at the end of the rainbow? From the way

you dress, it looks unlikely.'

'Don't worry, sister, that's just a disguise ... Wouldn't want to attract undue attention, would I?' he chuckled. 'I'm confident I am more solvent than you are on a librarian's wage.'

'Anyone would be.'

They reached the hotel and were dropped off by Massimiliano. Philippe and Sofia had been travelling for over 16 hours and went straight to their room, which was situated a floor above theirs, up the twisting stone stairway and with a balcony facing the same stark rocky hills against which the hotel had been built, sparse vegetation and weeds peeping timidly through the gaps in the stone and hardened earth.

'Sofia is odd, there's something out of time with her, or maybe her muteness is misleading me, but she looks pretty. Fragile. Not at all my brother's sort of girl,' Danielle remarked as Tristan retreated into silence, eager to manage to somehow spend time alone with her the next day in the hope of finding more about how she escaped the Island and the fate of the other children.

16

It took a couple of days before Tristan got the opportunity to spend time alone with Sofia, when Danielle and Philippe on a grey, windy day with pool lounging and beach out of the question, decided to take the bus into Palermo to explore the city. Tristan had never been much of a tourist and made his excuses, which were readily accepted as brother and sister were looking forward to spending time together.

The hotel bar area was empty, customers having to rely on a drinks dispensing machine. Tristan sat in a corner alcove with Sofia. Music played softly in the background. He was nursing a Coke while she sipped from a glass of effervescent San Pellegrino water.

'Can you speak or do you stay mute by choice?' he asked her.

Her eyes were wells of hurt, but she remained silent. Might she also be deaf, as Danielle had speculated the other day?

It then occurred to him to ask her the same question in German and there was a hint of recognition and her lips moved, though no sound escaped.

Tristan didn't know any sign language and guessed neither did Sofia.

He kept on interrogating her, a frustrating one-way dialogue. 'What happened to the other children? To my sister? Claudia? I remember you and her would often play together.'

She raised her left hand, waved it momentarily in front of his face, moved it up and down but the slow-motion gesture meant nothing to him. There was an air of resignation about her, of total passivity, barriers to her soul raised and impervious to any breach. Just a hint of a smile crossing her thin, pursed lips, as if understanding his frustration.

How did Philippe and Sofia communicate?

He asked him that evening, again in the bar which was now manned by the hotel owner's wife who had moved behind the counter in a swirl of cigarette smoke and was busy polishing long-stemmed glasses. Danielle and Sofia were sleeping in their respective rooms. Philippe was sampling some of the *grappa* varieties on offer.

'How did and you and Sofia meet?'

'That's a long story, Tristan,' he paused. 'A long and crazy story …'

'I'm all ears.'

Philippe sighed. 'In total confidence?'

'Of course,' Tristan agreed.

'Not everything I'm involved in back in Panama is legal, you understand.'

This came as no surprise to Tristan, from the little he knew and had so far observed of Philippe. According to his sister, he worked for a ship chandler in a managerial capacity, supplying food and other essential supplies to cruise ships from several large companies who docked in Panama's main port.

'You could call it a logistics business,' Philippe grinned. 'Demand and supply.'

Tristan nodded.

'Most items the company can readily provide, but then there are other commodities needed, if you see what I mean.'

'I think I get it.'

'Some of the cruise operators are more flexible than others when it comes to the bottom line. So I, and a few business partners, have a small enterprise going delivering alcohol and tobacco which might not necessarily have always filtered through the proper channels of taxation. We have suppliers down south. A few bribes here and there to customs staff grease the wheels of commerce; the poor guys are so badly paid by the government or the port authorities that anyone can be bought.'

'I'm sure that happens in every port,' Tristan remarked.

'Exactly.'

'So how does your extracurricular business relate to Sofia?'

'Well, it's not just the cruise operators we deal with. We have a good reputation for delivering safely in our field of enterprise and on occasions there's a demand for other … materials.'

'Such as?'

Philippe looked at Tristan with a sense of reservation, then decided he could be trusted.

'Drugs, arms …'

'Really? For cruise ships?'

'No. Other more clandestine customers. You know Central America is a place in turmoil. If we didn't do it, others would. But we know the sea routes, the coast guard and custom vessel routines, and how to operate under their radar. We're just delivery guys at the end of the day. We never venture as far as American territorial waters, we're not that stupid, we leave the merchandise attached to buoys at agreed coordinates just outside where other parties pick them up. A parallel network of distribution, if you like.'

'And?'

'Under a year ago, just two of us, a Honduran guy I trusted implicitly and myself, were doing a midnight run with some merchandise. An almighty storm broke earlier than we had expected, carried along by powerful winds, and caught us by surprise. It poured buckets and somehow our speedboat engine packed up. We weren't overly worried. Jesús was a hell of a mechanic and as soon as the storm passed, we would get the opportunity to get the engine going. We were in open waters, so no one would question our presence there or our cargo. We had to wait four hours though and, during that time, what with the strong winds we had drifted a fair way east deeper into the Caribbean. When dawn broke and Jesús finally had the chance to get his tool kit out, with the sea around us at last becalmed, I remember looking out at the sky and the rising sun and noticing a faint glimmer of land a few miles away, an island of some sort, but one I had never seen on any map of the area. I was intrigued and, once the boat's engine was fully operative again, we made a detour in the direction of that curious strip of land. However small it was, it should have been on at least some of our maps. I had actually been on the lookout for ages for possible uninhabited islands to use as possible way stations, places where we could store some product away from prying eyes, but the area up to a few hundreds of miles from the mainland had been well-charted, with some tiny islands even bought up wholesale by cruise companies as private leisure stop overs for their passengers, on which they built small amusement parks and facilities.'

'Let me guess,' Tristan interjected. 'It's on this island you found Sofia?'

'How the fuck did you guess?'

'It doesn't take much imagination to see where your story was leading.'

'Right. Anyway, we reached this small island and there she was, sitting on the shore, in an almost catatonic state, peering out at the sea. Saw us coming but didn't display any emotion. At first, I thought she might be some tourist left stranded there from a cruise ship excursion, you know when they drop couples off for a day on an uninhabited strip of beach for a romantic day, the desert island experience, but there were no hampers of food, or champagne bottles anywhere in sight. And the girl just remained silent, blanking all our questions. I'm sure you'll find this funny but for a moment I remembered that fairy tale, the Little Mermaid, and wondered whether like her, she'd had her tongue cut out! Strange thoughts, I know, but it's not the case. She just prefers not to speak or has some form of congenital speech defect. Jesús explored inland beyond the heavy vegetation that bordered the beaches. Burnt out huts, signs of previous life, logging, but no trace of anyone else. Anyway, as far as her pretty tongue is concerned, it's certainly present and I must say she knows how to use it, if you know what I mean,' he added with a lascivious smirk curling his lips. 'Although I've had to teach her a few extra tricks. But she was a quick, and willing learner.'

'How come you call her Sofia?'

'We asked her for her name and she somehow understood us, clumsily traced something in the sand ... S ... O ... P ... H ... That's where we got it from. And when we indicated we had to go she rose to her feet and just followed us. She's weird but also lovely, affectionate in her own way. I managed to get her some papers back on the mainland. Yes, we sleep together, but I swear I've never forced myself on her. She just moved in, so to speak. What can I say?'

'How long ago was this?'

'Just about six months ago,' Philippe stated. 'I couldn't leave her stranded on the island, could I? When Jesús and I decided to leave, she just followed and I've, in some bizarre way, taken her under my protection. On the first night back in Panama, she came to my bed and we've been lovers ever since but still she doesn't say a word and refuses to answer any questions, when I suggest she write things down. But I've become terribly attached to her. She's so different from the women I've known before. Innocent, knowing too, an enigma, as if she's running away from something …' His confession tailed off.

He ordered another round, sensing the bar attendant's impatient mood, and the fact we were the only customers present and she'd rather close shop.

His story made sense to Tristan, of course, but then again it didn't. If the children's island was actually located in the Caribbean, off the coast of Panama, why had we never been visited by anyone, discovered? Over the years it would have been inevitable. And if the Piper had come to a decision to make the Island visible to the rest of the world out of a later whim, what had happened to all the other children there, including his sister Claudia?

'So, you and Danielle, is it working?' Philippe asked Tristan, changing the subject.

'I think so,' Tristan replied.

'Good. She's been involved with a lot of wrong men in the past,' Philippe said. 'She's in need of a good one.'

'Can I ask you one more thing about that island?'

'Go ahead.'

'Do you maybe remember whether there were any birds present there?'

Philippe looked puzzled, taken aback by Tristan's question,

tried to make sense of it.

'Sure. Tons of them. Like any old island, especially in early morning, birds of all sorts, seagulls, all swooping up and down the beach dragging rotten kelp, hunting for crabs and all that.'

Tristan nodded.

It appeared as if the children's island had just returned overnight to the real world, all its impossibilities brushed away, reintegrating the march of time. Which still didn't explain Sophie's presence or provide a clue to the fate of the remaining kids. Or why she had been left behind? All part of the nefarious plans of the Piper?

That night he slept with a troubled mind, aware that the past was catching up with him after all these years hoping its memories would remain in exile and that he had turned over a new leaf.

Next to him, Danielle moved closer to his body, instinctively seeking out his heat, under the duvet. Sicilian nights were nowhere near as warm as they had expected. It had been a toss between coming here and, irony of irony, travelling to an all-inclusive resort somewhere in the Caribbean!

He placed his hand against her back, caressing the soft down cushioning her pale skin, could almost feel the distinct muffled thud of her heartbeat as it journeyed across the surface of her skin, her breathing a descant punctuating an indistinct melody.

She mumbled in her sleep, his name, the names of others. He felt no jealousy towards those who had come before him in her life, although he knew that the scars they had inflicted were still lying shallow beneath the surface, and could tear open so easily. He was unsure whether he was the one who could heal her properly. He carried too many memories of his own, centuries of memories, an eternity of anxiety, but most of all an abyss of unanswered questions that formed a core of absence in his heart. He even wondered at times whether he might not be hurting Danielle by supplying her with a false sense of hope. He had seen the white strips of flesh on her wrists where she had once cut herself. He had never asked her about them. They spoke a language he feared. Of attachment. Of despair. A place he never wanted to visit again since he had lost Katerina.

'I like it when you touch me that way,' she whispered.

Tristan hadn't realised she had awoken. It was still the dark of night, a full pockmarked moon floating outside the balcony of their hotel room, lighting the skin of her shoulders with deathly pallor as his fingers enjoyed her intoxicating softness, travelling with the slowness of wandering ants from the small of her back to the rise of her buttocks, closer to the core of primeval heat between her legs.

'Take me,' Danielle asked.

Sometimes, she would ask him to 'hurt' her, encouraging him to be rougher, to pin her wrists down as he thrust inside her, to circle her neck with his outstretched hands and lock her in a vice, something that scared him, worried his pressure would extend too far and might do her harm, feeling helpless at interpreting her needs, and the deep-seated reasons that lie behind it.

Danielle had told him from the outset that she had known many men before him and that they had been bad men, but that somehow she hadn't known how or wished to rebuff them. The only details she had provided one night after crying abundantly following their lovemaking, leaving Tristan puzzled as to whether it was out of joy or pain, was the story of an older man.

'How much older?' he had enquired.

'I was 19. He was 50.'

'Did he seduce you?'

'I think it happened the other way around. I seduced him.'

'But, surely, he was the one who took advantage of you, abused you even?'

'I'm not sure. It's not so clear cut. I wanted him. Made him want me.'

'How did it end?'

'Badly,' she pointed at the thin white scars crisscrossing her wrists. 'But I don't want to talk about it anymore.'

Tristan nodded.

The following morning both couples took breakfast together. It was a grey day, with a forecast of strong, surging sirocco winds later in the day.

As they sipped their coffees and nibbled at their patisseries and cold cuts of prosciutto and salami, Tristan could feel Sofia's gaze fixed on him. He held her stare, wondering what was going on in her mind, but she never broke the silent contact. He was the one who was forced to blink first. Did his presence and association with the Island scare her?

Danielle wanted to go into the city to visit the cathedral, the Palazzo Reale and the Botanical Gardens as there was no immediate prospect in store of beach or pool lounging. Tristan, although exhausted from lack of sleep and a long night of troubled thoughts, half-heartedly agreed to join her. Philippe wanted to stay at the hotel; he had some business calls to make to Panama. Danielle invited Sofia along but she silently declined the offer and retreated to Philippe's room.

'I just can't read her, you know,' Danielle remarked. 'I understand what my scoundrel brother sees in her but they just have nothing in common, let alone language. What do you think?'

'I don't think I have an opinion.'

'She looks at you in a strange way, I've noticed. As if she knows you from somewhere but I'm not sure whether it scares her or pleases her. Me, she just ignores altogether, though. Strange girl. But I'm certainly jealous of her hair; I'd kill for those blonde curls ...'

She was already legging it out of their room, heaving her small rucksack onto her shoulders, so Tristan was spared the obligation of replying.

The bus into Palermo stopped on the coastal road just

outside the hotel every half hour and was due very soon. They had to rush to catch it, which brought a welcome halt to their awkward conversation.

Tristan was bone tired by the time they returned to the Mondello outskirts by late afternoon. Culture tourism was anything but leisurely and he'd hated the crowds pressing against them at every church and museum they'd attended, as well as the lengthy queues outside the ice-cream parlours where they had sought respite. The strong winds had ebbed, leaving just a stir of heat in the air as they climbed the circular stone stairs to their floor, stepped into the room and both threw themselves down on the bed, after kicking off their trainers.

'Never again,' he muttered.

'You're terrible,' Danielle remarked, smiling broadly. 'For a man who loves books, you have a contradictory attitude to all other forms of art.'

'No one's perfect,' he retorted, a phrase he had borrowed from a Hollywood film he had particularly enjoyed, and which always made her laugh.

'And some are less perfect than others,' she wanted to have the final word.

They were enjoying dinner alone at the Puglian restaurant down the road when Philippe rushed in to the dining room and hurried to their table at the back, which overlooked a small garden.

'She's gone,' he said, slightly out of breath.

'Who? Sofia?'

'Yes, I took a nap after my calls and she was alone at the bar, browsing through some magazines, as she often does. When I woke up, she had neither returned to the room nor was any longer downstairs. I went down to the pool area but it was deserted. I even crossed the road and walked down to the beach, but there was no sign of her. I just have no clue where she might have gone.'

'She's probably just taking a stroll,' Tristan tried to appease him. 'She'll reappear soon.' Although a voice inside his head was doubtful she would.

'Just be patient. Dine with us, Philippe,' Danielle suggested.

'She has no money with her. Never does. Just always follows and relies on me. She wouldn't be able to go far ... I must confess I went through her bag. Her passport and it seemed most of her clothes were still there.'

'That's reassuring. I'm sure there's a very rational explanation. Maybe she went for a stroll and got lost?'

'Damn it,' Philippe said. 'Maybe I'd taken her for granted. You know how it is when you grow attached to someone. You just don't realise ...' He appeared quite genuinely distressed and unlike his usual buccaneering self.

By morning, Sofia hadn't returned. Philippe and Danielle were unsure what to do next. Tristan remained a bystander, unwilling to offer any explanation or make any sensible suggestion.

They lazed around the pool through the morning for lack of anything better to do, reluctant to leave the hotel should Sofia reappear out of the blue. The sirocco wind had lost much of its earlier intensity and the flimsy parasols remained in place. Philippe was restless and Danielle couldn't concentrate on the book she was reading, perturbed by the fact that her hitherto cavalier brother was so distressed.

'Should we get in touch with the police?' she enquired.

It was not a welcome suggestion. Philippe was inclined to avoid any possible contact with the law.

But the decision was taken for them.

A moment later, a uniformed *carabinieri* emerged from the stairs leading from the hotel reception area to the terrace where the small oval-shaped pool was, accompanied by the manager, who pointed them out to the official before swiftly retreating back to his office downstairs.

He spoke English with a strong accent straight out of a Hollywood comedy. He carried a large Carrefour supermarket plastic bag from which he pulled a crumpled set of clothing from the bag after introducing himself and checking on their identity.

Tristan immediately recognised the linen floral print dress

that Sofia had been wearing the last time he had seen her before they had left Mondello to visit Palermo the previous day. Danielle brought her hand to her mouth and held her breath. Philippe was utterly silent, colour draining from his face.

The policeman also produced a pair of pink Crocs, identical to the ones Sofia owned.

The items, he explained, had been found on the next beach along the coastal road, just a couple of kilometres away, by fishermen. The beach stood in a cove that made it difficult to reach on foot as it was surrounded by rocks, a tongue of the mountains flowing down towards the sea.

Someone had recognised the dress as belonging to a young foreign woman who was staying locally and this had led him to the hotel where the manager had pointed them in their direction.

'Was this *ragazza* part of your group? Family? A friend?' he asked.

Danielle took hold of the dress, reluctantly running her fingers along its hem.

'She is,' she confirmed.

'I'm sorry to inform you that she probably went out to sea and was unable to swim back. When the winds are in full flow, there is often a powerful undertow. That particular area, where her clothing was retrieved, is notorious for bathing incidents,' he pointed out.

They sat there crestfallen, trying to absorb the information. Tristan dug his nails into his palms.

'Did your friend have any mental issues maybe; suffered from depression? Was she happy?' the policeman asked.

'I don't think she would have committed suicide,' Tristan said. Something deep inside him was still somehow connected to the other children of Hamelin and registered the loss, knew the terrible event had carried a dreadful inevitability, but there was no reason to complicate matters for Philippe and Danielle, he reckoned. It would be better if they assumed it was just an accident. And as to Sofia abandoning her clothes, well skinny-dipping was not a sin.

'I'm sorry for your loss,' the *carabinieri* said. 'The authorities along the coast will look out for a body washed ashore, but the tides around here are unpredictable and it might never be found.'

Philippe silently rose and rushed away from the pool.

'She was his friend,' Danielle pointed out to explain his sudden flight.

'I understand,' the cop said. 'I will have to take down her details. I presume you have her papers, passport? We will have to open a dossier.'

'Yes,' Danielle said. 'I will go and fetch them.'

The policeman suggested they meet up in the lobby to go through the necessary administrative paperwork, apologising profusely that he knew the time was not right but that the authorities required him to obtain all the necessary information. Officially, it would be catalogued as a missing persons dossier, but he held little hope of Sofia or her body ever being found.

That night Tristan slept alone. Danielle was staying with her brother who had turned out to be more affected by Sofia's disappearance than she had thought possible, for a man who had discarded women over the years with gay abandon and little in the way of sentimentality.

Tristan was similarly affected, but for different reasons. He had somehow over the past years managed to partly banish his memories of the Island, Hamelin and even early days in Paris with Katerina, in an attempt to deny the core of pain that lingered inside his heart and mind. What was it about this new life he had escaped into and the way people faded so easily out of it? First Katerina and now, as he preferred to remember her, Sophie. Could the Piper be far behind, involved in nefarious ways, looking over him, an invisible but powerful supernatural presence, punishing him for his rebellion against the state of things?

Should he just passively sit back and wait for the next catastrophe to land along his path? Or should he react, fight back?

He felt torn, once again reminded that he was unlike others

and was literally a man of two worlds. Neither of which he appeared to properly belong to.

It took a further day for them to complete all the formalities surrounding Sofia's disappearance, leaving forwarding addresses and telephone details, and they were allowed to depart Sicily.

Philippe returned to Panama, while Tristan and Danielle made their way back to Paris. They parted at Palermo airport, their flights both leaving soon.

Paris in August was a ghost city, mostly populated by tourists, the sounds of a fifty or so different languages a dissonant soundtrack. Tristan had by now read all of Jules Verne and couldn't raise much enthusiasm for the other classic French authors Danielle felt he should read. Her work at the now sparsely-attended *bibliothèque* now bored her to tears, ever repetitive and unchallenging.

'I hate this place in the summer,' she remarked one evening.

'So let's do something about it,' Tristan suggested.

He would sell off another batch of his American technology shares. Their value kept on increasing.

She raised a slight smile.

'Where to?' she asked. 'I'm sick of this place. Even somewhere imaginary will do. Say Atlantis or Hy-Brasil.'

'I'm not sure if I can deliver the impossible,' Tristan remarked, with a wry smile.

17

Danielle before Tristan.

She had never thought of herself as a bad person. If anything, her brother Philippe had been the black sheep of the family, caught cheating at exams and being accused several times of distributing illicit substances first at school and later in the community. He was almost five years older and had always treated her as his pet. Their father was away on business one week out of two, and their mother was a drunk who spent her hours in a daze, blissfully ignorant of what was going on.

When she turned eighteen, Philippe began to introduce her to some of his friends. Whether he took money from them, she didn't know but it wouldn't have surprised her. At first, she had been curious, but soon it became a custom for them to give her small gifts. She acceded to their demands. First, she learned how to give blow jobs, and later agreed to be mounted.

Over two years, she slept with ten of Philippe's acquaintances and wore a different ring on each finger of both her hands. She knew none of them had much value, but they were like a seal, a manifestation of her perversity. Made her feel adult.

Between the older boys and men, she desultorily agreed to an occasional date with classmates, but found them all clumsy and naive in their words and gestures and eventually restricted herself to her sex dates with Philippe's handpicked acolytes. She knew other girls at the *Lycée* whispered behind her back that we was a slut but felt impervious to the growing rumours that never travelled beyond the school grounds. She was actually a model student in other regards, her teachers full of praise for her essays, her reading and keen interest in biology and plant life.

Danielle was fully aware she was being used but in a

contradictory way also felt she was in control, although the sexual acts she freely consented to actually provided her with little pleasure. Her mind rose above the filth she indulged in and, in the moment – and they were seldom lengthy in their perfunctory rhythm – she saw herself as a spectator to her own debasement, a detached, almost scientific observer of the sexual act and the fever it triggered in the bodies of men and women. She knew this phase would pass, that statistically she would one day enter into more meaningful and rewarding relationships, but for now this experimental phase was all she could afford, and there was no harm in it anyway. Everyone was a winner: Danielle was storing invaluable knowledge that would one day repay her in spades about what men wanted; Philippe took his pimp's commission and protected her; the men enjoyed their hasty fucks; nobody was harmed in the process.

Each ring on her fingers was different: a simple wooden one made out of oak, several silver ones with varying patterns, intricate carvings of flowers or a fine pattern of bonsai branches, one with a thumb-size skull that made her think of pirates in movies or in books she had read, another with a cross, yet another with a small diamond-like piece of coloured glass that caught the reflections of the sun when held in its direction, one a cygnet ring with a dark, black stone embedded in the dull metal, a wedding ring-like which was turning green at the edges and even a fragile pink plastic ring that could well have come from a vending machine or a Kinder chocolate egg in all its cheapness but for which she held some misguided affection as it had been gifted to her by the first boy she had willingly taken into her mouth to embarrassing effect when he had come prematurely and taken her by surprise. She looked down at her ringed fingers and only regretted the fact she badly chewed her nails which in a ridiculous way spoiled the whole thing.

After Philippe left home to go and work as a trainee for a shipping company in Marseille in the south of France, and she was left alone at home preparing for her *baccalauréat*, Danielle slowly disengaged herself from his friends and their simple demands, shedding them one a time with one pretext or another, and forcefully concentrated on her studies. She reckoned she now knew enough about the ways of men and did not require further lessons on their lusts and basic hollowness. She successfully applied for a grant and began a comparative literature course at the Sorbonne, during which time she also attended numerous lectures on botany in one of the university's great auditoriums by the Panthéon, even though she had not signed up for the actual course. She held a deep fascination for the life of plants and found their study compelling. So little demands on life but survival, unlike the needs and cravings of human beings in nineteenth century British and French literature or even real life as she had so far experienced it.

Two thirds of the way into her degree course, Danielle had arranged a three month Erasmus exchange program at Goldsmiths in London to both improve her English and study under the tutelage of a British academic who was a specialist of the works of H G Wells, whom she was hoping to write her dissertation on, comparing his vision of the future to that of almost contemporary French futuristic author Jules Verne, whose works she had cherished ever since she had been a child and had captured her romantic imagination.

The room for rent was in Ealing in north west London and was situated in a semi-detached two-storied suburban house with a small patio at the front and a large unkempt garden at the back, just a five minute walk from a convenient bus stop. The ground floor was used as a doctor's surgery. His name was Dr Patel. The cost of the rental was advertised on the uni's notice board twice as cheaper than other accommodation featured on the many cards pinned to the cork display panel in the student's common room, and Danielle who had been staying in a central youth hostel of dubious hygiene and suffocating dormitory atmosphere reckoned that, with a cautious approach to her food budget, she could just about afford it. The lower rent was explained by the demand for certain domestic tasks that would have to be undertaken, which didn't scare Danielle off. She had always been a tidy person and the prospect of some cleaning and dusting chores actually suited her. She found she could do those sort of things with part of her mind switched off, allowing her other thoughts, academic and otherwise, to prosper while she busied herself away mechanically.

Her initial interview was with the surgery nurse, a middle-aged woman of corpulent stature, and she didn't meet Dr Patel until a few days after she had moved in. He was in his 60s, copper-skinned, his dark, lustrous hair grey at the temples, and wore thick glasses. He introduced himself as they danced around the surgery's main reception area, Danielle with her duster and broom, he shedding his white coat after a day's consultations.

Danielle quickly saw from the way he gazed at her as she moved around and, later, when they sat down together to share a pot of coffee he had brewed, that his interest in her was far from benevolent. She knew men well enough by now. He was fascinated by the fact she was French, and complimented her several times on her English. She protested about her pronounced accent, which she felt unduly reminded her of Maurice Chevalier in old black and white Hollywood movies seen on late night TV. He brushed her excuses away. 'It's delightful, Danielle, absolutely.'

For several days in a row, they would meet up after his day's work and they would share a tea, a coffee or at his suggestion something stronger and he would interrogate her about France, her studies, the French and their way of life, with genuine interest. Ealing was too far from London's centre for Danielle to wish to travel into town in the evenings, even more so if she had commuted in and out of the city that same day for lectures, and his company was welcome for an hour or so before she moved back to her room to study or make notes.

It had been over four months since Danielle had been to bed with a man. He was a handsome man, and far more intelligent, cultured and subtle than any of her brother's friends (or clients) and she had decided that should he make a pass at her, she would not resist. The fact that he was almost three times her age was both attractive and worrying. Would his body, once revealed, display signs of decrepitude? Would his demands be different? He didn't live in the same house where he had his surgery but in Wembley, a few miles away, with an elderly relative. He seldom provided details about his life, but she had gathered he was divorced. An arranged marriage, set up by his family when he was still young, which had not worked out.

'Another glass, Danielle?' he offered to refill her glass of red wine. She had never been much of a wine lover, but Dr Patel was certainly under the impression that all French people were. She was already on her third glass and feeling just a little bit woozy.'

'The last one,' she said. 'I have to organise all my lecture notes later, and need to keep a clear mind.'

She raised her glass to him.

'Why all those rings, Danielle? Are you a hippy?'

She laughed. 'Nothing of the sort.'

'I understand having one or two,' Dr Patel said. 'But one on each finger is a bit much. Does it mean anything or is it a fashion statement?' he enquired.

Danielle was unsure whether she should reveal the truth. Her cheeks were reddening, from the wine, the heat in the room, the closeness of the man with his distinctive fragrance of citrusy aftershave and perspiration.

'They're symbolic.'

'Of what?'

'Each one represents a man I have slept with.'

There was a glint in his eyes as he processed the information.

'Very French,' he remarked.

'Not really. Just a silly quirk of mine.'

'You're still quite young,' he said. 'That's a lot of men, isn't it?'

'I have no basis for comparison. Is it?'

'Can I ask a personal question?'

'Of course.'

'I've come across reports in newspapers and magazines that

some students have had to get involved in forms of sex work in order to subsidise their studies. It's happening in England and the USA; have you come across this in France, maybe?'

'I suppose so,' Danielle said hesitantly.

'Would you?' he abruptly asked.

Danielle had never been with an older man and wondered briefly how different it might be, how much more confident the caresses would be, the rhythm unhurried and leisurely enough to detonate all those intimate triggers she held inside and which, she was aware, had never been properly engaged as younger men were too hasty in reaching for their pleasure and never emotionally engaged. Patel was handsome in an unassuming way, and had a touch of the night about him, of danger, of hidden knowledge. She was tempted.

The surgery waiting room in which they sat seemed to shrink as the tension between them rose. In one corner stood a large aquarium in which half a dozen small orange fish swam in dreamy procession.

She was about to respond when he spoke.

'I would love to sleep with you, Danielle, but that's not what I am offering though. Much to my personal sadness.'

He'd had a small laser operation to his prostate the previous year which meant he could no longer get hard, nor ejaculate, he explained.

'But it hasn't extinguished my love and desire for women,' he said.

'Far from it. I covet what I cannot have, strongly.'

'So what are you proposing?'

'I will not be offended if you turn me down,' he said. 'The room upstairs remains yours for the duration of your study term, and I'm sure I can manage some additional gifts in kind. I will find other suitable men for you and will watch, direct them, be involved, protect you. Even though I am unable to give you pleasure personally, I will do so by proxy.'

It sounded crazy, but a core of madness inside her had been set afire by the idea the moment the words had passed his lips. He was a medical doctor; it would be safe. There would be no emotional involvement, just a transaction. Or as she justified it to herself, an experiment. It was a situation she had idly dreamt of already, never believing it could come close to reality.

So began her love affair with Dr Patel, her landlord, her pimp, her protective father figure. The men would visit, mostly one at a time until the day he asked her whether she would accept more, which she did. She was always given the opportunity to turn any of them down once they walked through the door of his Wembley house, should she dislike any of them, which she seldom did. She guessed he found them on the Internet.

They would undress her under his instructions, slowly, almost religiously as if Patel was the conductor of a precise ritual, then they would mount her as he watched. Some were gentle while others could turn out to be rough, pinning her down on the bed, their weight pressing down against her body, making it difficult for her to breathe. They took her in every imaginable position as the doctor stood by their side directing them, sometimes holding one of her hands while the stranger thrust indiscriminately inside her, at other times drying the sweat pearling down her forehead or pooling in the hollow of her back. Sometimes, they would blindfold her, a few times they bound her hands; once she was laid on the living room table, the cold wood chilling her bare back, tied in a stance of crucifixion all limbs obscenely akimbo while hands unknown played with her for ages until she came with an almighty roar. Somehow the menu Dr Patel had devised for his pleasure and theirs, and on occasions Danielle's, was limitless.

After the men departed, they would sleep together in his bed upstairs, curtains by the window fluttering in the gentle spring breeze. Patel and her would both be naked, and he would keep her warm, his soft, large body spooned against her, his soft penis finding harbour between her arse cheeks. Generously, she would often volunteer to take it in her mouth or between her fingers should he so desire but it remained defiantly out of action, brown, thick but limp, a wonderful but useless decoration. He reassured her it was fine and he derived enough pleasure from watching her with others, and was even happier when she managed to orgasm.

Danielle's affection for the older man grew with every successive experience and for the first time ever she had an intimation of what love could be.

She even began to look forward to the weekends they would spend together, the silences floating between them, as they read in separate armchairs, he a newspaper and she, invariably, a book until the men arrived on cue to perform their assigned duties. She didn't know where he found them all and enticed them here, and she was curious how he advertised what was on offer, so to speak. The men said little once they arrived, before or after the bedroom; she assumed they had been ordered to remain silent by Dr Patel, and the only sounds passing their lips were the groans of lust they couldn't smother in the throes of sex, a sometimes cacophony of four-letter words, religious invocations of dubious worth and indistinctive grunts of a prehistoric nature. It was clear they had all been instructed never to kiss her on the lips, which they obeyed. No man ever visited twice. Nor asked Danielle for her name.

Her Erasmus exchange study term all to quickly came to a conclusion and she had to return to Paris.

Dr Patel and she agreed to continue seeing each other in this bizarre manner and he made arrangements for her to visit London every alternate weekend, paying for her Eurostar ticket on the early Saturday morning train, returning late on Sunday afternoon. This went on for several months until he suggested they might cool matters down and make her visits to London monthly instead. The thought tugged at her heart. Was he tiring of her? Had he found another impecunious student to agree to his devil's pact? Or was he no longer sufficiently turned on by the way his guests were violating her, her responses too artificial, her attitude now too detached maybe?

It was on the journey back to Paris, following a weekend of sex and awkward silence that she fell into conversation with a young American named Conrad. He was backpacking through Europe on a Railpass, and sought recommendations for his stay in Paris. He was pleasant, uncomplicated, and so unlike any of the men Danielle had been introduced to through either Philippe or Dr Patel. He was just a normal person. He wanted to be a journalist and had studied literature so they had a lot to talk about and compare. On his return to New York, he was hoping to find a job as a copy editor in newspapers or publishing. Like any student, his funds were on the low side and Danielle impulsively suggested he could sleep on her couch. He readily accepted.

Naturally, she took him to bed. He was clumsy but gentle, visibly wide-eyed at the thought he was sleeping with an actual French woman, unbelieving of his luck. His enthusiasm warmed her.

Conrad had only planned to stay in France a week or so but, at Danielle's insistence, remained longer, cancelling his initial plans to move on to Italy, Greece or Spain. It was still a fortnight before the new university year's opening term began and Danielle had time on her hands, which she spent guiding him around the city. It was late August and the streets were comparatively empty, even though the queues at the Louvre, the Pompidou Centre and the Musée d'Orsay were long, chattering in a hundred languages, none of which neither Danielle or Conrad ever seemed to properly identify, a fact they both found highly amusing. It was also a pretext to explore her own city and see places she had never been much bothered to visit before and to gain a new perspective on its streets, its flowering of small and large churches, gardens and hidden parks. And see it through the eyes of another person.

It was a strange parade of dying summer days and Danielle found that though she did enjoy almost acting like an ordinary person in the throes of a traditional relationship, she couldn't escape the feeling that she was also an observer of her own life and found it unaccountably drab, missing something essential. She knew it was her fault and not Conrad's. There was a core of craving buried deep inside her that scorned normalcy, that made her stick out in a crowd. She was convinced she was wired differently from others, a flaw that had always been present, had been in situ since birth, that kept on whispering to her that surely there must be something more to life than this. Or, when she felt sorry for herself, reminded her that things in books were different, and that maybe she had read too much and shouldn't live her life according to the rules of fiction.

It was a lazy late afternoon and Danielle and Conrad had just made love. Sprawled across her narrow bed, entangled in the sheets, he was now half asleep, one arm draped across her bare shoulder as she lay on her back watching the ceiling with its peeling paint and damp patches. Her apartment looked across to the nearby women's prison of La Roquette. It had closed a decade previously, but its proximity still ensured that rent was affordable in this part of the 11th *arrondissement*, which still resisted gentrification.

Danielle was daydreaming and smoking a cigarette. Conrad had, again, not managed to make her come despite his assiduous attention and efforts. His tenderness was, though, a saving grace despite her insistence that he should sometimes be more selfish and not be afraid of being more forceful, less focused on raising her pleasure rather than just his. Maybe other men had spoiled her in this respect, or even damaged her?

The telephone, on the bedside table, rang. Conrad stretched and moaned in his sleep, while Danielle extended her arm to pick it up.

It was Franck. She struggled to picture him. He was a man she had once been introduced to by her brother Philippe a year or so previously when he had been liberally offering her to strangers. She couldn't remember why but she had given him her number. He lived in the east of France, near Mulhouse, by the German border, and happened to be in Paris, he informed her.

'I'm in town and would like to see you.'
'Why?' she asked, although she well knew the answer.
'Because you're a good fuck. Why else?'
'I'm with someone right now,' Danielle replied.
'You mean permanently, in a relationship?'
'No. It's a friend. I'm actually in bed with him right now.'

There was a pause.

'Wonderful. The more the merrier, then. Where do you live?' Franck asked, quite unphased.

She remembered the evening Dr Patel had invited two men to join them, and how ashamed and degraded she had felt being shared in this way, although the memory of how Patel's eyes gleamed as he cheered their breathless endeavours on still flickered in her mind.

'So?' Franck insisted. 'Give me your address.'

She did.

He was knocking at her door a quarter of an hour later. She rose from the bed naked. Conrad half-opened his eyes. 'It's just an old friend,' she said to him. 'I won't be long. Just stay there and wait for me. Maybe best if he doesn't see you.' He looked up at her uncomprehendingly as if slowly processing the information, as she grabbed his shirt and slipped it on and walked out of the bedroom, her pale arse peering below the shirt's bottom edge.

Franck was as she remembered, shaven headed and stocky, with an assortment of tattoos trailing down his arms. He looked down at her, registering her dishevelled appearance and the fact she was barely dressed.

'You still smell of sex,' he said, pulling her to himself by her hair.

Danielle swallowed, then sputtered 'He's in the other room. He won't join us. We can go to the kitchen.'

'So I have you all for myself,' Franck said. 'That's fine with me too.'

Conrad's shirt was unbuttoned. Franck pulled it open, looking down at her breasts.

He kicked his trainers off and they both stepped barefoot into the nearby kitchen.

He pulled her up onto the small table, turned her round and quickly entered her.

A few minutes later, Conrad, holding one of the bed sheets around his waist looked in and uncomprehendingly watched the two of them coupling roughly on the table, all sighs, moans and frantic thrusts and squirming movements. Danielle knew how ugly the spectacle he was witnessing would feel to him. How he would feel utterly betrayed. But it was too late. She was aware she had reverted to nature, unable to halt her baser instincts.

Conrad said nothing. Franck was digging ever deeper into her guts and she momentarily moved her head round and caught Conrad's eyes. He was crying.

He was out of the apartment minutes later, quickly dressing and stuffing his belongings into his rucksack, the door slamming behind him. Franck was still pinning her down, pulling her hair back and viciously slapping her rump as he continued his business while she tried to overhear Conrad's receding steps on the stairs.

Later, after Franck's departure, having vigorously showered all the day's physical and mental filth away, Danielle swore off men altogether and decided she would become a new person from hereafter, a normal person. She stayed true to this promise to herself for a whole year, until the day Tristan walked into the library she was now working in, following her degree and a lack of teaching jobs.

18

Philippe had been living in Panama City for only three weeks when he experienced a vivid and memorable dream in which he believed he sold his soul to the devil.

The imagined event had never even taken the form of a nightmare, just an orderly transaction conducted in polite terms at the climax of which he had signed a legally enforceable contract in triplicate, witnessed in turn by a crowd of wild looking children with feral looks and shaky signatures. The devil had worn a three-piece suit and his hair had been slicked back with not a strand out of place and dark as night, his attitude unhurried and officious. He looked just like a stockbroker but a small voice inside Philippe's head sounded an alarm bell and reminded him that his interlocutor was actually a creature of the night.

When Philippe had woken up the following morning, he had felt much the same as usual, with no parts visibly missing, whether physical or mental. If he had sold his soul, he wondered, what had he exchanged it for? And dismissed the whole thing as just a curious and ridiculous dream of no consequence.

He wasn't sure whether he was made for the tropics, always sweating profusely whether day or night, skimming by the walls when he ventured out of air-conditioned buildings to avoid the fierce heat of the sun that towered above the city like a fat, dictatorial monarch with no regard for its subjects. He'd arrived here with a suitcase full of clothes better suited to mild and cold European weather and, once he could afford it, would have to acquire a whole new wardrobe of lighter, linen suits, jackets, trousers and short-sleeved shirts. The office work was boring, although he had quickly established friendships with some of the men, both local and Spanish-speaking in the large warehouse the company owned in the docks by the mouth of the canal, and had the germ of an idea that would make his bank account a tad healthier once the right contacts could be established.

The company apartment he had been granted use of was pleasant and well-located in an area of the city where most of the expatriates lived, on the ground floor of a stucco row of buildings surrounded by green vegetation with full-time gardeners ever on duty planting, trimming and watering the lawns. There was also a kidney-shaped swimming pool at the rear of the complex, which he hadn't been tempted yet to use over the slow week-ends, preferring the company of others in bars and dives in the less salubrious districts of the city, where the drinks were markedly cheaper if you didn't mind sidestepping the beggars littering the outside pavements, many of them refugees from civil wars in nearby countries who had managed to escape one form of hell for another.

Philippe had always had a difficult relationship with beggars and down and outs. When he had still been a child back in Paris, their presence in the streets of the *banlieue* where he had been brought up concurrently fascinated and scared him, particularly when his father, noticing his sense of discomfort, would remind him repeatedly that this could happen to him should he fail in his studies or ignore parental instructions. His nightmares became the stuff of horror, picturing himself by the banks of the Seine, pulling a torn and filthy blanket around his bloodless, pale body in desperate search of warmth, his hands brown and dirty, his nails broken, his knuckles bloody and his feet, peering out of the too short protection of the blanket, shoeless. That image dominated his youth and he determined at an early stage he would avoid that fate, would earn money by hook or by crook, or any means possible, even dishonest ones. This had included extracting monetary gain from introducing his younger sister to friends back in Paris. The girl was a dead loss, he felt, and they had little in common. She had taken to becoming a whore with a strange passiveness, as if her mind and body were two separate entities, going about the sex involved with splendid detachment and, apparently, little actual enjoyment, ticking off the experience as she did the countless books she read in the pages of her notebook, where she seldom wrote anything personal or important. Truly he didn't understand her.

He had become friendly with Jesús, who was a senior foreman in the warehouse and a welcome font of information in all things commercial and mercantile. A few years earlier, the Americans had invaded the country and deposed Noriega and still controlled a major zone around the Canal, which Jesús, through his network of contacts, had liberal access to. Much of the black-market transactions took place there, around the bars and clubs and the PX stores that supposedly only catered to the military and their families.

It was at the Puerto Aventuras bar where they had met up one weekday evening alongside Marieke, Jesús's Dutch girlfriend and a couple of Yank business contacts, that after a glass too many of contraband whiskey, the group noisily agreed to move on for the evening to what the Americans referred to as a good old titty bar, a down at heel strip joint hidden away and known only to connoisseurs of gentle depravity in the depths of the dock area, catering to sailors on furlough between contracts and passing rough trade. Even Marieke, a lanky redhead all bones and permed hair was curious about the place, deluging them on the walk there with lurid tales of the Amsterdam red light district with which she appeared to have had a close and personal acquaintance, although she strongly denied this and just pointed to youthful prurient interest.

The place was unimaginatively called Dreams, its name carved out above the entrance in glaring pink neon shouting out at the equatorial moonlit night. A couple of burly security guards lurked in silence outside, vetting visitors with dreamy indifference, their bulk blocking out the distant sound of a heavy bass beat filtering from the inner depths of a club as they approached it.

A couple of sultry-eyed and heavy-breasted strippers were cavorting on the central stage, merry-go-rounding between a set of rigid steel poles to the sound of a mariachi tune, their booties shaking on automatic pilot. There were few spectators around as Jesús and his group walked in and settled at a table at the back of the darkened room. In the glow of the single spotlight volutes of dust swirled like dwarf clouds across the stage floor.

'Is it always this empty?' Philippe asked as they sat down. He had expected the place to be buzzing with life from the tales he had heard.

'It's still early,' one of the men said. 'It livens up later. A lot …' he smirked.

Jesús had fetched their beers from the bar after a brief conversation with a wild-haired woman who was sitting on a stool there with a tall glass of clear liquid. Water? Gin? Philippe could only see her back. She sat straight; her pale bare shoulders draped by her falling curls.

When Jesús returned with his round, Philippe asked him, 'Who was that girl you were talking to? The next stripper to take to the stage?'

'If only …' Jesús sighed. 'I'd pay a lot of money to see that.'

'Just a customer? Works here?' Philippe persisted with his questions.

It was Marieke who answered between gulping down her already half-empty glass of beer as if she had just returned from a stroll in the desert and was desperate for anything liquid.

'She's a strange one, she is. Has become a regular here and sometimes does the odd job: cleaning up, washing glasses, moving stock around, always watching people come in as if she was waiting for someone special to arrive. She calls herself Katerina but she has another name on her papers, I was told by the owner, who had to check up on her to see if she was legal before she was allowed to work. According to her passport, she is also from the Netherlands. My arse! I once tried to engage her in conversation and she visibly didn't understand a single word of Dutch. Says she's Russian, but again the accent isn't quite right. She just walked in one evening months ago. We thought she was just a passenger from a cruise ship tempted to explore the sin zone, but she just sits around, lost in her own world.'

Philippe was intrigued.

'I see that look in your eyes,' Jesús said. 'Every single day when they realise she is unattached, men have invariably tried to pick her up. Offered her money, but she's not interested. Juan Antonio, who runs the place, also offered her the opportunity to dance and you know what; with her exotic looks she'd make a fortune in tips, but she just dismissed the idea outright. No one knows what she does for money as the work she does here cleaning up and such barely covers her bar bill, nor where she lives locally. She's never been seen outside of these doors, on her own, let alone with a man.'

The conversation moved on. Philippe had been studying how the system whereby orders for deliveries of alcohol and tobacco were forwarded on to the warehouse for delivery to the visiting cruise ships and thought he had spotted a glaring administrative loophole in the process. In order to exploit if, he would require accomplices in the warehouse. He cautiously set out his plan while the others listened. Together with Jesús, he had taken the measure of them a few nights in a row while they drank and caroused and knew they were not men of deep integrity but guys whose principles could easily be swayed with the right incentives on offer.

They were all immediately interested, after some initial protestations to establish the fact that though they had hitherto always followed the right path, a change of direction was not out of the question, as all in present company had monetary needs which virtue alone didn't cater for.

They huddled together like conspirators while a procession of strippers took to the stage. Philippe would throw them the occasional glance, but none were his type. Too Latina, thick-waisted, heavy on top and with dull eyes and large, prominent buttocks. He'd always had a thing for pale women. He knew his own weaknesses. Had Danielle been blonde, he might have well been tempted to avail himself of her charms, knowing she would have proven passive and accepted without batting an eyebrow, a slave to her inner submissive nature. But, fortunately, there had always been enough women around in

Paris answering his criteria and willing to bed him. Life was already complicated enough to add incest to the list of charges he might one day have to confront.

On her stool by the bar, the woman who called herself Katerina sat for a further couple of hours, curtly dismissing any approach by club customers, local businessmen on the prowl or sailors on shore leave, slowly nursing her drink and oblivious to her surroundings. Philippe noticed how she tapped her feet to the beat when some songs played, or stayed motionless like a statue when the music was not to her liking.

They had collectively reached a form of agreement over which step to take next to set up the scheme Philippe had proposed. Now, all they had to do was find willing buyers on the actual boats docking in port with both the authority to purchase outside the normal channels in the knowledge it was not completely legal. A task Philippe's position in the office would facilitate.

Philippe looked around to the bar, ready to conclude the deliberations by picking up the next round of drinks himself, and determined to see Katerina's face after being teased all evening by the pallor of her uncovered shoulders and the top of her back above the white cotton fringe of her low-cut blouse. But she had departed, her stool now occupied by a visiting sailor in crisp, starched white uniform, in conversation with one of the strippers, his fingers grazing her knees as he peered unashamedly down her gaping cleavage.

The fleeting vision of Katerina stayed in his mind for days. He visited the club on a few occasions during the following weeks, but she was not to be seen. He asked after her, but no one there even knew where she lived or what she might be doing during the day. She came, she went, making random appearances when night came and that was the whole sum of their knowledge.

He was busy fine-tuning the plans for the first illegal consignment of goods their group was preparing to divert, which the officer in charge of procurement for a large Norwegian cruise vessel had agreed to purchase when an acolyte discovered that, from the following day, the timing rounds of the customs staff at the docks had been adjusted. Although all the paperwork Philippe had set up for the operation should pass muster, it would still require someone be present to divert attention in some way from their nocturnal activities in case of any last-minute changes to that evening's roster. Antonio Cartano, an accountant in the chandler's office where Philippe worked and also a terrible gambler who had willingly been roped into their scheme declared he knew the perfect person for the job. A woman. Philippe had reservations. He felt any of the strippers or barmaids Antonio was likely to know would easily be recognised. The docks were a small world.

He was surprised when Antonio brought Katerina along to a bar where Philippe had agreed to interview her. Where did Antonio know her from? Her face was even more striking than the profile he had observed in semi darkness. Her hair was a tangle of blonde Medusa-like curls, her cheekbones sharp enough to cut glass but her green eyes observed him through a curtain of dulled sadness. She wore what seemed to be the same off the shoulder white blouse he had seen her with at the bar. It was more modest at the front than it was at the back, a vertical row of small ebony buttons topped by an intricate, old-fashioned bow. Her jeans were frayed at the ankles but stuck to her long legs like a second skin. He hadn't realised how tall she was.

She introduced herself. Marieke was right; she was not Dutch. As to her Russian origins, Philippe's knowledge of accents wasn't acute enough to pinpoint it. As it was, he spoke English himself with a pronounced French, one which made many of his colleagues invariably smile.

He explained what was needed of her. To distract attention should any customs official leave the two-storeyed control building unexpectedly. This by any means. How she managed it was unimportant.

'I understand,' she said.

'Are you certain?'

'If I have to, I deploy my charms. You don't have to spell it out ...'

Philippe smiled. He knew she had it in her. She was not overenthusiastic or boastful, but quietly confident in her remote way that she could deliver what was required, and could think on her feet, unlike some of the local girls Jesús had initially suggested.

There was also something else about the young woman that appealed to him, a sense of defiant vulnerability; Danielle had possessed it too. It drew the inner streak of control that he knew he harboured to the light.

He asked her many other questions about herself, her origins, what she was doing in Panama City, how she earned a living, but the young woman was evasive. It wasn't as if she didn't trust him, but preferred to be seen as a blank canvas, indifferent to the world she was living in.

They agreed on her fee should the operation prove successful, irrespective of whether she would have to intervene or not. At Antonio's suggestion, it wasn't much. She accepted; never even bargained.

The operation went off smoothly and was to be the first of many. The inside information about the patrols and customs officials' inspection rounds always turned out to be accurate, and Katerina's role always remained that of an observer, lurking in the shadows in her short skirt and lipsticked to the hilt, her smile in readiness.

Philippe wanted to know more about her, breach her defences and repeatedly invited Katerina to share a drink with him, whenever he came across her at the club. He didn't have a clue where she spent her daytimes, only venturing out at night; like a beautiful blonde vampire, he thought, although in his imagination vampires were always sleek and dark-haired.

'We're the only Europeans here,' he said, seeking common ground and a subject for conversation.

She nodded. She only drank lemonade, he had noticed.

Never touched alcohol. He'd asked her why, but she had not answered.

'In Paris, where I come from, they call it *citron pressé*,' he said. 'Most of the cafés have this machine in which you drop the lemons and they squeeze the juice out of them in a jiffy. Here, they do it by hand.'

'I know Paris,' Katerina, her eyes clouding, almost to the point of tears.

'Have you? That's wonderful, *magnifique*. I was born there, lived there all my life before I came to Panama, you know.'

She stared at him, lost in her own dreams.

'Where in the city did you live?' he asked her.

'I don't remember.'

'Really?'

'Something happened. I know I've been to a lot of different places, cities, countries, but I can't recall anything in any detail.'

'That's curious.'

'I've lost my past,' she said, wistfully, taking a deep breath to regain her composure. She was visibly perturbed when reminded of the situation.

He tried to humour her, hoping she wouldn't fall silent and cease conversing now that he had actually got her started and gleaned some minimal information about her and life.

'You've lost your past,' he said, grinning. 'And I've lost my soul?'

She looked at him with alarm.

'I had this strange dream in which I sold my soul to the devil,' he continued.

'What did the devil look like, in your dream?' Katerina asked.

Philippe described him, the way he dressed, his appearance as a wealthy banker.

Katerina visibly froze.

Philippe waited patiently for her to speak again.

She finally did.

'What does it feel like to be without a soul?'

'Much the same, I must say.'

'The same as what?'

Should he confess that deep down he was basically dishonest, untrustworthy, a man who saw no problem in exploiting others, women, cheating? He reckoned she already was well aware of this. And more. The way her eyes looked at him said it all. Had he been a man without a soul all along? The thought made him uncomfortable. A heavy silence settled between them.

One of the strippers was taking to the stage behind them. The loudspeaker crackled as the system was switched on, a prelude to yet another big beat tune for her to cavort to.

Katerina turned her head round and wistfully looked at the dancer going through the motions. She sighed.

'You've never done it?' Philippe asked.

'Done what?'

'Danced.'

'Not to that terrible sort of music,' she said.

She took a final sip from her glass, readied herself to stand up, picked her small handbag up from where it had been hanging on the side of the chair.

'Where do you live?'

'Nowhere.'

'Tell me more about you … Please …'

'There's nothing to know.'

'I'm sure there is. Everyone has a story. No?'

'I have a lot of stories but they all belong to me alone and are not meant for public consumption,' she said.

'Maybe I'd find some of them interesting?'

'I'm sure you would …'

He took hold of her wrist in an attempt to dissuade her from leaving.

'Tell me some.'

'Why should I?'

'Sometimes stories can be a burden, and telling them lightens the load.'

He didn't let go of her arm. She opposed no resistance.

'Just one?'

'The past is gone. It means nothing now.'

'What about Paris? We have that in common. What did you do there?'

'The only reason I know I've been there is finding a few crumpled receipts in my suitcase, labels on some of my clothes, the fading memory of the taste of a fresh croissant in the morning straight from the *boulangerie*'s oven, the churning of my guts when I see a photo in a newspaper or a magazine of the bridge across the Seine, but I am unable to fix on anything specific. The past is a blur.'

Philippe gazed at her. Her green eyes were veiled with mist or was it the onset of tears?

'You remember nothing at all?'

'No. Only the stuff of dreams.'

'Such as?'

'In my sleep, things, images, emotions return in fragments, rise to the surface, but they make no sense. There is a man and we meet in foreign places and he knows how to touch me and his voice is like velvet. But I have no idea what he even looks like. We are in a room in a luxury hotel in the mountains, the view from the window tells me it's a ski resort, and we take a bath together in a large white tub while I'm playing music by Pink Floyd and I melt in the embrace of his arms. Another night we are freezing in bed, the only warmth generated by our entwined bodies. I know we are in a medieval stone village in the hills outside Rome. I later looked it up, it's called Calcata. But a voice inside me tells me I have never been to Italy, and this is somehow someone else's dream. It doesn't belong to me. On yet another night of darkness and anxiety the man, whose face I am unable to recall in any detail, is with me in a hotel room in Barcelona and he is naked, his back to me, shaving, peering closely into the bathroom mirror as I watch him proceed slowly, and I catch him later in the corner of my eye, popping a triangular blue pill before he joins me in bed. Later, we are on a beach 30 minutes south of Barcelona and my bikini is ill-fitting and one of my nipples slips out and his smile melts my heart. But it is another woman's dream, as the subtle blend of pink and brown of the breast tip on view is unlike the shade of my own nipples, and again a voice whispers in my ear that I have never been to Barcelona or its neighbouring beaches … On another night, we share a room that overlooks New York's Washington Square and we have a terrible argument because I am jealous of his wife and I take refuge in a corner of the lobby bar until he finds me and his words soothe me. We always meet in hotels in places I have never been. My memories somehow belong to other women.'

Philippe was lost for words, as the stripper on the nearby stage finished her set, walked off into the wings and silence returned, bar the clinking of glasses and muted conversations at other tables.

Katerina stood.

'I have to leave,' she said.

'Another time, maybe?'

'Maybe.'

He never saw her again. They soon wound down the smuggling game anyway, as it couldn't be repeated too often without bringing attention to the growing gaps in the warehouse's inventory. By then, a cousin of Jesús had introduced them to someone in Honduras who was seeking a new network to move drugs into the area for onward travel North where the demand never ceased.

Katerina must have left Panama, as no one ever saw her again in the city or the club.

Life is a strange dance, Philippe reckoned. People stepped in and out of it in intricate patterns, some never to be seen again, while new faces came along to take their place. But who was playing the music whose patterns they all followed?

He quickly pushed the strange but striking young woman to the back of his mind. Put it down to a missed connection.

But he was strongly reminded of her the day they chanced on the curious island and found the mute girl, Sofia. Not that the two women looked at all the same. But they shared an aura. Of strangeness.

19

Tristan and Danielle travelled light, seeking the sun in all the expected places: on an atoll in the Maldives with fewer than fifty other holidaymakers on the island and the clearest sky at night either had ever seen. It was full of stars neither could recognise, an illuminated canvas of wonders that shed a glimmering light on sea and land and was a thing of absolute beauty.

When they tired of paradise, they moved on to another continent, travelling from the polluted heights of teeming Mexico City to the farthest reaches of Patagonia and Tierra del Fuego. They crossed landscapes of highs and lows, deep verdant forests and arid deserts, journeying on rickety coaches through endless nights and journeys that took days and nights to complete, sometimes interrupting their rambling itinerary by staying overnight in down on their luck isolated motels, where cockroaches and dust coexisted and the water from the bathroom tap ran cold and a dubious shade of pale orange.

But they were unable to settle anywhere for long. A sense of frustration accompanied them on their restless travel, the next destination always a few days away, like a promise to themselves that had to somehow be fulfilled. They were in no hurry, which was fortunate, as repeatedly one of them would succumb to a bug, become feverish and the road had to be interrupted between bouts of vomiting and diarrhoea until they regained their health and energy.

They were sitting in their room in a small pension in Valparaiso, a ten-minute walk from the seafront, both reading old well-leafed paperback books they had picked up in bus stations and motels along the way. Danielle's was a battered edition of an Aragon novel, while Tristan was absorbed in an American legal thriller.

'I need a coffee,' Danielle said, setting her book aside on the bedside table. 'I can't concentrate on reading any longer. I need something to keep me awake.'

'Sure. I'll join you.'

There was a bar they'd spotted nearby off the promenade, normally full of locals, just a beat away from the tourist circuit. They had been in town for ten days now.

'Another day, another town,' Danielle remarked.

'Yes,' Tristan said. 'Maybe this wasn't such a good idea after all.'

'So what do we do now? Return to Paris?'

'I don't know.'

'What would we do there? The same old routine?'

Their conversations were becoming sparser, full of silences, as if they had run out of things to say, or ways of expressing them. Tristan knew all too well that both he and Danielle still simmered inside with subjects best not raised, but it was never quite the right time to delve into those darker areas they both cautiously kept shielded from each other.

'I'm sure we can both find work in France again, if that's where you would rather go. The *bibliothèque* will, I'm confident, have you back and I can find something in the financial sector again.' He didn't mention the fact that he hardly needed a job any longer as his technology shares were exponentially growing in value and earning substantial dividends to keep them in comfort for a long time to come.

Danielle appeared to be in two minds. Far from enamoured of the prospect of returning to Europe but now weary of all the aimless travelling which had not turned out to be anywhere near as exciting as she had hoped it might be.

'I'll leave the decision to you. Whatever you choose, I'll be happy to go along with it,' Tristan assured her.

'I'll think about it,' she said.

'Just one thing …'

'Yes?'

'Before we return, though, there is one thing I'd like to do, as we're still out and about?'

A faint smile curled across Danielle's lips. 'I think I know what it is ...'

'Do you?'

'I've learned how to read you, Tristan. I should, by now. You want to visit Panama and see if Philippe can locate that island for you. Is that it?'

'Yes.'

'You and your islands ...' she grinned. 'Maybe you should make your life's work to explore every island on the planet, no? Although I guess that would take several lifetimes to complete.'

Tristan nodded. Once, he knew, he'd had lifetimes to spare, but this was no longer the case. He could feel it in his bones and looking at his face in the mirror, tracking the signs of ageing. Every day they grew stronger and more apparent. As this thought crossed his mind, he wondered if the same was now happening to Katerina, wherever she might be. He sighed.

'Would you come with me if I went?' he asked Danielle.

'Of course. I suppose we'd have to go to Panama City then, hook up with Philippe, as he's the one who knows where to search for the place.'

They didn't have much to pack into their rucksacks, some jeans, shorts, T-shirts; they always left the books they were reading behind, and the following morning they headed to the local airport where they caught a plane to Panama with a lengthy stopover in Recife, in Brazil, on the way.

Arriving late at night in Panama City, all the stores at the airport were already closed, so they took a room at a hotel overlooking the main runway. In the morning, they caught a cab into the port zone where Philippe lived, found a store selling cheap burner hand phones and Danielle was finally able to call her brother at his work. Neither of them had previously travelled with a phone, not having any need for one. They were told at his office that he was away on business for 48 hours, so they were left with a couple of days to kill. They moved on to a tourist hotel closer to the centre, where they decided to treat themselves the luxury of air conditioning and fragrant toiletries and a chance to wash away the grime of months on the road. The heat outside was unbearable, stifling and oppressive but they had no intention of visiting the city's attractions; they could see the muddy waters of the Canal, its fortifications and first set of enormous hydraulic locks from the window and terrace of their fifteenth-floor room anyway.

Somehow Philippe was not surprised to see them, once he had returned from his trip.

'I assume you've not had further news of Sofia?' he asked.

The police in Sicily had not made contact. Still, no body had washed ashore or any sign of her in the region. They hadn't expected any.

Tristan explained the purpose of their visit and their desire to try and locate the Island. Philippe was initially reluctant to assist them.

'You know we only came across it by accident and it isn't on any map. Maybe it's for a reason and it's not meant to be found again. It won't be easy. We did note down its location, but I'm not sure how reliable that might prove. Jesús made some enquiries about it after we'd been there and retrieved Sofia, but local sailors or fishing folk either disbelieved us or warned us off, as if the place was cursed.'

'I realise that,' Tristan stated. 'But that's yet another reason I must go there. Things in my past for which I need some form of explanation ...'

Danielle gave him a strange look. Back in Palermo, she had noted the curious affinity Tristan had found with Sofia, but had written the feeling off to just curiosity. He had never said more about the Island to her, whether before or after the disappearance of the young mute woman.

'I can pay,' Tristan said. 'For the hire of a boat, fuel and a goodly bonus on top.'

Philippe mentioned a likely sum which Tristan agreed to. Danielle found it outrageous, but kept quiet. She had long guessed that Tristan had access to money, but not to this extent.

'And I want to spend a night or two on this island,' he

added. 'We'll take enough food and water along, and some camping equipment. You can just drop us there and come back to fetch us at an agreed time, or stay,' he added.

Philippe opted for the second solution. Danielle felt aggrieved that Tristan hadn't even asked her opinion or given her the same choice, but recognised that Tristan was dealing with his own personal demons and she had always been along for the ride, even though she felt at times that Tristan had come to now take her too much for granted.

'I've a few other things to do first,' Philippe pointed out. A drop of merchandise off Florida territorial waters, to be left attached to a buoy with a signal transmitter. But the speedboat he would hire could be used on his return from that job to travel to the Island. It was also the beginning of the rainy season, so much would also depend on the weather forecast.

Tristan suggested they combine the two journeys. Initially drop off Philippe's consignment of drugs then travel straight to the island with no need to return to Panama in the interval. It might save them a day's travel or so. And avoid having to falsify yet another sailing plan to be lodged with local port authorities.

'That's a long time at sea,' Philippe pointed out.

'We can carry extra fuel and supplies, can't we?'

'I suppose so.'

They agreed on a date.

Stuck in their hotel room with little left to say, now increasingly uncomfortable with each other but wary of taking any rash decision about their future together, Tristan and Danielle waited for the day, both drowning in an ocean of deepest silences.

The surface of the Caribbean Sea was like a windswept desert of shimmering water as far as the eyes could see. They had been racing ahead for hours since the drop, Philippe constantly at the helm checking his dashboard screen to adjust their direction whenever they strayed from the dotted green light outlining their journey still to come on the flickering sonar screen. Behind the speedboat, the sea quickly closed its jaws on the carrousel of broken waves their progress along the surface created by the speed of their passage.

Ahead hung the unbroken line of the sky where it merged with the sea, their respective shades of stark blue blending effortlessly into a uniform and peaceful screen of cerulean canvas.

Tristan intensely fixed the line of the horizon as they sped on, although it never seemed to move or get any closer, contradicting all the sea miles they had already left in their wake.

At the back of the 15ft Cobra, Danielle was sunning herself on the narrow, wooden deck, clad in a white bikini, her skin growing redder by the hour despite the lashing of sunscreen she kept on rubbing into her limbs and face.

Time was at a standstill. Philippe had not expected the journey to take so long and was beginning to doubt the notes he had taken on his earlier foray when he had discovered the mysterious island.

'Are you sure we're heading in the right direction?'

'According to the coordinates I jotted down last time, we are,' Philippe confirmed.

Maybe the Island had now been swept off the map, Tristan speculated. It had briefly emerged into the real world in time for mute Sophie to complete her ill-fated escape and had now disappeared back into the folds of space and time where it had taken refuge for centuries. Nothing would surprise him any longer.

'There …' Philippe shouted out.

Tristan's mind had wandered off and he focused again. Danielle raised her head.

Tristan gazed out at the sea surrounding their racing speedboat.

There was nothing to be seen.

'I can't see anything.'

'At three o' clock, by the stern,' Philippe cried out.

The Piper's Dance

Tristan squinted; his vision impaired by the strength of the sun. He brought a hand to his brow to cut down on the glare.

A black dot in the distance, still miles away, interrupting the horizontal, gently undulating line where sea and sky parted ways.

'I see it now.'

'It must be the place,' Philippe said. 'There's nothing else on the maps around here for miles. And I can see a strip of land on the edge of the radar screen. We've made it!'

Their destination still felt as distant as the stars, though, as if the speedboat was wading through mud.

Tristan's heart skipped a beat.

Slowly, he felt progress finally being made: the small dot in the distance began to transform, its shape flattening until it betrayed a line of land that gradually came into view.

A rush of memories washed over him.

Danielle joined him where was standing at the prow of the speeding boat as it approached the land.

'It looks just like any other island,' she remarked.

It was true; there was nothing out of the ordinary about the place from their current perspective. All islands looked the same, Tristan reckoned. But he knew in his guts this was the one where he and the children of Hamelin had spent a childhood that had lasted centuries. An impossible place that made no sense.

'Maybe that's all it is,' he said. 'But this is where Sofia was found, so I was curious.'

The Cobra was now within spitting distance of the land and Philippe throttled down the speedboat's powerful engine and the boat began to slow, and soon came to a total halt. The Island was protected by a coral reef and they would have to step off the boat and wade through knee-deep water to reach the shore, as their embarkation couldn't come any nearer in the shallows.

Philippe had, after all, decided to join them, nervously protesting that he was unsure he could locate the Island again if he had to abandon them there for a day or more. 'Anyway,' he jested, 'maybe I can find myself another girlfriend, even one who talks, this time around ...'

They secured the speedboat with a series of ropes they attached to some of the rocky outgrowths of the reef, and disembarked, carrying their sleeping bags and a large wicker hamper each with food and water to sustain their sojourn.

Edgily stepping through the azure shallows, they made their way toward the beach, with Tristan leading, both eager and nervous to again set foot on the golden sands he remembered all too well, anxious to feel its texture, its warmth, the microscopic grains of sand moving between his toes, shifting imperceptibly under his weight, a memory carved deeply into his soul, a still beating echo of the past.

Once finally on land, he peered at the curtain of trees marking the borderline of the small forest that led to the interior of the island where the colony had once stood. There was a sense of familiarity, but also of uncertainty. He was unsure how much he recognised after the years away. Could it be another island altogether? He was beginning to doubt himself. Philippe sidled up to him, dropping his bags to the ground and answering his unspoken doubts. 'Yes, this is definitely the place. Look over there at those two parallel cuts in that tree trunk; I remember doing that with a machete.'

'So what now?' Danielle asked, catching up with them, and similarly unburdening herself. She bent over to wipe away the wet sand from her feet and slipped on the pair of white trainers she had hung by their laces across her shoulders. Philippe and Tristan were still barefoot. 'Do you have a plan? Or are we going to pretend we have been shipwrecked and be obliged to build ourselves a shelter by hacking away at the trees and playing Robinson Crusoe? I've read the books too ...' She was in a foul mood.

Tristan was indecisive. He turned to Philippe and asked, 'Didn't you say that last time you were here, you found some evidence of people having lived here at some stage, you mentioned burnt-out stuff in the interior.'

'Yes. But it could have just been natural, you know. Lightning igniting dry wood. I wouldn't call it evidence.'

'Well, while you boys stand idle, I'm bloody hot and I need to clean up,' Danielle said, throwing off her clothes and kicking off her Converse. 'I'm having a swim.' She stood defiantly naked by them. As she swivelled round and began to walk down to the shore, memories stirred in Tristan's mind of Katerina's splendid nudity in this very same place and a wave of guilt washed over him at the thought he was so unfairly comparing the two women.. Philippe similarly stood fixed to the spot, troubled by the vision of his naked sister; he might well have once pimped her to others but this was the first time he had seen her fully nude since they had shared baths as children. The sight both aroused and disturbed him.

Ignoring the two men, Danielle reached the water and jumped in headfirst, splashing around like a puppy, her pale body fading in and out of the intense green of the coral sea.

'I think I might join her,' Philippe said. 'I'm as sweaty as hell.'

'I want to go into the forest and see what could lie beyond,' Tristan said. 'Find that area you mentioned, where the fire might have taken place.'

Philippe nodded and pulled his T-shirt above his head.

Time and time again as he marched through the thick vegetation and deep silence of the coastal forest, Tristan would lose his bearings, as if the canvas of humid earth, sturdy tree trunks towering above him and luxuriant vegetation blocking his path at every step was conspiring to divert him in an unfamiliar direction. To think that once upon a time, he could walk this forest with his eyes closed and never lose himself! But slowly the inbuilt memories returned and he began to navigate himself towards where the colony used to be, lullabied by the rustle of leaves and the murmur of the faint breeze that managed to break through the brocade of trees and hanging branches.

He took a deep breath. He was home again, in the silence where no birds or insects were allowed to thrive, in that curious bubble that defied all the laws of physics.

He closed his eyes and kept on moving forward. When he opened them again, aware that he had moved beyond the forest, was no longer hemmed in by the impenetrable spider web of plants and trees, he found himself in the clearing where once the huts and habitations the children of Hamelin had found shelter in had thrived.

There was nothing left standing, just random mountains of debris scattered across the whole area, as if a hurricane had passed through and devastated the colony, and then whatever had survived had undergone a trial by fire, charred pieces of wood turning to crumbling ashes as he stepped across them, gnarly branches deformed by the intensity of the blaze distributed in almost geometric patterns across the ground as far as the eye could see. Had Tristan not know there had actually been dwellings here, it could have been yet another landscape after the battle, the natural order of the land disturbed by a series of familiar phenomena and up-ended topsy-turvy, now just waiting for the winds of time to blow away all traces of the storm and the conflagration and allow inert matter to revert to undisturbed normalcy. What had occurred here was still reasonably recent. Grass was beginning to grow back in isolated patches, branches of trees on the periphery beginning to sprout leaves anew, sap leaking through the dry bark of their tortured trunks.

Tristan sat down. He estimated he was close to where the Library had been situated. What could have happened to all the books? Had they burned too, surely there would be odd pages still lying, half-charred, torn, shredded amongst the mess of the clearing.

He tried to collect his thoughts, dampen his emotions and memories, capture again the unique silence that always characterised the place, even when the children had been playing noisily and running gently amok between the geometrical patterns of the buildings they had found awaiting them on their initial arrival on the Island. The characteristic silence that a mute wind and a total lack of birdsong birthed.

The Piper's Dance

He could feel his heartbeat slowing, his breath drawing down to a whisper, as he synced himself to the rhythms of the island.

Dusk soon fell, and he was unsure if he could find his way through the forest back to the beach in darkness, and resolved to sleep here. He knew Danielle and Philippe would not worry. They had planned to camp by the beach.

There was nothing to be found here and they would return to Panama in the morning, he realised. Coming here had been folly. There were no answers. The Piper's plans were never easy to fathom, and it was clear that, wherever he was, he was still in control and would not allow Tristan even a glimmer of hope. He realised that, deep down in his heart, he had dreamed he would come across some clue to Katerina's location by coming here. But this was not to be.

He closed his eyes.

The night was a desert of dreams.

On one hand, Tristan was all too sadly aware that he was on the island in the present day, while on the other part of him – the better part?- felt he was altogether elsewhere. Not so much in the past, but captive within another, new dimension in which he and all the others he knew and would ever come to know were just puppets on a string, dancers to the Piper's tune on a ballroom floor whose dimensions were impossible to comprehend. A feeling of absence within a presence, of presence within a core of absence.

One moment the sky was a wall of stars, both familiar and unfamiliar, their configuration changing like oil spreading through water; the next, it was pitch black and moonless, a wall of sheer darkness as the worlds shifted between yesterday and today, and dimensions in motion.

Still in the realm of dreams, he caught sight of the golden pipe, floating through the air, waltzing through nearby branches like an elongated bird of just one colour.

A moment later, he felt the closeness of Katerina's body, her smell, feral, dripping with all the pheromones of lust, but when he opened his eyes, it was gone, leaving a terrible void in his heart and mind.

He had an epiphany in which a diorama of beaches was unveiled in his presence: the Island where he had once been exiled and had now returned to, the beach in Sicily where Sophie had disappeared, another he and Danielle had wandered endlessly up and down on when they had visited the Maldives, yet another somewhere in the Caribbean where they had to dodge a canal of effluent and waste draining into the sea. A beach in France where everyone wandered naked, every body on display a catalogue of beauty; a strip of sand isolated between rocks south of Barcelona where mostly men also paraded in the nude, their genitalia pierced, ringed, fierce in length and girth.

Beaches.

A fleeting vision of the Piper's face, his lips curled into a half-smile that spoke of both benevolence and cruelty.

The fading memory of the unearthly, discordant sound of the golden pipe they had followed so full of innocence.

The Piper's eyes, talking to him silently in the very depths of his dream.

Talking to him of beaches.

Past ones and others still to come.

Maybe it was a message? A map to where he might find Katerina, liberate her from hell like a present-day Orpheus. Or a road to oblivion.

He re-joined Danielle and Tristan as dawn broke. They were both still sleeping, trussed up in their sleeping bags under the shadow of an outlying tree where the forest met the sand.

He woke them.

'I think we're done here,' Tristan announced.

'Did you find anything?' Danielle asked, rubbing her eyes.

'No other mute girls?' Philippe jested.

'There was nothing left,' Tristan said.

A dawn chorus of birdsong was rising across the canopy of the island's interior forest as the sun peeked over the horizon out at sea.

They gathered their belongings, gingerly stepped into the sea and waded through the shallows towards the reef beyond which the speedboat was moored.

'A nice early start,' Philippe stated, looking down at the Rolex he wore on his wrist and checking the time. 'We could be back in Panama City by mid-afternoon.'

20

Tristan and Danielle soon made their way back to Europe.

Neither returned to their previous jobs. She no longer had any desire to catalogue books at the *bibliothèque* nor he to spend time in a drab office developing financial analytic programs alongside colleagues he had little in common with. They could live easily enough on the ongoing dividends from his technology shares if they didn't splash cash around.

His familiarity with the future evolution of these investments, gained by his readings in the Library back on the children's Island, had not passed unnoticed and he had quietly set up a small consultancy service, which also generated some further income from corporate sources.

The silences between them grew deeper and longer lasting, as they both struggled with the respective ghosts from their past assailing them.

The small apartment where they now lived, by the old La Roquette women's prison, was becoming increasingly claustrophobic. She was letting her parents' old house. The intensity of the sex they now rarely shared had lessened, and had now become more of a routine than a need.

'We can't go on like this,' Danielle remarked.

He looked up from his laptop. 'Do you want me to move out then?' he asked her.

She'd been sitting on the sofa for the past two hours with not a word exchanged between the two of them, trying to read an old 19th century novel by J K Huysmans and unable to concentrate on its pages for more than a few minutes at a time. She just lacked the clearness of mind to abandon itself to its subject and dubious forms of mysticism, but then she recalled she had been unable to take more than a passing interest in any book, even pulp San Antonio thrillers, ever since they had returned from Central America and their fruitless wanderings.

'I'm not sure,' Danielle said. 'But clearly, we're both unhappy, Tristan. we never communicate. We coexist together like strangers. You don't want me anymore; you don't touch me. It's no way to live.'

'I know,' was all he could say. She had been hoping for more of a response. His continuous passivity was increasingly becoming a matter for profound irritation. He was deep in thought.

'Maybe we should go travelling again?' Danielle suggested. 'There's nothing of importance keeping us here, is there?'

'Where to?'

'No particular destination in mind. Maybe we can join some cruise and see where chance takes us. If some place along the way catches our fancy, we can just walk off the boat and stay there? A bit like a throw of the dice.'

Tristan couldn't think of anything better.

A month later, they departed on their journey.

The *SS Montana* was embarking on a round the world journey which would take just under six months, leaving Tilbury, in the Thames estuary in the UK, and sailing south. Its first port of call was Ponta Delgada in the Azores followed by the island of Madeira, before it crossed the Atlantic, with random stops in the Caribbean and the Dutch Antilles, before crossing to the Pacific via the Panama Canal.

'On our day onshore, we can meet up with my brother,' Danielle suggested.

Then the boat sailed down the Pacific through French Polynesia until it reached the New Zealand islands, and then the Australian coast. Tristan and Danielle had booked passage until Sydney, hopeful that along the way, they would settle on somewhere that felt serendipitous.

'It all sounds so glamorous …' Danielle remarked as they leafed through the paperwork the travel agent had sent them.

'Or terribly tedious …'

'We can stock up on sea sickness pills, just in case. I'm told the Bay of Biscay can sometimes be rather choppy.'

The ports were mostly pleasant, the *Montana* surprisingly steady, like a vast city on water cutting through the waves at a leisurely pace. It swept forward with heavy grace, with its roster of over 1,000 passengers and as many crew. The turbulent waters of the Bay of Biscay were soon bypassed when the Captain sped through the night to avoid its troubled waves, and any nausea it generated quickly passed as they slept through the passage.

They enjoyed the winter sun on the observation deck, sitting in their deckchairs, reading books chosen at random from the ship's library and lazily sipping cold drinks which would have cost them half the price on land. As ever, they avoided the company of others. They still didn't communicate much, but enjoyed sharing the experiences: the flavoursome vegetable soup they shared at a roadside table in a narrow alley in Funchal before rushing back to the port; the Moorish squares of Gibraltar; the loud Hawaiian shirts they both chose for each other in a Curacao store while they waited for the drawbridge which cut the city in half to be reopened. By no way were they typical cruisers, a species they forensically observed at close range with both disdain and a faint touch of horror. And there was nothing more pleasurable, Tristan found, than studiously coordinating his gentle thrusts inside her when they made love to the inner rhythm of the boat effortlessly cutting though the waves like a knife through butter, the minimal sway and movement of its massive bulk surging ahead in silent triumph, dividing all resistance in its path and almost attaining the majesty of flight.

At one stage in their maritime journey, they had seven or eight days in a row between ports of call, moving invisibly along the wide, limitless seas.

At twilight, on the forward deck, waiting for the call for dinner in the main restaurant, gazing at the ocean unfurling with no end in sight and blending with the horizon as the sunset faded, their eyes fixed on the endless horizon, Tristan remarked. 'It's truly amazing, isn't it, that there could be so much water?'

'Yes, so much. Hard to get the brain around it. And then you recall that such a large proportion of the planet is just that: water. More than land surface, in fact. The mind boggles. And all that secret life underneath, too …'

'Makes you think, doesn't it?' Danielle said.

'Yes …'

'How insignificant we are the scheme of things.'

Tristan nodded. He had felt personally insignificant for years now in that very knowledge. He suppressed a smile. But, there was no denying, there was both a majesty and quiet form of serenity to the moment as they gazed at the sea moving from day into night, a low mist floating above its moonlit glittering surface.

He turned to Danielle, looking into her grey eyes with their evanescent speckles of green, like miniature jewels sparkling in their depths at irregular intervals, depending on her moods.

They were miles from civilisation, even the smallest of islands, heading on a straight nautical line for Polynesia, isolated, plains of water in all directions. She was pensive now, more so than he had ever seen her before.

'Makes you think, eh?' Again.

'Yes,' he agreed.

They remained on the cruise all the way to Sydney. They had been tempted to alight in Tahiti and had actually packed their bags in expectation, but something about the tedious early morning sail through its container port had promptly stolen all the magic the place had held in their imagination, all industrial landscapes, reservoirs, refineries, grey metal and petroleum smells. It was so unlike what they had expected. Once on shore, there was more disappointment in store: the place had evolved into a mere tourist trap, Papeete a down at heel town where glittering designer shops coexisted with rundown stores, feral kids and alcohol-sodden natives hawking junk around the perimeter of a central gallery of stools selling unappetising food produce or outrageously-priced black pearls. Nonetheless, he bought her a small necklace, more of a choker, which circled her pale neck, a delicate contrast of shades that pleased him and made him recall the early days of their relationship. Before Philippe and Panama. And the return to the Island and the ghosts it had conjured.

It was raining buckets when they reached Auckland and they didn't even disembark.

The *SS Montana* docked at the Sydney White Bay cruise terminal, miles from the city. They were totally unprepared for being there, having assumed on their departure from Europe that by now they would have settled for some other port along the way, another country, another city. All they knew of Sydney was the countless photos of the harbour and the Opera House they had come across in movies or books.

A line of cabs sat, engines purring, by the walkway they emerged onto after passing immigration. They stepped up to the first one. The driver was from Israel, he explained, a biochemist still waiting for his work visa and biding his time driving a taxi. Asked where they could go, he suggested a well-known local beach, known for its hedonistic lifestyle and surfers. It was also a long, expensive drive away but Tristan and Danielle agreed, for lack of alternatives.

They booked themselves into a small boutique hotel on the promenade.

After such a long period at sea, it felt disorienting to be on terra firma, not having to adjust for the delicate sway of the boat and the unsettling sameness of days on end at sea. Like an astronaut returning to Earth after a trip through space.

After a few days exploring the small town, they decided it was as good a place as any to stay a little longer and as the local summer was ending managed to get a short let on a small holiday apartment in the heights leading away from the seafront. Danielle, throughout their search for a place to settle down momentarily, insisted to all the realtors shepherding them around, that it should feature a balcony from which she could watch, contemplate the sea in all its splendour above the roofs of the adjoining buildings, hotels, eateries, gift shops and clubs that littered the promenade.

They briefly argued between each other -Tristan wouldn't have minded staying in the hotel closer to the beach- negotiated with the property agent, calculated, dithered and then signed the lease on the dotted line.

Already, the sea was calling out to her. A feeling Tristan was all too familiar with.

Day by day, locked into a monotonous routine, they began to drift further apart. As if the scenario of their inevitable parting had been written long ago and they couldn't cheat their fate.

Tristan could work from anywhere on his financial consultancy. Have laptop, can travel but Danielle was now idle and left to her thoughts. While he typed away, she would spend hours on the balcony gazing out at the changing colours of the ocean or would walk to the beach, sit herself down for hours, eyes fixed on the horizon, deep in contemplation. When he asked what was going through her mind on these lengthy occasions, she could never express herself to any degree of satisfaction, mumbling, stumbling on words, and then falling silent again.

By now, he knew all too well that her ghosts had returned, tendrils from her troubled past which she had never truly revealed in full to him wrapping their insidious roots deep down inside her mind, burrowing like a knife in a wound.

The summer season faded away.

As did the tourists and the surfers.

The gulf between them grew deeper with every passing day. He was working to a deadline defined by the time difference between Australia and France. Danielle now spent increasing hours away from their apartment. Often, when Tristan stepped over to the balcony for a breath of fresh air, he might observe her in the distance towards the end of the beach, where the rocks rose, sitting motionless, like a matchstick woman on the plain of sand, with her back to him, entranced by the swell of the nearby waves and the ebb and flow of the water swirling by her feet.

One day as he watched her in the distance, he spotted the elongated silhouette of a man emerge from the sea, ambling towards her. Tristan sat frozen to the spot. Something about the silhouette's blurry movements reminded him of the Piper. The man reached her, standing tall beside her and the image froze, both Danielle and the stranger fixed like statues. Squinting hard as he was, Tristan was unable to make out much of the unknown man's features, let alone what he was wearing, his image shrouded in eerie darkness, just a sombre silhouette, his shadow falling on her lanky form, the warm, brown shades of her now-tanned skin offset by the white of her skimpy bikini.

They were immobile for an eternity. In conversation, probably.

A call of nature stole Tristan from the balcony and, by the time he rushed back, the man was no longer at her side and he could see Danielle slowly walking along the beach on her way back to their place. The stranger was nowhere to be seen. Returned to the sea where he had come from?

'How was it?'

'It was good. The sea is always so beautiful.'

No mention of the man she had fallen into conversation with. Probably because it meant nothing, just an idle encounter not worth mentioning.

For the following four days, Danielle returned to the same spot on the beach and, invariably the man emerged from the sea at some point and joined her. He never sat. Danielle never rose. What could they be talking about?

'Saw you chatting with someone. Anything interesting?'

'No,' she looked him in the eyes, almost defiant in her response. 'Just someone. Nothing of importance.'

Tristan bought a pair of binoculars at one of the gift shops on the promenade where they also sold giant, embroidered towels, swimwear and an assortment of surfing accessories at extortionate prices.

He stood on the corner of the balcony, ashamed, furtively

watching her in the distance. Lines of white on a sullen sea echoing the streaks of her bikini against her tanned skin.

A dark blur upon the breaking wall of waves and the man appeared, as if from the very depths of the sea. Tristan adjusted the focus of his instrument. His heart seized. The stranger Danielle had met up with was stark naked. His attention was inevitably drawn to his cock, thick, long, straight, dangling proudly between his massive thighs as he cut through the flow of the water lapping its way towards the edge of the beach. Tristan swallowed hard next: much of his body appeared to be covered in shiny, dark scales, his ebony hair fell to his scaled shoulders, wet, dripping with salt.

He looked like a magnificent beast roused from the deep, both human and inhuman.

He reached Danielle.

She stood to greet his arrival.

Tristan watched their lips move through the lens of the binoculars, his breath tight and irregular, the cold metal cutting into his unshaven cheek. Neither of them even spoke.

Do mermen even have a language or the capability of speech?

Danielle unhooked her top which fell to the ground, while the stranger tugged at her bikini bottom and pulled it down to the sand.

Tristan wanted to close his eyes, but he just couldn't.

He watched them make love. The beach was almost empty bar a few passers-by, who didn't appear to notice the rutting couple, as if they were shielded by an invisible wall.

Tristan tried to feel detached but couldn't pull his eyes away. The merman was brutal, unrelenting, a master of the fuck. For a brief moment, Tristan recalled the beach scene in 'From Here to Eternity' with Burt Lancaster and Deborah Kerr. It was an incongruous thought and what he was witnessing was in another dimension of sex altogether. Primal. Elemental. Savage.

How long Danielle and the stranger's sandy union lasted, he had no clue about, but he had to eventually stop watching, as every successive thrust was a further stab to his heart and gut. Somewhere inside him, he had always known that Danielle and he wouldn't last forever, but he would have never predicted it would happen this way.

Like a film you can't unremember, abominable images had been carved deep into the back screen of his brain. The porcelain white of her skin scraping relentlessly against the off-green texture of the stranger's scales; the massive girth of his erection, his penis a rainbow mix of azure colours, its glistening, darker tip digging into her slit, parting her labia with ferocity until it was swallowed whole. Tristan wanted to close his eyes, throw the binoculars and their shocking focus away but could not find the will power to do so, entranced by the spectacle of the mating, conjuring in his ears the noises of the sea, the lapping of the waves surrounding their rutting bodies. Witnessing the O of her mouth as he ploughed into her, the V of her hard nipples as he played her body like an instrument. Tristan came watching them.

That night she did not return.

Nor the following day. Tristan had already reached a resigned sense of acceptance. Then, on the morning of the third day since he had witnessed her in the arms of the merman, the key turned in the front door and she walked in.

She wore a thin sundress, almost transparent against the rising light cavalcading through the window and the white cotton curtains. She was visibly nude underneath.

He looked at her.

She was flushed.

There was a length of thick gauze plastered along the right side of her neck.

'What is that?' Tristan asked.

'Nothing,' Danielle said.

'It's not,' he replied. 'Show me.'

She did.

There was a raw, deep scarlet scar running along the ridge of her long neck. Between it, a new mouth, a dark maw that gaped open.

'What the fuck?'

'It's not what it seems,' Danielle stated, her gaze defiant.

'Did he do it?' he asked.

'No, he sent me to a doctor in the hills who was willing to perform the surgery.'

Tristan fell silent.

Danielle then walked past him and made a beeline for the bedroom.

'You're leaving, aren't you?'

'Yes.'

'Why come back at all?'

'I wanted my jewellery. The black pearl necklace from Tahiti, and some baubles. That's all. You can donate all my other stuff to charity. Any charity. It doesn't matter.'

They hadn't even explicitly mentioned the merman and what Tristan had observed on the beach. As if she was aware he had witnessed it all and was quite unconcerned by the knowledge.

Once again on the balcony, Tristan was holding the heavy military-issue binoculars to his face. Following from afar her deliberate path along the promenade, then down the stone steps to the beach and her steady progress toward the Eastern rocks where the beach turned into the sea.

The merman emerged from the water. Danielle shed her sundress and, wonderfully naked and free, took a step towards him. He opened his arms, took her then by one hand and pulled her towards the harbour of the sea. Soon, the water was up to their knees, their waist, their necks until they were fully submerged and Tristan caught a brief glimpse of their legs scissoring the waves, fluttering as they both swam under to travel to the merman's unfathomable world. Where she could live, now that her body had been surgically adjusted and she could survive under the sea, the gills in her neck like a beautiful newly-sculpted cunt.

He suppressed a tear.

It felt for a moment like a map to the future had opened up, on a world in which events repeated themselves endlessly, a desolate waltz in which partners made brief contact before inevitably drifting apart never to see each other again as they drifted to all four corners of the globe and seas, fated to commit the same mistakes over and over again. Unable to break a cycle inscribed in the night stars. The curse of the Piper, he guessed; the price he had to pay.

First Katerina – had it also been a merman who had stolen her away or some other fantastic creature of legend, unless it had been a mere mortal – and now Danielle.

'Damn this world,' he muttered. It would have been better, he reckoned, if he had remained on the Island, whiling away the meaningless days, oblivious of other possibilities, free of wanderlust, never growing up, if only not to have known the emptiness that now filled him to the brim, the black dog mining his soul, leaving him bereft and, worst of all, helpless.

So what was his future now? He couldn't remember much beyond the next decade, beyond the plague that would strike the world, the small wars and famines, the natural catastrophes and political upheaval. He should maybe have devoted more attention to sporting milestones; at least, he could have bet ahead on them, not that he was in need of further funds.

When the lease on the flat expired, he abandoned the apartment they had shared and moved back to the small hotel on the seafront. Was even given the same room, its window opening onto a mezzanine roof from which he could observe the sea. He fell into a routine, waking daily at the break of dawn to observe the early surfers gathering on the edge of the water with their multi-coloured boards, catching the strong, morning waves in a ballet of grace and constant motion. By mid-morning, when families took over the beach, he retreated to the room and spent a couple of hours on his laptop, monitoring the stock market in Europe and contacting his handful of clients with relevant investment tips. He would venture out at lunch and snack on boiled shrimp and salad at the small Asian bar tucked between a shoe store and a pharmacy, and then spend most of the afternoon walking the coastal trail. Evenings, he queued diligently amongst the noisy crowds at the steak restaurant along the promenade and ate alone. Then, back at the hotel, he would read. Danielle had left her books behind but he soon ran out and found a gallery-shaped bookstore in town where he could replenish his stock. He chose books at random, no longer thirsty for knowledge as he once had been, but keener on the emotions that ran between the lines on the pages, where characters lived, played and died. At times, Tristan felt, he was becoming a character in a book himself, trapped in the story and unable to affect its progress, tethered to the plot and the narrow road that dictated his journey to the final page.

The world was full of stories.

Maybe he should write his own? He thought of it but was unable to raise sufficient enthusiasm or the will to do so. It would prove unbelievable anyway, he thought, too far-fetched and unrealistic.

Weeks passed. Months.

He found some form of inner peace, now resigned to his fate. No longer resistant to the narrative that had been assigned to him by the Piper, whose presence now felt oddly distant, resigned to whatever the future – a personal future of which all knowledge was obscured – brought along.

One day, he had a telephone call from Philippe. When he informed him that his sister and he were no longer together, the Frenchman was unsurprised. 'She was always flighty,' Philippe remarked, unperturbed by losing touch with her when Tristan informed him she had left no forwarding address. He did not inform Philippe about the merman.

'And no further news of Sofia?' Tristan enquired.

'Not a word. She was strange. Those were strange times. I no longer think of her; there would be no point.'

It was a patchy connection. Philippe mumbled something about new, profitable business in, of all places, Patagonia. But Tristan was no longer listening properly. Patagonia, he knew, was the end of the world. A place he had instinctively been avoiding all along to visit.

21

A fog of lassitude loomed over him.

Tristan had no wish to return to Europe, even though the beach resort now invariably evoked painful images which he could not erase from his mind. He met his assorted deadlines, socialised as best he could in bars and with fellow lodgers at the hotel, lived quietly from day to day with a lasting pain in his heart and sharp pangs of memory piercing the night sky as he unsuccessfully attempted to reach the peace of sleep and untroubled dreams.

He now made a daily pilgrimage to the area close to the eastern rocks where Danielle had first encountered the merman and later departed with him for marine parts unknown. He knew that in the latter part of their relationship, their mutual sense of wanderlust had constantly sabotaged their feelings for each other, even as they had held on to the illusion of love like buoys scattered at sea. He had tried to satisfy her, but it had not proven enough. He hoped she was happy now. But he missed her so much. Damn it he did! And wondered what life must now be like for her, how things functioned under the sea or on the exotic faraway islands where she and her merman and others of his kind maybe lived, took refuge. Had they ventured far beyond the coral reefs, maybe travelled as far as the Caribbean where the Island appeared to be, close to the legendary Sargasso triangle? Surely an apposite place for extraordinary creatures to live.

Time lost its meaning. Weeks passed, seasons ticking away with metronomic regularity, possibly even more than a year, in a state of despondency, half alive, submerged by sadness. Once again, he appeared to be living in a bubble, observing the world and its inhabitants from afar. Tourists at the hotel came and went, staff changed. He would often go drinking at a shady tavern to the left of the rocks in the unfashionable part of town, where you could be morose with no one making any objection and ignore the slumming crowds, remaining seated in splendid isolation. But alcohol had no effect on him, did nothing to affect his lucidity.

It was long before dawn. The beach was still deserted.
The sun was just a lonely speck rising in the west. The wind was mild and travelled across the land like a gentle caress. Tristan was nursing a mild headache, through lack of sleep and recurring nightmares. Sitting cross-legged in the humid sand. Watching the sea, unfurling in front of his eyes eternal, steadfast, imperial.
He blinked. Caught a fleeting shadow darting across a dying wave before it crashed against the nearby shore and then flowed back, its undertow yearning for the open sea.
He opened his eyes wide.
The blurred apparition gained focus. A shape formed.
He blinked again. His throat tightened.
It was a woman. She was naked. Her heavy, dark-nippled breasts swaying gently in the muddy water that washed across them. She had brown hair, falling wet to her shoulders, a trailing strand of seaweed snaking between the wide, wet valley of her breasts. Her eyes were emerald. Not Danielle. She stopped. Looked across at him, with the hint of a smile
Tristan waved at her, hoping he wasn't scaring her. Maybe she was an early morning swimmer enjoying the innocent thrill of a skinny dip who hadn't expected to come across anyone around at such a premature time of day? She appeared foreign, different.
She began to move forward in his direction, gliding with uncommon elegance through the incoming tide until the sea swayed sideways as her midriff was revealed. He held his breath. The young woman had no legs. Just a scaled mass of flesh. A mermaid.
She wriggled onto the shore and settled by his side with all

the grace she could muster. She stared at him in silence and he wondered if, like Sofia, she was also mute.

He spoke his name. Introduced himself, gesturing with his hands in an effort to communicate.

But, she could speak. As he quickly found out.

He was instantly entranced by the sheer alien code of her beauty. She told him her name was Liv Lisa.

It was unbound lust at first sight. At least as far as Tristan was concerned.

As if his stuttering journey through life, from Hamelin to this windswept section of the Australian coast, now made sense, compassed by an inner logic that had led him to this moment, despite the anguish, the losses and the overall shadow of the Piper.

All too soon, the sound of old diesel-powered vans parking beneath the promenade and lanky surfers unloading their boards ready to catch the early morning waves disturbed their initially hesitant conversation.

'I have to go,' Liv Lisa said, 'It's better if I'm not seen by too many people.'

'I understand.'

'But we can meet again,' she suggested.

'I'd like that,' he said. 'There are so many things I want to ask you. Difficult to know even where to start.'

'Same time tomorrow?'

'Here?'

'Where else?'

He gazed in amazement as she made her way through the sand, elegantly dragging her body, towards the ebbing low tide water.

It occurred to him he hadn't even enquired about the merman and whether she knew him. And his current paramour.

For several weeks in a row, they would meet at the same spot on the deserted winter beach and talk endlessly. Tristan would tell her about his life, the impossibilities, the cities he had seen, the places he had been, the things he had done. Nothing he revealed ever surprised her, as if she, too, was a citizen of a realm of improbability. She would, her voice imbued with all the dizzying softness of a musical instrument played by a virtuoso, talk to him of the distant islands she came from, her folk, her legends, encouraging his hands to stray across her body, the silk of her skin, the damp firmness of her regal breasts, the hypnotic texture of the scales covering the lower half of her body, her tail. She openly welcomed his seduction. Prompted it. As if it were the most natural thing in the world. He never even bothered to ask her about Danielle or the mermen; what she had to say was so much more fascinating. That was the past and this was the present. And Liv Lisa now reigned at its centre.

They became lovers. Bodies on a beach before the sun rose.

Never had a woman, let alone a mermaid, taken his cock inside her mouth with such care and devotion, the wetness of her tongue and its salty surroundings like a balm, the movements of her deft tongue like a snake of lust enveloping him in her grasp, as her body danced to the song of his resurrected desire. Never had his anus been fingered like an obscene melody on a piano, the movements of her supple fingers in harmony with the travails of her busy mouth, orchestrating the rise of his engorged fluids through his balls and helpless cock like an experienced conductor who'd entranced every concert hall in the world.

But, most of all, it was the spectacle of Liv Lisa's face hypnotising him in a well of primal attraction when she looked into his eyes, kissed him, played with him, readying his shaft for that ineffable moment when she pulled him inside her and the abominable warmth that surged around his penis and spread like an out-of-control virus through his whole electrified body at the point of union, captured him in her web of desire, and immediately transformed into the unforgettable. A thing of beauty, both naive and wanton, childish and as old as the world at the same time, her deep azure eyes reflecting every shade the sea contained, trailing behind its eternal tides of lust.

The sheer perfection of her breasts, like the unfolding of

geometry in slow motion.

The magic touch of her hands, her wandering fingers.

The curve of her arse where it merged imperceptibly with scales and her tail.

The aching phosphorescence of her body, its light bathing them in a field force that existed out of time as they merged, made love, fucked, fought, enjoyed each other inasmuch as they could.

Every successive day when the sun had finally risen properly over the far horizon, Liv Lisa would retreat to the sea with a sigh of regret, always promising to return the following day. Which she invariably did.

By miracle, their beach assignments were never spied on by others or interrupted as if Liv Lisa was capable of conjuring a force field that isolated them from surfers, bathers or other passers-by.

'The seasons are turning, the weather will soon change a lot, and it will be too hot for me to safely swim these waters,' Liv Lisa said to him one morning.

Tristan knew what this implied: that he might not see her again, or at any rate until the circle of seasons had completed its travels around the sun. A prospect he truly feared. She now meant too much too him and he could not bear the prospect of separation.

'Maybe I could travel with you to those islands you talk about so much,' he pointed out. 'I'd be happy to. Not to lose you.'

'It's too much to ask,' Liv Lisa said.

'Nothing would be too much,' he replied. 'There's nothing that keeps me here. He had explained over the course of their conversations how he had come here, even going as far back in his story to Hamelin and what had happened afterwards. She had not appeared surprised. She was accustomed by birth, it seemed, to the unfathomable mysteries of the world.

'I was human once,' she had revealed to him, but not provided much in the way of detail.

'But you're not capable of living under the sea. Your biology will not allow it,' she stated.

'I think there is a doctor who could operate on me, modify me appropriately,' he declared. That was how Danielle had engineered her own departure towards the depths, with her new marine lover.

'I know,' Liv Lisa sighed. 'But for any man from the land to join us there, he must also pay a tribute. It's our tradition. It's not just being able to survive. And, if you were to prove willing and be accepted amongst us, you would be a different person. There would be no turning back.'

Tristan nodded. He couldn't think of anything worse than no longer being able to see Liv Lisa. It wasn't just the sex, however wonderful and savage it had become, but the fact he felt such a strong emotional connection to her.

'Whatever it takes. I will do it,' he declared.

She explained.

His gut churned as he digested the information and all its implications.

Indeed, he would become a very different person if he agreed.

'We wouldn't be able to mate,' he pointed out.

'Not your usual way. But we will, I promise you. It will be different, but as fulfilling. There is so much you don't know about the ways of the sea and its creatures,' Liv Lisa said. 'Bodies adapt in curious ways, you'll see.'

They agreed to meet on the night of the spring solstice by the Bay of Sharks in Nuku Hiva, in French Polynesia a few months hence. Tristan knew there was a regular boat service to the island. It was a long journey but Liv Lisa informed him it would be halfway to the marine grounds where she normally lived when not roaming the waves.

After they parted, Tristan came to realise that never had Liv Lisa, during the course of their odd relationship, expressed what her feelings towards him were. She willingly accepted his touch and gave herself unreservedly to him, but it always had been her topping him from below, giving him the impression that he was the one in charge when actually she was leading their intricate sex dance in subtle ways. She was not the one who suggested he join her, change himself. The longer he spent separated from her, the more he realised how she had been manipulating him all along. As if their initial encounter had been planned. But this realisation did not change his resolve.

He made enquiries about the doctor who had clandestinely performed the essential surgery on Danielle but initially came up against a solid wall of silence. No one would admit knowing his identity or his place of work. And describing the intervention he sought was awkward without attracting undue attention.

He woke up one morning with a bad toothache. There was a small dental clinic in one of the small roads on the side of the hotel, leading away from the beach. He was given its address by the night manager at the hotel and walked over to be the first client of the day. The gums on the lower left-hand side of his mouth were badly swollen and throbbing with pain. The dentist lanced the infection and gave him a prescription for painkillers and antibiotics. Tristan was settling the bill with the surgeon's assistant in the front office. She was a willowy tall blonde, with outrageously permed curls which looked so out of fashion they became a fashion statement in their own right. She kept on looking up at him as she scrolled a receipt, inviting his attention, or was she flirting? She was not his type at any rate. But he was encouraged to ask.

'I'm glad I found your surgery. Hector, at the hotel, sent me … I'm also seeking a doctor around here, have been told he sometimes takes on … unusual work …' He fell silent. Hoping she wouldn't come to the conclusion he suffered from some sexually transmitted disease or something worse. 'As you know, I'm not local, so not covered by health insurance, but have no problem paying privately …'

She smirked. Suggested they meet up somewhere to talk privately later. Her name, she said, was Aurora.

'I think I know who you mean,' she said, that evening after agreeing to meet him for a drink at the Argentinian bar near the mall. 'He's a bit shady; I have a friend from nursing college who once assisted him. He paid her off the books. That's how I heard about him. He certainly doesn't advertise his services. A man of discretion.'

Aurora supplied him with a name and an address.

The doctor's practice was in the hills a few miles further up the coast. It didn't sound like the particular doctor Danielle had consulted and who had successfully operated on her but it was the only lead Tristan had after weeks of being fobbed off and being passed from post to post in his quest for information. He turned down Aurora's suggestion of further drinks or coffee at her place, but left her a large bill instead which she happily swept up into her purse.

The nearby town was precariously perched towards the top of a steep hill. The doctor's premises were behind a shuttered storefront on a cobbled street on the outskirts. Most of the buildings on either side of it were festooned with graffiti. No name on the door, but definitely the address Aurora had given him. There was a buzzer, which Tristan rang.

It took what felt like an eternity before he heard steps inside the shop and then the door opened halfway.

'I've been told you're a doctor who doesn't ask questions,' Tristan said.

In the semi darkness, he could see the small man was balding, wore a smock in shades of grey, was barefoot and kept his wire-rimmed glasses elevated between forehead and scalp. Somehow he reminded Tristan of the Piper, although he was half the physical size, many times older in appearance and didn't have a luxuriant hairdo by any conceivable means

'Who sent you?' he asked Tristan.

He mentioned Aurora, explaining she knew someone who had once assisted him.

'I don't mean her,' the doctor said. 'She wouldn't have a clue as to the types of surgery I perform. I assume someone else pointed you indirectly in my direction.'

Tristan hesitated. He just hoped he had come to the right

place or person and wouldn't be laughed out of town.

'A mermaid sent me.'

The man opened the door wide and indicated he should enter.

'Good,' was all he said in response.

He had finally tracked the right man down.

He explained what he wanted. The surgeon showed no surprise.

'I wouldn't, if I were you,' he said. 'Mermaids are extremely unreliable. That's a well-known fact. They lure you to unholy places until there is no turning back.' They were sitting in a bright, neon-lit office, sipping strong coffee.

Tristan stood firm. Told the doctor he was ready for the consequences.

'So be it,' he said.

'When can you perform the necessary surgery?' Tristan asked, now eager to be transformed so that he might gain the capability of breathing underwater, as Danielle seemingly had been able to. He expected the doctor to say he could do the work in a few days, but he surprised him.

'Now,' he said.

'Here?'

'I have the facilities at the back. Don't worry, they're fully hygienic, sterilised, quite modern, Anyway, it doesn't require that much equipment. And I've performed this particular adjustment many times. You'd be surprised at the amount of foolish men who've been trapped by the lure of mermaids and taken the jump … You won't be the last either.'

'I wasn't expecting this to happen so soon,' Tristan pointed out. ' | I haven't brought any money with me,' he pointed out.

'No need,' he said. 'I'm paid by the mermaids, not the client.'

Tristan was still trying to process the information, as the doctor stood and waved him in the direction of the back door of the study towards his operating theatre. He was right: it was modern, a barrage of whiteness and bright lights and gleaming steel surfaces amongst the galleries of sharp steel instruments scattered across the immaculate metal surfaces.

'Come,' he said. 'You'll be back on your feet by mid-afternoon.'

Tristan underwent the delicate operation that would allow him to breathe freely under water; the cut along his neck that would match Danielle's, and then having the filter installed that would prevent the sea waters surging into his lungs. This, the small doctor managed with just a local anaesthetic. He awoke briefly and was quickly put under again. 'There's something else your mermaid wanted done,' he heard the doctor say, as he succumbed to drowsiness. And wondered momentarily how come Liv Lisa and the particular doctor knew each other already.

Then, Tristan went under for the other part of the surgery.

This was infinitely more complex. As Tristan would discover later, the procedures he suffered were a penectomy and a bilateral orchiectomy. If you wanted to be technical about it.

When he woke, he initially experienced no localised pain but to his surprise discovered that the doctor had expunged his genitals. The tribute Liv Lisa had called for.

He had been castrated.

It later felt sore but he well knew that physical pain always passes. Initially, the shock was more mental; a complete shock that obliterated the initial and rapidly growing discomfort in his loins.

Raising himself from bed where he had been left to rest and recuperate following the surgery, Tristan looked down at his body. It had been scrubbed clean, pale and smooth all over, this new corporal landscape almost natural because of the absence at its centre. Not that he'd had that much use for his cock for some time, he consoled himself. Not since that final coupling with Liv Lisa.

As agreed, the doctor's bill did not have to be settled. But he had unilaterally taken payment in kind. For the fruit of his labours, he would retain Tristan's now severed penis. For his specimen collection, he pretended. Little did Tristan know that he would later pass the small flask in which it now floated, shrivelled, small and pitiful to Liv Lisa. That they had a deal in place and it wasn't the first time she had mischievously pointed a man in his direction. At least he had not been lying and spoke from experience when he had informed Tristan that mermaids were not to be trusted.

Tristan reached Nuku Hiva several weeks later and made his way quickly to the Bay of Sharks after disembarking. There was no sign of mermaids, let alone Liv Lisa. Somehow a small voice inside him whispered to him that he had been duped and that Liv Lisa would never manifest herself and he was on a fool's errand. But he held hope against hope.

He returned every single day for several weeks, but she never made an appearance and questions around the small settlement that lived on selling cheap jewellery to cruise ship visitors elicited the fact that not a single mermaid had been sighted around the archipelago for centuries and were believed to be the stuff of legends, or what fishermen lie about when overly drunk.

He came to spend long hours on the narrow beach of the small cove, where sharks were similarly illustrious by their absence.

A dreadful emptiness showered across his soul. By now the area on which he had been successfully operated had fully healed and the inconvenience of its absence was no more than the wind of a fleeting memory, just a slight burning sensation on the occasions when he had urinated through the small passage that had been created for that purpose.

A whole year went by and he returned every day before dawn to the beach, but no one came to join him. Ever. Apart from stray dogs detached from their leashes and owners, and weeds, shard of wood, all flotsam washing up from the sea.

One night at a local tavern, Tristan met Volker, an elderly German ship's mate hailing from Hamburg. As two of the only Europeans presently on the island they became friendly and were drinking together in a smoky corner of the sticky-floored joint when, out of nowhere, the subject of fantastic sea creatures came up.

'I believe in them,' Volker said, with a deep sigh. 'Most don't, believe me. But I have incontrovertible evidence.'

'So do I ...' Tristan nodded.

The German sailor fixed him in the eyes, as if doubting him.

Tentatively encouraged by their respective reaction to the way the conversation was developing, they both hinted at a close personal experience with such creatures.

This is how Tristan learned about the legend of Liv Lisa, the beautiful, seductive mermaid who stole men's cocks and, reputedly, had them hanging from her necklace. It was said she now had two handfuls of penises strung along her coral necklace. No other mermaid in the hemisphere it appeared had harvested as many, a testimony to her incomparable beauty and powers of seduction.

Ages later, now back on the Australian mainland, having given up on Polynesia and any hope of the corrupt mermaid manifesting herself again, Tristan had visited an occult library in a forgotten Outback town where he was told that rare books about legends and the sea were stored in abundance. He had to bribe the librarian to be given access to the rare book section, where forbidden texts and images were kept. There, he found in the second edition of a Zafon classic, a collection of sea lore, engravings actually depicting Liv Lisa and her kind and the necklaces they harvested on their dangerous journeys. There was a striking image of a cock necklace and the image captivated him. The adornments came in all sizes, some small, others large. Some veiny, some smooth, all conserved by some dubious miracle of science at the pinnacle of their erect size through meticulous taxidermy, it appeared. It was both a morbid and a fascinating sight, not that he could ever recognize his own lost attribute any longer, even if it was actually featured in this particular, detailed illustration.

But he knew all too well that, now, one of them must surely be his, not so much a stellar but probably an undistinguished addition to Liv Lisa's dreadful collection.

And was Volker's too? He was evasive when he probed him,

but there was something of a faraway look clouding his face with sorrow when he had evoked the subject at their last meet before abruptly changing the subject of their conversation.

Neither had ever returned to the tavern the following days.

Tristan set out on his travels.

He lounged on the beaches of Spain, Thailand, Bali, some of the Maldives islands, crossed the Panama and the Kiel Canal, navigated the Florida Keys, lingered on Bora Bora and tramped down the Yucatan Peninsula. Never discovered where mermaids and mermen might lurk. Every trail he followed ended up a dead end and all his questions evinced were incredulous looks which at times made him doubt his own sanity.

He often wondered how he could summon the Piper but realised he had no idea how. And what would he have asked him anyway: was it all part of your plan? Do you also have the power to make me whole again? Haven't I suffered punishment enough?

22

Considering how much sex had once played a role in his life – having it, thinking of it, seeking it – it was a great irony that it just never occurred in Tristan's dreams. Nonetheless, those unwelcome night adventures of the mind were frequent and potent. Strictly speaking, the dreams were more like nightmares, but then he had never quite been able to make out the difference between the two states. All too often, he would wake up in the middle of darkness, his heart beating wildly, often drenched in sweat, stomach tied in knots, emerging from yet another dream riddled with anxiety, his thoughts racing in ever desperate circular motion, a loop he couldn't escape from, disturbing, gasping for air, his chest in a vice of oppression. He was already exhausted, both emotionally and physically, before he even rose out of bed.

The actual events making up the fabric of the dream would quickly dissipate, like clouds melting into the event horizon, but random, flickering images, emotions, fragments, feelings would linger for a short while and only later in the day would he recall some of the elements, the building blocks of the dreams.

Most of them, or at any rate the more, albeit briefly, memorable or affecting ones, surprisingly now involved beaches.

But none he had actually visited in the years since Hamelin.

Real-life locales seldom made an appearance in the theatre of his dreams. The settings for his panic dreams were generally anonymous, long tongues of sand, squashed between emerald seas and dense inner forests, mostly uninhabited, littered with seaweed, squashed plastic bottles, driftwood and the usual detritus washed in by the waves. Like a movie of desolation after the end of the world as we know it, dead landscapes draped beneath the ever-blue sky, silent, a stage for a movie still without a script, waiting for him to assemble the jigsaw that would make it complete, meaningful.

The beach returned in the screening room of his unconscious mind in the early hours of morning and he woke up, fingers gripping the edges of the sheet, vistas of sand like flies in amber dominating the landscape, his body short of breath, his mouth dry and sweat pearling down his collar, the panic attack slowly fading as he thought he heard either Katerina or Danielle's voice shouting out at him from the next room.

Which was, of course, empty.

He looked at the ceiling, seeking out shapes, meaning. It remained blank. Just another room in a rundown housing estate at the shit end of Patagonia. *I'm hearing voices now*, he thought; *can it get any worse?*

Soon after that morning, he prepared a rucksack with spare clothing, and drove off. Leaving his few possessions behind. He had no plan to return.

By the end of the day, he was several hundred miles away, two tanks of gas, a couple of chocolate bars and half a dozen cans of Pepsi to the better, already approaching the coast.

It was winter. Both the downcast sky and the sea conjugated shades of grey and he was sitting in a bar off the town's main promenade squeezed between bed and breakfasts, overlooking a pebble beach where only dog walkers and shell hunters walked at this time of morning.

The barman brought him his cup of chowder.

'It'll warm you up,' he said.

'Thanks.'

'It's better here in summer,' the barman added, in a vain attempt to cheer him up. 'Not tropical, but you know what I mean. We're not climate blessed down here. Don't get many visitors these days. Well, not at this time of year ...'

He looked up at the man. He was in his fifties. His hair was thinning and his shirt had once been white.

'I think I already knew that before I came here,' Tristan said, dipping the heavy silver spoon into the cup, stirring the thick, hot soup.

'So what brings you to these parts?'

'Travelling. Researching …'

'Really?'

'I read somewhere about the beaches of Patagonia and thought it would be interesting to visit.'

The expression on the barman's face, as he rolled his eyes, was one of incredulity.

'Damn, I'm surprised anyone from outside the region would even know about that goddam place. Sure not a tourist hot spot,' he indicated.

'There are stories.'

'There sure are. I don't even know why it's even called a beach. No sand, just pebbles, rocks, waves. Centuries ago, it was said that pirates would light fires on the promontories to attract vessels into the shallows in the hope of shipwrecking them. And it's halfway round the world from anywhere. Go figure!'

'I'm hoping to write a book about unusual beaches,' Tristan replied, which was a total lie, a thought that just happened to cross his mind at the moment as he tasted the chowder which was much too salty and tasted more of potato than clams.

'Well, it's a couple of hours drive south. There won't be much traffic, I reckon.'

'I'm in no rush. I'll get there some time,' he said, concluding the conversation.

It had been three months since he had taken off and he had visited a dozen or so beaches so far, and still didn't know where he was headed or what he was actually seeking. It wasn't as if the sandy, blue-skied, coral beach of his past dreams could even be situated this far south, even if it existed anywhere but in his mind. But he was in no hurry. Since he had begun to travel, the circular nightmares and regular panic attacks had finally ceased and all he dreamed about now was women's bodies. He could live with that, although waking every morning with a raging imaginary erection made him feel like a hapless character in a Thomas Pynchon novel. It could be worse, he supposed. Yes, it was, he no longer had a penis, he sighed.

He lingered in that particular town a further two days before he travelled to the unnamed Patagonian beach.

He arrived at dawn in the middle of a storm.

The rain was pelting down, playing a ballet of dissonances over the hood of his metal grey BMW, droplets skipping along in gay abandon like ants across an open fire. The wind had a sharp bite about it when he opened the door and he decided to remain inside the car until the weather calmed, even though the second-hand car's heating was on its last legs. He would have to find a garage soon, if he remained much longer in these inhospitable parts, and get it fixed.

By midday, the curtain of rain obscuring the beach and sea parted slightly.

The actual beach was narrow but deep, lengthy tongues of land venturing into the sea and its procession of high waves, as if probing the ocean's defences. There was a ragged beauty to the vista, a forlorn sense of brutality and desolation, an echo of the dead souls who had seemingly been shipwrecked here in times of old and witnessed their broken bodies washed onto the unyielding stony shore to be buffeted over and over again by the savagery of the waves. Much too cold for mermaids, he knew, to venture this far. He had long given up on that possibility.

The sky had cleared and was now the colour of washed-out denim as he finally exited his car and stood on the edge of the small chalk cliff that towered over the beach. There was a red stain in the distance at the far end of the pebbled carpet separating the hills and the ocean. He peered ahead as the dot moved, slowly expanded, came into focus. He blinked.

A human silhouette bent over at the knees.

He made his way down to the beach. She was wearing a red plastic-like anorak and was scooping pebbles into a variety of small pails, marking each rescued stone with a thick marker pen in fluorescent ink. She saw him coming and looked up, her long, wet hair spilling from her hood.

'You're probably wondering what I'm doing?' she asked

him, as he approached.

'Not so much what but why,' he remarked.

Her smile was crooked, full of mischief.

'I'm a geologist. Taking samples,' explaining herself and her presence here.

'It's a god-forsaken place to have to come and work,' he told her.

'I go where the work is, where the beaches are,' she acknowledged and stood up. She was half a head taller than him, green-eyed and wore no make-up. 'What about you?' Her skinny jeans adhered to her long legs.

'Just another beach hunter,' he said. 'We come in all sizes,' he remarked.

'So you do.' She set one of her pails down and advanced her hand. 'Dr Trish Vaughan.'

He extended his. Her handshake was firm and confident.

He introduced himself to her.

Later, he gave her a lift back to the small nearby town once they discovered they were staying in the same hotel. She'd walked all the way to the Patagonia beach, had to rely on local buses and trains. Trish was good company, and they shared a meal.

'What's your next port of call?' he asked her after she'd confessed her work on this specific beach had come to its natural end.

'It's a resort on the west coast called Vermilion Sands. It was once a huge development but I understand it's fallen on hard times and most of the complex has been abandoned, and what's left of it is in good enough nick and has been turned into an artists' colony. There's been a lot of dredging in the sea nearby and the beach has allegedly acquired some interesting geological configurations through the redirection of the tides and the university have given me a brief to investigate further.'

'How are you getting there?'

'About three trains I've calculated, and some lengthy pit stops if the time tables prove correct,' Trish said.

'I'll drive you there,' Tristan offered. 'I've nothing better to

do and the place sounds fascinating.'
'Are you sure?'
'Of course.'
Dr Trish Vaughan accepted his offer.

To describe the resort as run down would have been an understatement. The tall, concrete towers which once housed thousands of sun-seeking holidaymakers in their architectural heyday were actually crumbling, roofs caved in, balconies detached from their facades or, in some instances, hanging precariously by an iron girder with countless shards of masonry balancing above the void below, as if battered by some hurricane or typhoon just the day before, wounded giants standing blemished against the azure blue of the spring day.

The more exclusive stucco villas dotted between the Le Corbusier-styled towers were in better shape but far from habitable. There was no electricity, water, and mould and vegetation appeared to be winning the war, gradually wrapping the buildings in a thick, impenetrable coat of decay.

The dozens of Olympic-size swimming pools which had once been one of the resort's main attractions lay empty, scattered with detritus and the pitiful remains of dead animals causing the smell of decay to hang in the air. There was no sign of the artists who were allegedly active here.

As for the beach, it no longer existed at high tide, fully swallowed up by the encroaching sea and no more than a landing strip of damp sand when the waters retreated.

'There's nothing for me to do here,' Dr Vaughan said, with a sigh of exasperation. 'It's too late. Maybe a year ago or so, I would have been able to analyse the flows and counterflows of the tides through the strata's of the beach, but it's beyond repair, so to speak.'

It felt to him, as he looked out at the bruised landscape, that any trace of civilisation here couldn't have occurred here a year back, let alone a century ago.

'I wonder where all the supposed artists have gone?' There

was no trace of their presence.

She gave a few calls.

'They left just a few weeks ago,' she informed him. 'I asked a friend in my department to look it up online. Seems they've gone east seeking a volcano or something of the sort. It didn't make sense to me, some sort of psychic search. Not my area of expertise.'

They drove back up the coast, mostly in silence.

Sometimes they stayed in small pensions and shared a room both fully-clothed, lying in bed, barely touching, sleeping in the warm glow of each other's body, content with just the companionship. On other occasions, they dozed in the car. His finances were running low and he knew that all too soon, his credit card would get declined down at a petrol station and that would be the end of the road. Trish was content to let him pay for gas and snacks, and didn't appear to be lush with funds either. Both travelled light, just a few spare clothes and some toiletry, and various small pieces of scientific apparatus in her bulging rucksack, test tubes, syringes, pipettes, multi-coloured sample cases.

They reached the Golden Littoral and Balmins Beach.

'Do you have any work to do here?' he asked her.

'No. My research is done. But I'm no rush to go home. There's not much waiting for me there,' she said.

'Same here,' he said.

'A few more beaches to explore then?' she suggested.

'Why not.'

Balmins was rather notorious, not just a tourist hot spot, but also a gay haven and renowned for its isolated nude bathing area, situated between the glittering lights of the sea front promenade with its posh hotels and seafood restaurants, and the old port, which was now evolving into a somewhat exclusive marina for pleasure boats, many of which appeared to be owned by absent Russian oligarchs.

They were on their way back to the Port Balmins Hotel after a meal in the hills behind the beach, by the town cemetery, of grilled fish and polenta.

'I'm sorry,' he said to her, 'I like being with you but I'm also not a great social animal. Do I bore you?'

'Not at all. You're just a man of silences. I don't mind. I'd rather that than the opposite.'

'You don't have to stay with me, you know. If you want some time off, feel free, no need to have me tagging along all the time.'

She considered the offer and suggested she might go off on her own for a few hours, try a bar, a disco maybe. She felt like dancing. He agreed.

When she returned to their room hours later, well past midnight, she was not alone. The man escorting her was stocky, in his late 40s, he reckoned, impeccably dressed in a smart dark three-piece pinstriped suit, looked a little like the actor Benicio del Torro, but without the sneer, not a dark hair out of place, ebony eyes, with an air of uncontested authority which hung above him like an aura.

Tristan was sitting in their hotel room's only armchair, distractedly leafing through a foreign language magazine he couldn't understand, nursing a glass of water, when they arrived. Trish's face was blotchy, the alcohol she had imbibed betraying her excited state of mind.

'Who's this?' the stranger asked, indicating Tristan. 'Your husband? Your boyfriend?'

'Just a friend,' she answered boldly.

'Hmmm ...' the man said. 'I'm going to fuck her,' he continued. 'Do you want to leave or stay?' His tone of voice was full of impregnable confidence.

He felt a rush of adrenaline surge through his body, but before he could answer, or ask any questions, he was interrupted by Trish.

'I want him to stay, and watch,' she said.

'If that's what you two want, that's what you will get,' the man said. 'But on my terms.' He ordered the partly inebriated Dr Vaughan to sit on the edge of the bed and walked over to him, ordered him to rise from the armchair and stand by the far wall where he bound his hands tight with the belt he had deftly pulled from his jeans.

'Don't want any interruptions, or risk you having any second thoughts,' he pointed out. 'Just stand there and watch, or close your eyes if you prefer, but don't fucking move, understood?'

Tristan nodded.

There was no fear, just a prurient curiosity and expectation.

'I think she wants you to see how she should be properly treated. Teach you, and her, a lesson.'

The stranger quickly stripped Trisha and positioned her on all fours on the bed, undid his own trousers and roughly mounted her with no fancy preliminaries. She moaned, and watching in dreadful fascination as he did Tristan was unsure whether the sounds that escaped her lips were the product of pain or lust.

By morning, she had been used more than he ever thought anyone could, soundly beaten, verbally abused, hurt and a parade of bruises marked a crooked road across the geography of her pale skin, choke marks around her throat, broken in body and soul. But from the sketch of a smile birthing across her lips, blissfully content.

Standing, hands tied, by the wall just a pebble's throw away, he had watched in abominable fascination throughout, trying to understand, to process the events unfolding in front of him in all their crude horror, knowing that Trish was not just complicit in what was happening but also badly craved this repetitive pattern of degradation and humiliation. Not that in his emasculated state, Tristan had ever offered her the solace of sex.

'Benicio' left early in the morning, slamming the door behind him, not bothering to untie his wrists. He had to ask Dr Vaughan to drag herself off the bed, still reeking of sweat and sex, to do so.

She then moved to the bathroom, and stood silently in the shower, cleaning away the excesses of the night. No humming or singing.

She wouldn't look him in the eyes after she returned to the room.

'How did you come across him?' he asked.

'He found me,' she replied.

'Where?'

She didn't answer him directly. His eyes were drawn to the bruises on her small breasts, and the scarlet bite marks on her neck.

'Women like me,' she said. 'Some men, that type of man, they smell it on us, they see it even if it's invisible to others, the craving for submission. It's an illness and they are the doctors …'

'It's happened before?'

'Yes, an addiction, I know … but …'

He gazed at her. For a moment, he thought she was about to burst into tears.

'He wants me to go with him later, to the beach. He wishes to collar me …'

'Will you?'

'Maybe …'

After he walked down to the port to fetch some bread, jam and a bottle of mineral water, and returned to the hotel, she had gone. As had her rucksack.

A pattern with women Tristan had become familiar with.

He briefly thought, later that day, to amble down to the nude beach where the eastern quadrant was occupied by the gay community, with their tattoos and extravagant piercings and the 'free' area where all genders paraded as nature intended. But he did not do so.

That night as he tried to sleep, he couldn't help imagining the stocky man brutally pulling a naked Dr Vaughan along the fine sand on a leash connected to a dog collar around her neck, her parts rouged, her eyes lowered as if in modesty, exhibiting her and then gifting her to other men in turn in full view of the whole beach and its denizens, before allowing her to be ritually devoured, consumed like in a Tennessee Williams play.

He departed Balmins the following day.

While the waves roared just fifty metres away, he watched a group of locals kneeling in the sand, in a ceremony to honour the dead from the tsunami that had submerged the beach five years ago to the day. Their plaintive chant spiralled through the air; a sad lament orchestrated by a shaven-headed Buddhist monk in orange rags. The smell of incense reached his nostrils. The sound of tiny bells ringing.

Behind the beach halfway to the small road that traversed the village and its procession of bars, tailors and cheap bed & breakfast establishments, stood a rectangular granite monument on which the names of all the victims were carved. Next to it, a narrow canal serpentined its way across the back of the beach area, parallel to the shore, swollen once a day by refuse pouring down from the hills or dredging a torrent of mud after each rainfall.

A gaggle of street vendors littered the slightly elevated path that ran along the beach, hawking umbrellas, silk scarves, gaudy bikinis, and coconuts.

It was out of season on Tsunami Beach, still too close to the rainy season for the tourists to have arrived in droves. There was just a scattering of European retirees who enjoyed the clement weather and the depressed state of the local currency, and some gap year students seemingly all spat out from the same mould: identical dirty blonde hair, blue or grey eyes, sunken features, and on a continual high from the cheap and easily available weed.

He sat on the ledge, watching the waves break and a few tentative surfers treading gingerly with neither the talent nor the guts to tame them properly. Their boards were too new and their tan betrayed the fact they hadn't been around these parts for long.

'Just another fucking beach,' Tristan said quietly, with no one around to hear him.

Even the waves were nowhere like Bondi, but at least the place was cheap. His cash was running out, as were his options but he felt no desire to return home, to his own country, his old life. He had no place to call home, anyway, he reasoned.

He didn't think he could stay here much longer and realised he was overstaying his mental welcome. More than a month already. Time to move on.

He didn't even enjoy the heat that much.

'Do you have a light?'

Someone had sat down next to him, furtively, taking him by surprise.

'Sure.' He pulled out his lighter.

In exchange, the newcomer offered him a hand-rolled cigarette and brought another to his chapped lips. They both took an initial puff. The stuff was strong, odorous. Tristan had never been particularly partial to it, but saw no point in being rude and refusing to partake. It wasn't as if he had any immediate plans and ending up high this evening wouldn't kill him, would it?

'I'm Kem.'

'Kim?'

'No, Kem with an E.'

'Ah.'

Taking a closer look at his interlocutor, he realised it wasn't a teenager. He was older, grey hair flowing elegantly long down his shoulders, a bushy hipster beard moving between ginger and white covering the bottom half of his face. His shorts were washed out blue, his patterned Hawaiian shirt a carnival spread of shells. His tan was deep, ingrained. There was something familiar about him, Tristan felt. Although Kem in no way resembled the Piper, he shared a similar aura.

'Seen you sitting here a few days already?'

'Yes, I like to look at beaches.'

'Don't blame you. There's nothing like the beach life, man.'

'But I don't think I have yet found the right one, the perfect beach,' he confessed, 'Maybe I've been looking in the wrong places. Haven't tried any actual small islands yet. Might like them more. Commune with nature and all that. Earth, sea, sky, you know ...'

He knew he was just spouting the sort of nonsense the guy would expect. Blame the potency of the grass.

'Ah, I know of a beach I'm sure you've never come across. A traveller's secret,' Kem said.

'Tell me,' Tristan asked, if only to be polite.

'It's not easy to find, but if the stories are true, it's a hell of a place. Apparently, there's even a legend surrounding it. A hiding place, a base for the last mermaids remaining in this particular ocean.'

'Mermaids?'

'Indeed. Did you know that no breasts feel as exhilarating to the touch as a mermaid's tits? It's unforgettable. Even a young virgin's buds aren't as magical, they say.'

Tristan briefly felt dizzy.

'It hasn't even got a name,' Kem said. 'They just call it the Last Beach.'

'And how do I get there?' Tristan asked his newly-acquired bearded companion.

His credit card was declined a hundred miles off the beach when he pulled into a gas station, so he'd had to abandon his car there and walk and hitch the rest of the way. It took him over a week. The road was a forgotten one, with barely any traffic, just a lone vehicle or two every hour.

He reached it at sunset, emerging from the trees that obscured the beach from the interior plains, the sharp orange orb of the sun sinking gracefully into the horizon, while storm clouds gathered above it.

His joints ached, he hadn't shaved in an eternity and must look like the parody of a caveman or a scarecrow, his clothes dusty, caked with sweat, his shoes falling apart with every new step.

The beach was just like a dream.

Desolate but beautiful in its loneliness. Empty.

He stepped out of his shoes, then his trousers, which he dropped to the floor of fine, yellow sand. He unbuttoned his once-pink shirt and pulled its starchy material off. Then his socks, and the glorious sensation of the unique texture of millions of grains burnished by an eternity of sea crunching under his bare feet.

He slid his boxer shorts down to his ankles and trampled them into the ground.

Took a deep breath and advanced towards the muted roar of the faraway waves, dipped his toes into the tepid water still harbouring the day's heat, advanced further until the sea reached upwards and rose to his waist, a dip in the sea floor and the water retreated upwards past his midriff, drops dripping from his navel across his lower, smooth stomach, like a procession of pearls and then he continued his advance into the ocean.

His shoulders.

His neck.

His chin.

His eyes.

For a brief moment, he thought he should say something but nothing came to mind and he stepped forward until he was fully submerged. And found himself swimming in the cold waters with the agility of a fish. It was actually the first time he had tested out the success of the operation to help him live in water that he had undertaken all those months before at Liv Lisa's request.

It was an exhilarating feeling, and Tristan was sorry he hadn't actually ventured out swimming before and taken advantage of his new talent.

When darkness cast a cloud over the sea and the beach, he waded back to the shore.

A woman was kneeling in the sand, close to his pile of discarded clothes. She was wearing denim dungarees and was barefoot. Behind her, the sun was disappearing behind the crest of the distant hills and, through the dying glare, Tristan had difficulty making her out.

Water dripping from his body, he approached her.

She looked up, her eyes fixing on the blank area where his genitals had once been, but expressing no surprise at his emasculated state.

He knew those eyes.
That wild, unkempt hair.
Katerina.
He ran to her. Cried out her name,
But she looked at him blankly.
She didn't recognize him.
They were together again.

A man with no cock and a woman with no memories of their past life together.

But it felt like Eden all over again.

Wherever he was, the Piper closed his book. This dance had finally come to an end.

ABOUT THE AUTHOR

Maxim Jakubowski worked for several decades in publishing and later owned the Murder One bookshop. He has written 20 novels (including 10 under a collaborative pen name, several of which made the *Sunday Times* top 10) and 5 collections of short stories. He is recognized as a major expert on popular fiction and reviewed crime for 12 years each for *Time Out* London and *The Guardian*, and won several awards in the mystery and SF & fantasy field. He is also a major editor of bestselling anthologies, and has been translated widely. He is currently Chair of the Crime Writers' Association. He lives in London.

PRAISE FOR *THE PIPER'S DANCE*

'Maxim Jakubowski's ominous and hypnotic new fantasy spans time, space and the infinite part dream and part nightmare, it thrills and compels.' DAVID QUANTICK, Emmy-winning writer of *Veep* and *The Thick of It*

'A brilliant and unique novel! Wildly creative, wildly erotic, *The Piper's Dance* is a rich blend of journey, discovery, myth and lore – modern and ancient – told in Jakubowski's masterful, evocative style. The clever plot speeds through time, place and dimension and is filled with heartbreak and joy, sensuality and horror, and characters who come truly alive on the page. This is a novel that will stay with you long after you finish the last page.' JEFFERY DEAVER

'Maxim Jakubowski has long been one of our most inventive as well as prolific writers. Like all his work, this book surprises and delights' PETER JAMES, author of the bestselling Roy Grace Crime Series

'I might kill to get the movie rights for *The Piper's Dance*. It's that gripping.' MIKE HODGES, director of *Get Carter*, *Flash Gordon* and *Croupier*

'An emotive and beautifully told fantasy exploring good, evil and the grey areas in between.' SAMANTHA LEE HOWE, *USA Today* bestselling author of *The Stranger in Our Bed*